THE WHISKEY KILLING

THE WHISKEY KILLING

A NOVEL

H. R. WILLIAMS

FIVE STAR
A part of Gale, Cengage Learning

GALE
CENGAGE Learning

Detroit • New York • San Francisco • New Haven, Conn • Waterville, Maine • London

GALE
CENGAGE Learning™

Copyright © 2008 by H. R. Williams.

Romans 13:4 scripture taken from the New King James Version. Copyright © 1982 by Thomas Nelson, Inc. Used by permission.

Five Star Publishing, a part of Gale, Cengage Learning.

Set in 11 pt. Plantin.

Printed on permanent paper.

LIBRARY OF CONGRESS CATALOGING-IN-PUBLICATION DATA

Williams, H. R.
    The whiskey killing : a novel / H. R. Williams
      p. cm.
    ISBN-13: 978-1-59414-662-6 (alk. paper)
    ISBN-10: 1-59414-662-4 (alk. paper)
      1. Merchants—Crimes against—Fiction. 2. Police—Arkansas—Fiction. 3. Murder—Investigation—Fiction. 4. Revenge—Fiction.
    I. Title.
    PS3623.I5567W48 2008
    813'.6—dc22   2007036339

First Edition. First Printing: February 2008.

Published in 2008 in conjunction with Tekno Books and Ed Gorman.

To Bilbo
Thanks for everything

For he is God's minister
to you for good. But if you
do evil, be afraid; for he does
not bear the sword in vain . . .
　　　　　　　　　—Romans 13:4

PROLOGUE

Edwin Mayhew lay flat on his back in his own front yard and anyone could see him if they cared to look. It was one o'clock in the morning, but Edwin didn't know that. He couldn't move his left arm to look at his watch. He couldn't move his right arm either, or any other part of his body. Earlier, he'd tried to yell, but all that came out was a high-pitched whine, and that frightened Edwin, scared him even more than the four bullet holes in his chest.

The bastard had walked around the corner of the house and met him as soon as he got out of the car. Never said a word, just stood there for a moment. Then, he'd raised the rifle, holding it stiff-armed in front of him. Edwin knew about guns and he could see it was a .22-caliber semi-automatic. He couldn't see the person nearly so well. Whoever it was wore a wide-brimmed slouch hat and the face was hidden in shadow. Then the stranger did an unexpected thing. He reached out and touched the tip of the rifle barrel to Mayhew's chest. Mayhew heard a sharp crack, like a brittle branch breaking. He felt a sudden jab at his chest and a searing pain in his lungs. The same thing happened again and Mayhew sank to his knees, then toppled onto his back. The stranger bent over and the rifle touched Mayhew for the third time. Edwin knew what was coming now and squeezed his eyes shut. The bullet plunged into his chest and Edwin groaned. The fourth bullet followed immediately, and Edwin's legs straightened in a quick spasm. Just before he lost consciousness, the old man felt something splash down on his face. He looked up and saw the gunman standing over him with a foot on either side. He's pissing on me, thought Mayhew. Then the smell hit him and he knew that it was whiskey. The liquor rained down on his face and neck and onto his chest and burned like fire when it found the open wounds. Edwin Mayhew moaned, lost all feeling, and passed out.

He was conscious again, but there was no pain. Edwin felt as if he were floating above the short grass, and suddenly he was truly afraid. Why had this happened? Why would no one come and help him? He made an effort to fight off the fear and tried to remember everything. He'd closed his liquor store at midnight and that seemed like hours ago. Before going out the door, he'd turned and looked over the darkened store. The bottles were lined up on the shelves and the place was clean and neat, the way he always kept it. The cash register drawer was left open so a burglar would know there was no money inside. Wait a minute. After cleaning out the drawer, he'd put all the currency in the two outside pockets of his coat. The old man tried and tried again to move either hand, just enough to touch the pockets. It was no use. The hands would not obey him. He couldn't feel anything.

What had he been thinking about? It was getting harder to think. Oh yes, he'd left the store, climbed into his car, and driven up the long length of Court Street. His house sat at the far end. He'd parked out on the street and noticed that all the windows in the house were dark. Lavonia had probably gone to bed. The nightmare started when he got out of the car.

Nobody heard the shots, he thought. The creep was using a .22, probably had "shorts" in it. They're the smallest shell you can buy. Don't make much sound. Lavonia wouldn't have heard it. She was older than he and slept like the dead.

Edwin slipped closer to his own death and his thoughts

wavered and wandered. Was Vonnie dead? No, she was alive. She was alive when he left her that morning. Laura, the other sister, she was dead. Ruptured appendix. No time for an operation. His mother and father were dead. Edwin was sure about that. They'd died years ago, as had his older brother. Was Lavonia the only one alive then? Was everyone else in the world dead? No, the customers he'd waited on today were alive. They were alive somewhere and drinking their beer and bourbon.

The old man lay still and stared up at the starry heavens. A full moon had risen and was nearing a patch of clouds. He was amazed at the vivid hues: blazing stars and milky clouds and a crimson moon, all set against the blackest of nighttime skies.

Slowly the colors faded and darkness grew. Edwin lay very still. The darkness came closer, cascading down and flowing over him and into him. Then, all became darkness and Edwin Mayhew died.

★ ★ ★ ★ ★

Book One: The Killing

★ ★ ★ ★ ★

ONE

A small town gets as quiet as the countryside when it's two o'clock in the morning. It was even quieter in Billy Walker's bedroom, and the jangling of the telephone seemed as loud as a fire alarm bell. Walker lifted the receiver on the second ring. "Walker," he grunted, voice husky with sleep and too many cigarettes.

"Captain, hate to wake you." The police dispatcher's voice was crisp and cool, an alien tone at that hour. "Looks like a shooting. Edwin Mayhew's sister just called. She found Mayhew in their front yard. Says he's got blood all over his chest. An officer just got there and called back in. He says they're bullet wounds."

"Is this Pruitt?" Walker asked. He thought it was Pruitt's voice.

"Yessir."

"Has an ambulance been called?"

"Ten four, Captain . . . hold on!"

Walker could hear voices in the background, first Pruitt, then someone on the radio, then Pruitt's voice again. The dispatcher came back on the line.

"That was Officer Polk at the scene. He says the ambulance is there and the EMTs are working on the victim."

"Okay Pruitt. Tell Polk to let nobody in that front yard but the EMTs. I don't want him or any other policemen in there either. Tell him now, then get back on the phone with me."

"You got it, Captain."

While he waited, Billy Walker fished on the bedside table for a cigarette, then felt around for his lighter. He lit up, took a deep drag, and thought for a minute. Mayhew. Old Edwin Mayhew. He'd owned that liquor store at the end of Court for a lot of years. Always took the day's proceeds home with him, too. Walker knew about that. He wondered how many other people knew. Probably quite a few, and one of them had . . . Nope. That's wrong. Don't project. Don't get a mind set. Take it as it comes.

"Captain." Pruitt's voice again. "Polk's got the word."

"Good. Now I'm going to stay on the phone for a minute longer, and I want you to try and find out one thing for me."

"Yessir."

"Is Mayhew dead or alive?"

Billy waited and listened to Pruitt's voice on the radio. If Mayhew was alive, he'd meet the emergency medical team at the hospital. Maybe Mayhew could name who shot him. If Mayhew named him and then died, that was good evidence. A dying man's confession was rock solid in court. If the victim was dead, he'd go to the scene. The body might be gone; EMTs always rushed a victim to the hospital, regardless, just to protect themselves, but the crime scene would be fresh. That is, if Polk did his job.

"Just talked to Polk, Captain. He's dead all right. Both EMTs say so, but they're gonna ten thirty-nine him out anyway."

Ten thirty-nine. Radio code for expedite using siren and red lights.

"Okay, I'm getting ready to leave. Call Hull and Claggert. Tell Claggert to go to the hospital and stay with the body until the coroner gets there. I need Officer Hull at the scene with me." As an afterthought, he added, "You did good, Pruitt."

"Thanks, Captain. I'll make the calls now."

Billy Walker hung up the phone and stubbed out his cigarette. His wife had been awake through it all, but she never interrupted a police call.

"Old Man Mayhew?" she asked.

"Yeah, looks like he's dead."

"Want me to make some coffee?"

"No, I'll get some later." Walker leaned over and kissed his wife on the forehead. "Go back to sleep."

A few minutes later Captain William R. Walker, head of criminal investigation for the Medford Police Department, was in his car and en route to the front yard of Edwin Mayhew. He'd just informed the dispatcher, who had responded, "Ten four, Captain. Both parties called as requested."

Captain Walker reflected on the two parties. One was Bob Claggert, the newest member of the CID team. Tall, thin, and growing bald, the man looked older than his thirty-five years. Thin lips pressed tightly together, hardly every smiling, Claggert reminded Billy of a Klan member he'd once known. The Klansman believed he had a divine mission, too. He doesn't have the instinct for it, Billy thought. And he's not learning fast enough.

Then there was Cordelia Hull.

Two

Another dark bedroom, but in this one soft music played on a radio. A lone female lay on her back in the bed, arms flung out to either side. When the telephone rang, she flipped over, opened her eyes, and gave the phone a malevolent stare. It rang once more. "Shit," declared Cordelia, and glanced at the bedside clock. Almost two thirty. She gave a soft groan and reached for the receiver. Lifting it, she suddenly became all business. At this hour of the morning, it was a pretty sure bet who was calling.

"Cordelia Hull," she said.

"Sergeant, it's Pruitt. Did I wake you?"

"No Pruitt, I was doing my ironing. What's up?"

"Looks like a homicide. Old Man Mayhew got shot, right in front of his house."

Cordelia swung her long, dark legs over the side of the bed and sat up straight. "The liquor store owner?"

"Yes ma'am. EMTs are taking him away and the Captain is en route to the scene. Says he wants you to join him there."

Got to be dead, thought Hull. Otherwise, Walker would be going flat out to the hospital.

"Okay, Pruitt. Tell the Captain I'm on my way. Claggert's your next call, right?"

"Ten four. Captain Walker wants him with the body."

"Right. I'll call you when I'm in the car."

Cordelia hung up the phone, visited the bathroom, and headed for the closet. It was a walk-in, which was one of the reasons Cordelia (an unredeemed clotheshorse) had picked this apartment. Inside hung two rows of dresses, skirts, and pant-suits. Boots, shoes, and handbags lined the two upper shelves. Cordelia picked out an orange pantsuit, brown boots, and a hip-length, brown vinyl coat. Her wide mouth twitched in a smile. The perfect early morning murder ensemble.

Walking over to the dresser, she opened the top drawer and withdrew the .38-caliber handgun. Called a Chief's Special, it was small and compact and fit easily into her hand. She pushed a metal tab forward and the cylinder swung out, revealing five shells. She snapped the cylinder back in, and, as always, felt a little foolish. It seemed so melodramatic, yet she did this each time she went on duty. Next thing you know, she'd be twirling the damn thing around her trigger finger.

Going out the door, Hull picked up the portable fingerprint kit. The Captain didn't always have one in his car, but he sure expected her to.

Cordelia locked the front door behind her and walked to the unmarked police car. The full moon cast shadows across the yard. She looked up at it and gave a small shiver. As long as she'd been a cop, other cops had told her that more violent crimes were committed during the full of the moon. They'd even quote statistics to prove it. Well, Mayhew was now one of those statistics.

Old Man Mayhew. Hull knew him to speak to. She would drop by his store, occasionally, to pick up a bottle of burgundy. Mayhew always made it a point to chat with her for a moment. Hull figured it was because she was a cop, but then Mayhew would stare at her in his cold, steady way, and Cordelia would wonder. She'd heard things about Edwin Mayhew: stories, rumors, vague allusions.

"Medford, this is CID Two." Hull drove south toward Court Street. The CID contained three officers. She was number two and Claggert was three. Walker, of course, was CID One.

"Go ahead, CID Two."

"Ten forty-six, crime scene." The numbers meant expedite without siren or blue lights.

"Ten four, Sergeant," responded the dispatcher.

"I know it's on Court Street. East end, right?"

"That's affirmative."

Cordelia lived three blocks north of Court. When she reached it, she turned left and saw the blue lights flashing. She parked behind the patrol car, maneuvered her way through a small group of people, and approached Mayhew's front yard.

At first, she thought she was seeing things. Captain Walker was down on his hands and knees, and that wasn't all. He seemed to have his nose thrust into the short grass. In her two years on the force, Hull had never seen her boss do anything undignified, and now this. She reflected that Claggert would look natural in that position.

The young woman walked over and said, "Hi, Captain."

"Sergeant Hull" (he always called her sergeant when civilians were present), "kneel down there and tell me what you smell."

Say what? But instead of speaking, Cordelia followed instructions. She heard a few snickers from the crowd. At first, the only scent was that of earth and dry grass. Then, something else. She couldn't make it out, at first, because it was mixed in with the other smells. Then she knew. Hull got up and brushed her knees.

"Smells like whiskey, Captain."

They stood where Mayhew had lain. The spot was obvious. The EMTs had dropped bits of gauze and instrument wrappings while they worked on him.

"I've already looked for the bottle, searched the whole area but didn't find one."

Hull knew he was telling her this, not only to explain what

he'd done so far, but to add a bit more to her training. The bottle may have been the killer's. Find the bottle, you find the killer's fingerprints.

"What about footprints, Captain?"

"Not much chance on this lawn. Why don't you start walking it again. Go slowly. Anything that bears on this, pick it up. Do you have evidence bags in your car?"

"Always, Captain." Walker counted on her for the details and she hadn't let him down yet.

Smiling at her, Walker said, "If you're real lucky, you might find the weapon. I think it's a twenty-two-caliber rifle, the kind that fires short rounds."

Hull gave him a questioning look. Her boss lowered his voice and said, "This time, Cordelia, I brought my own evidence bag. It's in the car. Inside are four shell casings, all twenty-two shorts. They were lying next to this EMT crap."

"But what makes you think it was a rifle," she asked, then felt like an idiot because she already knew the answer.

"You tell me," demanded the Captain.

"Because almost all twenty-two handguns are revolvers and revolvers don't spit out shell casings."

Walker nodded and said, "Okay, get started. I told Polk to hold anybody who saw or heard anything. I'm gonna see who he's got. I'll talk to you when we finish."

"Captain, about that whiskey bottle. Maybe it was Mayhew's. It could've been in his pocket. Maybe it got broken when he fell."

"I don't think so," said Billy. "It's just something I happen to know. Lavonia didn't allow the stuff in the house, hated it with a passion. And Mayhew didn't drink."

THREE

Medford Hospital sits on the western edge of town and serves a threefold purpose. First, it's a point of embarkation for people suffering from really serious accidents or illness. Here, they're superficially treated and prepared for transportation to one of the large facilities in Memphis, usually the Baptist or Methodist Hospitals. That's an hour's drive from Medford. The hospital's second and broadest function is as a treatment center for lesser cases. Lastly, it's used for convalescent care, more often than not by the patients who were sent to Memphis in the first place.

There's another small service the hospital provides. It's a temporary depository for the town's murder victims, who all end up in the same stark room. Called the Cold Room, it's located at the southwest corner of the building and is normally used as a storage area for the hospital's perishable articles. A large wooden table stands in the exact center of the room, surrounded on all sides by medicines, food items, and sealed boxes.

Edwin Mayhew lies face up on that table, clothed in a khaki shirt, khaki pants, and a worn plaid sport coat. Scuffed brown shoes are still on his feet. His hat has been removed and Edwin's gray hair sticks up in several thick clumps. His face retains some color, but the eyes are a dead man's eyes. One is fixed on the ceiling and partly covered by the eyelid. The other is fully open and rolling to the side, as if seeking another attacker.

Bob Claggert opened the door to the Cold Room and stepped

inside. Surprised by the refrigeration, he reached down to zip up his police jacket. Bob wore civilian clothes under the jacket and a ball cap on his head. That was against regulations. In CID you wore all civilian or all police, no mixing. Claggert knew that, but decided that at two thirty in the morning, he wasn't going to worry about it.

He glanced at the thing on the table, then looked away again. Slowly, he brought his gaze back and let it rest on Edwin Mayhew. It was really him. Claggert couldn't believe it. Many a night he had stopped off at the old man's liquor store to pick up a pint of vodka. Sometimes, if the pint ran out and he wanted some more, he'd make a second stop. Mayhew would always say, "Why didn't you get enough to last?" or something like that. Told him that's what drunks did, bought one small bottle at a time. No harm in the old man, though. Bob believed Mayhew kind of liked him.

Sometimes he'd hang around the store and they'd talk. Edwin would tell him stories about the time he was a bootlegger and running booze over into Mississippi. Mississippi was dry at the time and Edwin would load up the trunk of his car with whiskey, cross the river at Helena, and deliver it to a place outside Greenville. Bob would narrow his eyes and try to look hard at Mayhew and Mayhew would smile and say, "The law can't touch me now. Too many years have passed."

When Edwin was in a good mood he'd also spin tales about the women he'd known, that is if you could call them women. Mayhew liked the young ones, the younger the better. He'd describe a certain girl, get a faraway look in his eye, and say, "Bobby, I swear she wasn't a day over sixteen."

Claggert didn't know whether to believe him or not. After all, Mayhew was an old man. But, every once in a while, he'd see sweet young things in the liquor store. They weren't Mayhew's granddaughters and they damn sure weren't old enough to buy booze. Something else, too. The old man had a way about him. He'd fix those gray eyes on you, and all of a sudden you didn't feel like doubting him. Claggert wouldn't admit it to anybody, but actually you felt like believing anything he told you.

Walking around to the side of the table, Claggert stopped and looked down. The policeman felt his nerves start to steady somewhat and he squatted down so that he was eye level with the corpse. God in Heaven! The dead man's eye was very close and it was staring right at him. Bob straightened slightly and saw the other eye looking upward. He gave a shiver and thought: What if that eye turned to stare at him, too? What if it moved so that both dead eyes were on his face, and then the whole head would slowly turn toward him and start to rise from the table, and . . .

"Shit," he breathed as he stood up and backed away. Then the door behind him swung open and touched him in the back, and a soft voice whispered, "Bobby?"

"SHIT!" he yelled and whirled around to face the young nurse standing behind him.

Reba Martin laughed as she looked into his pale face. "What's the matter, Bobby? You look like you've seen a corpse."

"Damn, Reba," Bob said. "You know I'm always nervous until I get some coffee down me."

"No, I don't know, since I've never been around you before coffee time."

The policeman leered at her and said, "Well, maybe we can talk about that."

"Sorry, Bobby. I'm spoken for. I just dropped by to tell you the coroner's out in the parking lot. I saw him through the window."

"I'll go out and meet him," said Claggert.

"Of course you will," said Reba, looking from him to the corpse.

Claggert followed Reba out the door and closed it behind him. He started down the hall with her, then saw Donald Reed coming toward him. He stopped and waited.

Donnie Reed was the coroner for Simpson County, duly elected to that office six months previously, and enormously proud of the fact. At the time of the election he'd had only one thing going for him, an endorsement by Scott Shannon, the district attorney. This proved to be enough. Shannon had been reelected to his office for the past twelve years and was a power in East Arkansas politics. Donnie Reed wasn't a power anywhere, and certainly not at home, where he was relentlessly dominated by a wife and two teenaged daughters. He owned a small furniture store on Court Street. It was moderately successful, but Donnie let out too much credit and his workers largely did as they pleased.

Of medical experience and knowledge, Donnie had zero. Of course, as a county coroner in Arkansas, you didn't need any. Coroners didn't perform autopsies. That was done by the state medical examiner. The coroner's job was to perform a few simple tasks in regard to the murder victim. After that, the body was transported to the state crime laboratory at Little Rock. Donnie had once confessed to his friend, Scott Shannon, that he didn't even like to be around dead bodies. They gave him the willies.

This morning, as he approached the CID officer, Reed looked anything but eager. He straightened his skinny frame, shifted the briefcase around, and stuck out his hand.

"How are you, officer?" he inquired.

"Doin' fine, Mister Reed. You ready to look at the body?"

Reed cleared his throat and said, "Yeah, let's get it over with."

Claggert opened the door and ushered Donnie into the room. The coroner walked to Mayhew's left side, and Claggert went around the table and stood facing him.

Donnie glanced at the policeman's name tag and said, "Okay, Officer Claggert, we've got to do this by the numbers." Secretly, he breathed a prayer of thanks to Billy Walker. The CID chief had drilled him in this procedure about twenty times. "First, I'm going to empty his pockets."

Donnie reached his hand into the victim's left coat pocket and drew out a roll of twenty-dollar bills. His eyes widened slightly as he counted out four hundred dollars. The other pocket yielded three hundred and fifty in ones, fives, and tens. Claggert drew a brown paper evidence bag from his jacket pocket and Reed placed the money inside. He signaled to Claggert and they removed Edwin's coat. The shirt pockets were empty, but the pants pockets held a clasp knife and a leather wallet containing two credit cards and a driver's license. These items were placed with the money. On the evidence bag's side were designated lines for certain information and Reed filled in some of the blanks. The two men proceeded to take all the victim's clothes off, lifting and turning the body as they did so.

The corpse lay naked and ashen on the rough, wooden table. It appeared slightly luminescent under the ceiling lights. The four bullet holes, stark and prominent, ranged across its chest. Dried, blackened blood was smeared around them.

The coroner now produced two bags of his own, which he'd picked up at a grocery store. He slipped them over Mayhew's lifeless hands. The ME wanted it that way. Sometimes much could be learned from what was on the hands and under the fingernails. Reed secured the bags with thick rubber bands. He made a bundle of the bloody shirt and other clothing and set it beside the body. Some final notations were made on the evidence bags and they were placed next to the clothes. Drawing a coroner's report from his briefcase, Donnie filled it out and gave it to Claggert to sign.

"Well, that's about it," he said.

"Shouldn't we cover him up with something?" asked Claggert, as he handed the form back.

"No, the Captain said . . . I mean the proper procedure is to leave him unclothed. The people from Little Rock will put him in a body bag."

Donnie Reed started for the door and Claggert followed him. As they were leaving, Bob glanced back at the motionless figure. Strange. He felt like maybe he should say something, something fitting. The policeman gave a rueful grin. Right, he thought. Like what? Have a nice day? Both men went out and Claggert closed the door behind them.

FOUR

Walker watched Cordelia begin her slow methodical pacing across the front yard, then motioned George Polk over.

"Anybody worth talking to?" he asked.

"Got a couple, Captain. They might have something for you."

"Keep them with you for a minute, George."

Billy strolled over to the small clutch of spectators. "I'm Captain Walker," he announced. A man and woman walking toward their car stopped and wandered back over. "I know Officer Polk has already questioned you, but please call me if you remember anything more about this, anything at all. Some of you were close by when it happened. Maybe you heard an unusual sound. Maybe you saw something that didn't look normal. Was someone running or walking fast? Was there a vehicle parked on the street with the motor running? If anything occurs to you, just call the station and ask for me. I'll get back to you." He surveyed them once more and added, "Now please return to your homes."

The spectators started drifting away and Billy walked back to Polk.

"Captain, this is Mr. and Mrs. Johnson," said the officer. "They live in the house next door."

"Howdy, Captain," said the man, sticking out his hand. Walker shook it and heard the woman murmur a greeting.

"Hello, folks. Anything you can tell us that would help?"

"Well, I dunno," said the man, making that wet sound that

28

bespoke false teeth. He and his wife appeared to be in their seventies. They both wore housecoats and Walker noticed that the man was barefooted. "It was the dog barkin' that woke us up. Rex won't bark unless there's somethin' around. When I got up to see what it was, I heard a car door slam. The old lady heard it, too."

Mrs. Johnson was nodding her head up and down. "Soon as it slammed, the motor started up," she said.

"Do you know what time this was?" asked Billy.

"I looked at the clock," said the husband. "It was twelve twenty."

"What did you do then, Mr. Johnson?"

"Well, I couldn't see anything wrong in the back yard so we went back to bed. A while later, the police ruckus woke us up."

"Did you say 'back yard'?"

"Yessir. That's where old Rex is, in the back yard."

"And where do you think the car was?"

"Oh, it was back there, too, parked in the alley."

Billy turned to the patrolman. "George?"

"Already taped, Captain. Did it soon as Mister Johnson told me. The alley's secured three houses down on both sides."

"Good man," said Billy. "Mister Johnson, that might have been the killer. The time is right. You never saw anything at all?"

"Nope," said Johnson. "The back fence was too high, but we could hear the car pull off up the alley."

"What did it sound like?" asked Walker.

Mr. Johnson looked confused.

"What do you mean?" asked his wife.

"I mean, was it a loud sound, for instance? Did the car sound like it needed a muffler? Did it sound like the motor was missing?"

"If the motor was missing, it wouldn't make no sound," said Mrs. Johnson with a cackle.

George Polk turned to her. "No ma'am. The Captain means . . ."

"She knows what he means," said her husband. "No, the motor just sounded ordinary, smooth and quiet. That's the reason I think it was a car. 'Course it could have been a pickup."

"Well, thank you, folks," said Billy. "We may be talking to you later. In the meantime, if you happen to think of something else, give me a call."

He turned and walked over to Cordelia, who was finishing her inspection of the yard. "Cordelia, the alley out back is secured, too. Give it the same once-over, tape to tape. When it gets daylight, we'll come back and do it all once more."

"I heard what Johnson said. That alley is asphalt, isn't it?"

"Yeah, no chance for a tire print, but there may be something else."

"I'm on my way," said Cordelia. "Where'll you be?"

"Inside," answered Walker, heading for Mayhew's house. "It's time to talk to the sister."

FIVE

Billy slowly climbed the steps to Mayhew's front porch. His body felt stiff and heavy. Getting up in the middle of the night came harder to a forty-five-year-old man, especially one who smoked too much and exercised too little. He glanced at his watch. Four thirty. Two and a half hours had gone by. His head ached and he needed a cup of coffee. Come to think of it, he really needed a cup of coffee. A chill wind touched the back of his neck and the Captain glanced upward. The full moon had traveled further west and was approaching a heavy cloudbank. The wind blew stronger and its breath had grown colder, a November wind, full of frost.

As Walker stepped onto the porch, he heard the short beep of a car horn. Turning, he saw Bob Claggert pulling up to the curb. Claggert got out and hurried over.

"The coroner just got finished, Captain."

"Did you take notes?" Billy would see the corpse and other evidence himself before the night was over. He might not even look at Bob's notes, but Bob needed the drill of procedure.

"Got 'em right here," answered Claggert.

"Hold on to them. We'll meet in the office at ten o'clock. Go home and get some rest."

"Okay, Captain. You want me to tell Hull to go home, too?"

"I'll tell her when she can go, Bob."

"Sure, Captain."

"By the way, one question."

"Yes sir."

"Did you smell anything unusual on Mayhew or on his clothes?"

"Smell? Why, no sir. I don't think so."

"Okay Bob, see you at ten."

Bob had almost reached his car when he saw Cordelia's flashlight in the alley. He walked to the rear of Mayhew's house and stood watching as she came toward him. Hull was in the middle of the alley, taking slow steps and swinging the flashlight beam from side to side. Her eyes were on the pavement.

"What's goin' on, Cordy?" Claggert asked.

Cordelia didn't look up from what she was doing, but her voice reached Claggert, low and soft. "Bob, I've asked you half a dozen times not to call me Cordy. Now, either you're too dumb to remember, or else you're a total asshole. Either way, I'm gonna make you a promise. Next time you call me Cordy, I'm gonna call you Shithead. And I won't care if it's in front of the Captain or the mayor or a bunch of Campfire Girls. Next time you say something like, 'Hey Cordy,' I'm going to say, 'Yes Shithead.' And I'm going to keep on saying it till I get tired of it. You do believe me, don't you, Bob?"

"Well, hell, Cordelia. If you're that touchy about it, I'll call you anything you want."

"Just call me by my name, Bob. See, I call you by your name. Your name is Bob and I call you Bob. See how that works?"

"Okay. Okay. Turned up anything yet?"

"Not yet," said Cordelia, easing up on him. "People next door say they heard a car back here. Couldn't see it because of the fence around their yard." She glanced at Claggert. "You just leave the Cold Room?"

"Yeah, I just reported to the Captain. I don't think he wants to discuss it till we meet tomorrow. I got my notes," he added, patting his police jacket.

Cordelia eyed the jacket and the civilian pants beneath it. "That's nice, Bob. By the way, I see you're still into cross dressing."

"Very funny. What are you got up for, a sunrise service?"

"What? In this old thing? Why, I just threw this on. Now, if you'll excuse me, I need to get back to my job."

"Okay, CID Two," Bob declared. He turned and walked stiffly toward his car. A sudden gust of wind whipped the ball cap from his head. Bob chased it down and stuffed it in his jacket pocket.

Shaking her head, Cordelia turned back to the alley and continued on her way.

Six

Billy walked across the wooden porch and rapped lightly on the front door. No answer. He started to knock again, but the door swung slowly inward. Lavonia Mayhew stood there in an old flannel nightgown. Her gray hair hung loose and the withered lips were pressed firmly together. Billy didn't imagine that was to keep from crying. That's just the way she kept them. Lavonia wouldn't cry. Walker had first met her better than ten years ago when he was a street cop. He and his partner had gotten a call to Lavonia's house, family disturbance. She was a Sutton then, married to a plumber named Maurice Sutton. When they arrived, the aforementioned Sutton was out in the back yard, cowering under a shrub. Lavonia stood over him with a baseball bat. As they came up, Billy heard Lavonia say, "Now Maurice, I won't brain you with this bat if you'll do one thing for me. Move your sorry ass inside the house and get your things together. Then get out of my sight and never show your face around here again." And Maurice had done it. As far as Billy knew he'd left town that same night, just drove away in his plumber's truck. Shortly after that, Lavonia, who had to be in her seventies, went to live with her younger brother. She dropped the Sutton name and signed everything "Lavonia Mayhew" from then on. She and Edwin, who was divorced, had lived in this house ever since. Over the years Billy had met her here and there and passed the time of day. Now in her eighties, she stared at the policeman with sharp, inquisitive eyes.

Walker smiled and said, "Hello, Miss Mayhew."

"Hello, Billy. Figured you'd get around to me sooner or later."

"Sorry I took so long. I was afraid the other witnesses might disappear on me."

"Did any of 'em see who did it?"

"No ma'am. I'm afraid they weren't much help."

Lavonia turned and said, "Come on inside, Billy."

Walker entered the dimly lit living room and Lavonia closed the door behind him. The wind blew against the door and she had to push hard to make it lock. She motioned Billy to a couch and then sat down in a straight-backed rocking chair. For a minute, neither spoke. They sat listening to the wind, moaning around the windows.

"Miss Mayhew, I'm very sorry about this. If you're not up to talking right now, I can come back later."

"It's all right. You've got a job to do and the sooner you get on with it, the better. Just catch him for me, Billy."

"You have no idea who it might have been?"

"Nope. I imagine it was a robber. Edwin always brought the store's money home in his pockets. Was the money missing?"

"I don't know. I'm going to look at the . . . I'm going to the hospital when I leave here. I'll find out then."

A large orange tabby cat walked across the living room floor. It looked at Billy and disappeared into the kitchen. The policeman followed it with his eyes.

"You want some coffee, Billy?" asked Lavonia. "I got some on the stove."

"I don't want to trouble you, Miss Mayhew."

"No trouble. It's ready. I'll be right back."

Lavonia went into the kitchen and Walker could hear the clinking of cups. The cat had come back to the kitchen doorway and was staring out at him. Walker's gaze wandered around the shadowy living room. The Mayhews lived in an old house and its interior showed the years. The wallpaper, once beige with red roses, had turned yellow and the roses were faded rust. The ancient fireplace, fireless now, looked sooty black inside, and the mantle above it was cracked and stained. Several pictures sat on the mantle. One showed some children, gathered around a dusty Model A Ford. In another, a man and woman sat on a porch swing. And, off to itself, stood a picture of Edwin Mayhew. He looked much younger and sported a dark mustache. Mayhew was leaning against a huge tree trunk and he was smiling. The sun shone on his face and you could see the white teeth.

"He was a nice-looking man back then," came the voice from behind him. "All the women thought so."

"Miss Mayhew, I . . ."

"Call me Lavonia. I always call you Billy." Lavonia handed him his coffee and they both returned to their seats.

"Mind if I smoke," he asked.

Lavonia shook her head and Billy lit a Winston. He took a deep drag and said, "Lavonia, what can you tell me about tonight?"

"Well, there ain't a lot to tell. I was by myself and I watched TV till about ten. Then I drank a glass of warm milk and went to bed. I don't know why, but I woke up at a quarter of two. Somehow, I knew Edwin wasn't in the house. I got up and looked in his room and the bed was empty. He usually gets in a little after twelve. This wasn't his poker night, so I figured something was wrong."

Lavonia stopped and looked at Billy. His dark brown eyes stared back at her with unwavering attention. His face remained impassive.

"Well, then I went over to the front window and looked out. I could see Edwin's car parked on the street, so I walked out on the front porch. That's when I spotted him. He was laying on his back in the front yard. I ran over to him and knelt down. I could tell that he was dead. There was blood all over his chest. He wasn't breathing and he was cold when I touched him. And his eyes, Billy. They were open, but they weren't seeing anything."

The old woman stopped talking and stared at the picture on the mantle. Billy got up and walked over to the smiling Mayhew. He picked up the photo and held it for a moment.

"Where was this taken, Lavonia?"

"Not far from here. Our daddy owned a farm. Me and Edwin would drive out on a Sunday. That elm tree was behind the house."

"What did you do after you touched him?"

"Touched him? Wha . . . ? Oh! I came back inside and called the police."

"Did you go back out to the yard?"

"Naw, I just sat here till they knocked on the door. I didn't want to go back out there."

"Are you sure you woke up at a quarter to two?"

"Yeah, Edwin gave me a clock. It was one of them things that shines the time up on the ceiling. I could tell what time it was as soon as I opened my eyes. Edwin gave it to me for my birthday."

They were both silent for a moment, and the knock on the door, though soft, made Lavonia jump.

"I'll get it for you," said Billy.

Cordelia was there. Billy stepped out on the porch and closed the door behind him. The wind had weakened, but the cloudbank had arrived, bringing a spatter of raindrops. They slanted down, glinting silver against the street lights. His assistant was brushing the moisture off her sleeves and shoulders.

"Sorry, Captain. I didn't find a thing."

"Okay. Go on home and get some rest. We'll meet in the office at ten. What time is it anyway?"

"It's four o'clock." She hesitated a moment. "You could use some rest, too."

"Soon as I look at the body."

"Want me to go with you?"

"No. No need." He gave her a tired smile and took a final drag on his cigarette. He started to flip it onto the front yard, but then thought better of it. Cordelia reached forward, took the butt between thumb and forefinger, and carried it out to the street.

"See you at ten," she called back over her shoulder.

SEVEN

Cordelia sat in the cruiser and watched her boss start back inside. His shoulders were slumped, but he straightened them and raised his head when he opened the door. Hull put the car in gear and pulled away from the curb. Driving home, she thought about Billy Walker.

The Captain had come to her three years ago and asked her if she'd like to be in CID, just like that. Her reply had been an immediate yes. CID people got more money and received special treatment. They were allowed to wear civvies. They had their own police cars and they reported only to Captain Walker. Walker reported only to the Chief, and from what Cordelia could see, he didn't do much of that. Mostly, it seemed the other way around.

Walker was a class act. No doubt about it. Hull had heard all the stories. He'd been an executive for some oil company, but he'd resigned and returned to his hometown. That was ten years ago. The company must have laid some heavy money on him because he'd bought a nice home and didn't do much of anything for six months. The general opinion was that he didn't have to worry about working again. Then, to the amazement of everyone, he joined the Medford Police Department. He was thirty-five years old and they made him radio dispatcher. That was the job they gave all the new boys until they went to the police academy at Camden. At the academy, Walker gave away ten years to the oldest recruit there, but he sucked up all the physical sessions and even set a few records.

Training was in two segments, academics and proficiency with weapons. Billy graduated number one in both of them. No one had ever done that before. Nobody had managed to do it since, either.

When Walker returned, promotions came quickly. In two years he was a lieutenant, and a year later the mayor and city council met, made him a captain, and placed him in charge of CID. The Chief didn't like being bypassed, but he was too intimidated by Billy to complain. Besides, he liked Walker, too.

The force's Criminal Investigations Department was a joke, but Walker proceeded to make it a model for the whole state. Investigators from other towns came to Medford for their training. She remembered they even sent some from Little Rock, for Christ's sake.

Memphis tried to recruit Walker, as did other cities. Some of the offers were great, but he turned them all down. Medford was his home and where he wanted to stay.

Cordelia was drawn to him and knew it, but she didn't quite understand why. It wasn't just his intellect or his accomplishments. What the hell was it then? Father figure? The young, black woman had to laugh at that. Natural leader? Sure, but that wasn't it either. No, she supposed it was just because she saw him for what he was, an honest to God original, complete within himself. Something else, too, in case anybody was interested. She'd probably take a bullet for Captain Billy Walker.

EIGHT

"Lavonia, if you had to make a list of people who might want to harm your brother, what names would you put down?"

Lavonia rocked slowly back and forth in her chair. "Billy, I caint make a list like that, 'cause I never knew that much about his life. My brother was private. He was private in everything. He didn't even tell me who he played poker with. And he never talked about business. I know he did other things to make money, things besides the liquor store, but I don't know what they were. He told me once that he had some investments." The old lady stared at Walker. "Now, I don't want to speak ill of Edwin, but I'll tell you something else. If he had even one friend, I don't know who it could be."

"All right, Lavonia."

"If the money's missing, it won't matter anyway, will it? I mean, then it's robbery and any low-down skunk could've done it."

"Yes ma'am. That could very well be true."

There must have been a pendulum clock in one of the other rooms, because Billy could hear the tick-tock, tick-tock of its regular beat, ticking off the minutes and the hours and the years, ticking off the span of a man's life.

"I don't even really know what kind of man he was," Lavonia was murmuring softly, "but he was a good brother."

Walker got slowly to his feet and placed his hand on the old woman's shoulder. "I won't bother you anymore tonight," he

41

said, "but I may need to talk to you later."

The sister looked up at him, her face filled with sadness. "I'll be here," she said.

Billy walked toward his car and noticed it was raining harder. Turning his collar up, he watched the fat drops splatter on the car roof. A scattering of soaked leaves lay in the yard and they glistened in the light from Lavonia's window.

On the way to the hospital, Walker had to turn the windshield wipers from slow to fast. He got out in a downpour and ran the few steps to the hospital entrance. Inside, he followed the hallway leading to the Cold Room. About halfway down, Reba Martin sat behind a desk, filling out a form. She looked up as Walker approached.

"Hi, Billy," she said.

"Hello, Reba. How are you?"

"Like I always am on the graveyard shift, tired."

"Well, you look pretty as ever," said Billy, giving her a smile.

"Why thank you, Captain," Reba answered as she led him down the hallway. If another man had said that, the nurse would have thought it flirtatious, but she understood that Walker was only being gallant. He was ever the gentleman.

They came to the Cold Room door and Reba inserted a key. "Kept it locked like you told me."

Billy nodded and stepped inside. He glanced back over his shoulder and said, "Thank you, Reba." The nurse closed the door behind him.

Walker stood over the body and let his eyes run slowly from the feet up to the head. The four bullet holes looked out of place, unnatural. Murder wounds always did, and, of course, they were. He bent over for a closer look. Not much blood, but the flesh around the holes was puffed up and split in several places. Picking up the evidence bag, he saw an amount written on the side. Of course, the Captain could have learned about the money back at Mayhew's house. All he had to do was ask Claggert. That went against Walker's practice. He believed it was best to know something only when it was time to know it. If he'd gotten that information from Claggert, then maybe he wouldn't have been as free and loose in his conversation with Lavonia. Walker opened the bag and reached inside for the wallet. Going through it, he found Edwin's driver's license. According to that, the victim was seventy-two. His birthday was in February. Walker closed the bag and took a step backward. He tilted his head sideways as he peered once more at the chest wounds. Then the Captain lifted Mayhew's shoes off the clothing and raised the bundle to his face. He took a deep breath before laying it back down by the body. Carefully, he replaced the old man's shoes. The smell of whiskey still lingered in his nostrils.

The eastern sky was lightening when Billy Walker reached home. He took off his shoes and tip-toed into the bedroom, holding them in his hand. Sammy was asleep on her stomach and the policeman quietly removed his clothing before lying down beside her. The bedside clock read five o'clock. Billy set the alarm for nine and sank back down on his pillow. Within moments, he was asleep.

NINE

Bob Claggert sat by himself in the CID office and waited for the others. He fiddled with a pencil and listened for the sound of footsteps on the metal stairs outside. He had arrived first intentionally, just one more proof to Walker that he was on the ball. He was sure that Walker knew it by now, but a little insurance wouldn't hurt. Bob knew that the Captain made note whenever anyone went that extra step. Walker might have some faults, but the man missed nada. He didn't even glance at my clothes last night, Bob thought, but I guarantee he noticed I had the police jacket on. And sooner or later, I'll hear about it. Well, when he sees me already at it this morning, that'll cancel out the uniform crap. I'm still ahead of the game. He wondered if Cordelia would get here before the Captain. That was his biggest obstacle, right there. Cordelia Hull had the seniority, and Bob had to admit that, for a woman and a nigger besides, she did a pretty good job. Hah! He remembered how his old man knocked the shit out of him once for saying "nigger."

"I don't want to hear that word come out of your mouth again," his pappy had yelled. "They caint help how they are and you ain't some redneck trash. Say 'colored,' goddammit."

Bob sat at his desk, fiddled with the pencil some more, and stared at the door. Well, one thing for sure, Cordelia wouldn't be around forever. All he had to do was keep his nose clean and wait. An old police sergeant had told him once that, sooner or later, if you watched a black person long enough, the "nigger would come out" and they'd steal something, or fail to show up for work, or spin out on drugs or liquor. At the very least, they'd forget and start talking some jive-ass nigger rap or join a civil rights protest. Bob had listened to what this student of the black psyche told him and had agreed with every word. Yep, sooner or later the nigger would come out on Cordelia, and little Bobby would be right there to see it.

Three metal desks stood in the CID room. Two were shoved together so the occupants faced one another. Claggert sat at one, which held a phone and three plastic trays marked IN, OUT, and FILE. The OUT tray was empty, but the other two held an assortment of envelopes and letters. Cordelia's desk, across from him, featured another phone, a small vase of flowers, and the same type plastic trays. All three trays were vacant. The Captain's desk stood alone at the rear of the room. It was slightly larger and held only a telephone and a nameplate, reading CAPTAIN WALKER. Bob had watched CID One at that desk. He'd bring a piece of work there, quickly finish it, and make it disappear. That is, when he worked at the desk, which wasn't often.

A wide work shelf ran along the left wall. Two computer consoles rested on the shelf with their keyboards at the ready. You could use them to call up almost any criminal record or other law enforcement information in the country. Not generally known was the fact that you could also call up a great many details about the average citizen. All you needed was a license plate number or some other scrap of data. Sometimes Bob would see a cute little fox driving around town and come back and punch in her LPN. There, glowing on the screen, would be her name, address, phone number, and a bunch of other stuff. Bob wrote the phone numbers down, but he hadn't gotten around to calling any of them yet.

A two-way mirror was built into the other wall and a door

marked INTERROGATION stood beside it. This opened into a small room containing a rough wooden table and four wooden chairs. A tape recorder and a metal ash tray sat on the table. Nothing else was visible. Another door, located along the same wall, displayed a sign reading EVIDENCE. This opened into an even smaller room crammed with guns, knives, dope, and stolen items, all the residue of crime. Everything from spent bullets to a pilfered wheelchair were neatly stored and labeled. All three rooms were without windows. Sunlight did not intrude here, and very little noise. Out of the silence, Bob heard talking and the sound of footsteps, coming up the stairs.

"Hello, Bob," said Walker, as he followed Cordelia through the door. "Been here long?"

"About an hour, Captain."

"Working on anything?"

"Just going over the notes I took last night."

The Captain turned his back to Claggert while he hung up his jacket, and Bob desperately tried to fish the notes out of a side pocket. For one heartsick moment, he thought he'd left them at home. Cordelia was looking at him, a slight smile on her face. The Captain went behind his desk and they both sat down.

He turned to Bob and said, "Any ideas on who did Mayhew in?"

"Well, it wasn't robbery," answered Claggert, glancing at his notes. "There was almost eight hundred dollars on the body. The killer had something else on his mind."

"You mean a different motive."

"Well, yessir."

"What do you think it might be?"

"I dunno. Maybe somebody had it in for him. He was a nice old man, but he could've had enemies."

Nice old man, thought Cordelia. If Edwin Mayhew was a

nice old man, I'm Tinkerbell. She could see where Walker was taking this and she waited for the hammer to fall on poor old Bob.

"You could be right about that, Bob," mused Billy in his quiet way. "But you're wrong in saying there had to be a different motive than robbery."

"But the money . . ."

"Yes, the money was still there, but that doesn't necessarily mean the motive wasn't robbery. Maybe it just wasn't a successful robbery. The killer could have been scared off before he got his hands in Mayhew's pockets. He may have seen something, heard something, and just took off."

"Yeah, I guess you're right," said Claggert.

"Bob has a point," Cordelia said, giving him a little boost, "but attempted robbery looks like our only route so far."

"Yes we have to work along that line until something else turns up. I've been here ten years," said Walker, "and seen close to twenty killings. Most were done on the spur of the moment, acts of passion, often by a family member. About a half dozen happened during a robbery. Not one was for revenge. Of course, there's always a first time."

Billy's voice died off and he was quiet for a moment, staring over their heads. "Mayhew followed a pattern," he went on. "He always closed at midnight and he usually took the day's receipts home with him. Usually, he reached home about the same time, and he went the same route every night. I believe the killer knew Edwin's pattern."

"You still want to go back over the crime scene?" asked Cordelia.

"Yes, but let's give Bob a chance. Maybe a fresh eye is needed. Bob go over there and walk it the way I showed you. Cover everything between the yellow tapes. Anything looking out of the ordinary, pick it up. Do you have evidence bags?"

"Got 'em in my car," said Claggert, heading for the door and stuffing the notes back into his pocket.

Billy watched the door close and lit up a cigarette. He slowly blew out smoke and looked at Cordelia.

"You didn't tell him about the whiskey," she said.

"Well, I didn't want to overload his mind."

That was the first time Hull had heard her boss say anything even vaguely disparaging about Claggert. It was vague, but coming from the Captain, it sounded like the voice of doom.

"The thing about the whiskey doesn't make sense, does it?"

"No," he said.

"Well, I guess we don't have to make sense of it. Just find the killer, right?"

"That's right," Billy said. "Anyway, if the killer was drinking from the bottle, he may have poured some on Mayhew, just for the hell of it."

"And while he was doing that, something scared him off."

"That's the way we're going to go with it, Cordelia. It's the logical course."

Cordelia saw it that way, too. She also saw the small frown, the furrow between the eyes. Logic was fine but he wouldn't neglect the illogical either. The frown deepened and Cordelia imagined that intuitive mind, tuning in and focusing on all the unanswered questions and the overall mystery of Mayhew's murder. They all said he was the best. Even the governor had said so, and maybe he didn't know anything about police work, but come on, the governor? Cordelia figured they were right, and when she thought about Mayhew's killer out there, she almost felt sorry for the poor bastard. She really did.

TEN

"I am Susan," she cried aloud, and her echo sounded along the empty corridor. I am Susan, she thought, and listened for the echo in her mind. Silence hung over her and then she heard, "I am Susan," and didn't know if it was her words or her thoughts or just the echo by itself. Someone had called her "Susie" once, but now she was Susan and she had been in this place for the longest time.

She knew that crazy people lived here. They stood out on the grass and made howling sounds beneath her window and she made the same sounds back. Sometimes she sang her song to them and sometimes she just screamed. Everyone but Maude was outside now and Maude was watching her walk up and down the long corridor. Maude's clothing was starched and white and she always stayed behind after the others had left. When they came back, Maude would take Susan back to her narrow room and lock the door behind her.

Susan walked to the entrance door and placed both hands on the smooth wood. There was a key slot but no door handle. She pushed hard, but the door wouldn't move. She felt that she would never go outside this door.

The young woman stood facing the entrance for awhile, her hands still pressed against its surface. A faded shift hung loosely on her body. She sank slowly to the floor and lay flat on her back. Then she carefully folded both arms across her chest and hummed a song her father taught her long ago when she was

Susie. The tune played inside her head. She knew all the words, too, and that was good because it was her very own song.

Maude heard, once again, the melody to "Yes, Jesus Loves Me" issue in a small girl's voice from the grown woman's throat. And she watched as Susan began rocking back and forth on the hallway floor, rocking back and forth and humming softly to herself.

ELEVEN

A chill wind blew across the police parking lot as Walker and Cordelia came out the side door and headed for Walker's car. Low, heavy clouds moved just above the treetops and a dark mist filled the air. Billy swung the big Ford out onto Court Street and drove toward Mayhew's house. As they approached, he could see Bob Claggert standing in the front yard, talking to Lavonia. She was up on the porch and went back inside before they reached the house. Bob saw them coming and stood waiting by the curb.

"Turn up anything?" asked the Captain as he parked beside him.

"Nossir, but I've still got the alley to look at."

"What did Miss Mayhew have to say?"

"Wanted me to give you a message. I think you're gonna like it." Bob's face wore a grin. "She's decided to put up a reward. A thousand dollars to whoever fingers Edwin's killer."

"I see."

"I figure that's enough to make one of his friends maybe not so friendly. Anyway, she just got back from the *Medford Gazette.* It'll be in the newspaper tomorrow."

"Well, it may be a help," said Walker.

Claggert gave the Captain a quizzical look.

"It's not all good news, Bob," he said, looking up at the deputy through the open window. "A public reward can cause a lot of hassle because it makes a lot more people aware of the crime. Some see it as a chance to name an enemy, settle a grudge, and perhaps make money at the same time. It also prompts a few false confessions. Sometimes, though, it produces the real article."

"How can you tell the real article from the false one?"

Billy stared at his man for a moment. A sensible question with no bullshit around it. Unusual. "You can't at first," he said. "You might suspect, but you won't know until you investigate each lead. That's where the hassle comes in. You waste a lot of time."

"Well, I got a knack for knowing when somebody's lying to me," stated Claggert, hitching up his pants.

"You may get some chances to test it," said the Captain with a hint of weariness in his voice. Beside him, Cordelia slumped down in her seat and stared out the opposite window.

"Bob, when you get through with the alley, I want you to go to every house on the block, both sides of the street. Ask the usual questions and be sure to ask if anyone saw the same car more than once. It would have been going slower than usual, or parked in two different places."

"The killer casing the joint, right?"

"Right," said Billy. Cordelia sighed.

They pulled away and she murmured, "A weekday night. After midnight. Not much chance. They were probably all asleep."

"Yeah, it's remote," replied Walker, picking up the radio mike.

"CID Three?" He glanced into the rearview mirror and saw Claggert hurrying toward his car.

"Go ahead, Captain," came the slightly breathless voice.

"Skip the Johnson house next door. I've already talked to them."

"Ten four."

"Still, four shots," she continued. "It was a twenty-two but it made *some* noise."

"Well, the killer muffled them a little. I think it was intentional. Each time, he placed the muzzle right up against Mayhew's chest."

Cordelia turned slowly in the seat. "Is it quiz time again?"

"Uh huh."

"You could tell by the wounds. The muzzle blast had puffed up the flesh and ripped it around the wounds."

"Very good, Sergeant."

"And the clothing would show burns."

"Of course."

Cordelia looked closely at her boss. "Any other little tidbits you haven't told me."

"Nope. Now you know as much as I do."

"That, I very much doubt." She noticed that Walker's face wore that small frown again. She decided not to press it. "Where are we going, *mon capitaine?*"

Walker had made a right turn and was heading south.

"Going to one of your favorite places," he said, "the Line. And there we'll do one of your favorite things, talk to Uh Oh Earl."

TWELVE

All the houses in the south part of Medford showed their age and most were run down and weather-beaten. This was not, however, the oldest part of town. That distinction belonged to the brick colonial, tree-lined, quietly dignified eastern part. But South Medford was the second oldest and ran a clear first in poverty, crime, and despair. In summer, its asphalt streets, hot, soft, and black, lay in sharp contrast to the wooden shotgun houses, bleached pale as old bones in the searing sun. A few chinaberry trees, spindly and thin-leafed, grew along the sidewalks, and it seemed that every other driveway held a disused, rusted-out vehicle, set up on blocks. In winter, the wind gusted across muddy, water-pooled yards, and swirled litter against the plastic-covered windowpanes. Many of South Medford's residents used space heaters and a cold snap generally brought business for the fire department. A small dwelling would blaze up with a fire engine answering the call, roaring up the street, tires bouncing in and out of the potholes, siren wailing, and usually arriving too late to be of any benefit. The dry wooden buildings burned quickly.

A railroad ran from east to west across this area and acted as a dividing line between the black and the white residents. Just north of the railroad lived the poor whites, and this part extended up into the town proper. The even poorer black community was grouped along the south side of the tracks, and that section had always been called the Railroad Line, or "the Line," by everyone in the town. The railroad itself was no longer in use and weeds grew among the crossties.

The Line, though within the city limits, was a place apart. The defunct railroad was its northern border and its inhabitants looked out across those twin rails into another country. Three streets ran across the railroad from Medford and disappeared between the ramshackle houses of the Line. The middle street, named Crescent, supported the neighborhood's few businesses. This amounted to a couple of bars, a liquor store, a small grocery, and a nightclub. All the regular shopping was done in Greater Medford.

Earl Gilbey owned the nightclub. The building had once been a railroad storage house, belonging to a gentleman named Snooks Brownlee. Snooks, in a series of failures to fill outside straights in one of Earl's floating poker games, came to owe him a few thousand dollars and offered the building in payment. Earl snapped it up. Everyone thought he was crazy, but Earl had plans and he could see the building's possibilities. Six months later, he opened up his Hawaiian Club and had been making good money from it ever since. So good, in fact, that he'd basically given up gambling, which had been his living before. Earl was more than happy to do it. Running three gambling dives had become a pain in the ass and hazardous besides. There was always some bastard ready to cut you because he didn't think he'd been given a fair shake, or one of your dealers was cheating you, or the competition was trying to move in. Also, he had the law to worry about. Tough, but before he became respectable, Earl had handled it all. He stood six-feet-four and weighed about two-eighty, a big man. A sizable belly protruded from lower chest to groin, but men who punched him there discovered that this was as firm as the rest of him. He fought hard, fast, and dirty and always seemed to make an appearance when trouble was brewing. Soon, just making the appearance was enough and it wasn't long before they gave him a nickname that stuck. If a game began getting a little too noisy or a player was becoming rebellious, someone would see Gilbey coming through the doorway and say, "Uh oh, there's Earl," and things would suddenly get peaceful again. Or he'd hear about some rogue poker game going on in one of the neighboring bars; the players would look up and see that immense black figure looming over them and you'd hear one of them mutter, "Uh oh, it's Earl," and the game would quickly fold. Sometimes, too, those words would be the last ones you heard before losing consciousness. So he became "Uh Oh Earl" everywhere along the Line and in some surprising places in Greater Medford also. He'd been an informant for Captain Walker for years and Billy had always found his information reliable. In return, Billy usually let Uh Oh's games function unmolested, and on the day Earl opened the Hawaiian Club, Billy told him to keep it clean and under control and he wouldn't see any blue uniforms. Earl hadn't seen any, but he had gotten an additional glimpse of Billy Walker's power.

Walker and Hull pulled in front of the Hawaiian Club and Billy spoke softly into the mike. "CID One, Medford."

"Go ahead, CID One," came the dispatcher's voice.

"CID One and Two are in the Line and at the Hawaiian Club. Will inform you when we leave."

"Ten four, sir."

Generally, CID people didn't tell dispatch their whereabouts; they preferred their movements remain secret. However, the Line was dangerous territory and Walker had issued standing orders that his people must always let the department know when they ventured inside its borders.

As Billy got out of the car, he noticed a short, thin black man standing in Earl's entranceway. He knew him only as "Slim," and while he watched, Slim disappeared into the darkened interior. "Well, Earl knows we're here," he murmured to Cordelia. They entered the building and he was struck, as always, by the size and cleanliness of the place. A polished wooden floor stretched off into the distance and supported a collection of tables and chairs. At the rear, a bandstand sat on the edge of a large dance floor and contained some drums, amplifiers, and microphones. Light sparkled off the chrome and tile bar, running along the right wall. Uh Oh stood behind it. He was working on a ledger, but looked up as the two investigators entered. A huge grin spread across his face.

"Well, well, well. If it ain't the illustrious Captain William R. Walker and Curvaceous Cordelia, his loyal assistant." Earl came around the bar and shook hands with both of them. "Looking good, Captain," he boomed. "And you, Miz Hull, are looking fine as wine."

Cordelia grinned at him. You couldn't help but respond to the man. It occurred to her, not for the first time, that if he had electric hair, he'd look like Don King, the fight promoter.

"Let me offer you a drink," said Earl, walking back behind the bar. "Knowin' that the captain drinks scotch. I got some twelve-year-old Glenfiddich here that ye canna put doon." The brogue was perfect, coming from the grinning black man, and Cordelia had to laugh.

"No thanks, Earl," she said. "Offer it sometime when we're off duty."

"As if you're ever off duty together. The captain's a happily married man, and besides, we don't want no race riots."

Walker had been quietly watching this exchange and Earl's face grew less jovial as he turned to face him. "I take it this is something other than a social call."

"Yes, it's business," said Billy.

"Sheila, we'll be in the office," Earl called to a short, plump woman wiping tables nearby. She nodded and Earl led the way to a side door. Billy saw Slim get up from a table and move back to the entrance. The trip was silent and swift, and Billy, suddenly, for no reason at all, sensed danger. He glanced around. There were no customers. Of course, it wasn't even noon yet. Still . . .

"Come on in, folks," Earl called from inside the office. Billy, with his neck hairs still prickling, followed Cordelia through the doorway.

Walker sat down in a leather chair facing Gilbey's desk. He looked over his shoulder at Hull and said, "Cordelia, keep an eye peeled out front. Earl and I will be finished in a moment." The young woman gave him a questioning look, but went outside and closed the door behind her.

Billy got up, reopened the door a crack, and peered outside. Cordelia was standing by the bar. She looked back at him and her eyebrows raised. Then, she quickly looked at Slim. Walker knew she was with him now. He left the door open and returned to his chair. Earl, sitting behind his desk, lit up a cigar and watched the Captain closely.

"You know about the killing last night, Earl?"

"Yeah, I heard about it. The liquor store owner."

"Shot in the chest. His sister found him in the front yard."

"Robbed?" asked Gilbey, blowing a stream of smoke across his desk.

"Could have been attempted," said Billy, "but he still had quite a bit of money on him."

"Well, that makes things tougher. If he'd got the old man's receipts, I might've heard something."

At the word, receipts, Billy's head came up, but Earl continued on. "You know, somebody who never has any money, and all of a sudden he starts spending a lot, it gets noticed."

"Who down here, besides you, knew that Mayhew carried store money home with him?"

"Nobody that I know of. Guess that makes me a suspect, huh?"

"You knew Mayhew for quite a while, didn't you Earl?"

"Yeah, we go back a ways. Edwin was into, well, other things besides selling booze. What I mean is, he'd branch out every once in a while. I don't think you know this, but he ran some gambling up in Big Medford."

"No, I didn't know it."

"Oh yeah, Old Edwin ran several card games, just like I did. Of course, his operation was more genteel, always inside a player's home, or in a hotel room, white folks gambling."

"You never told me any of this before."

"Well Captain," said Gilbey, placing his big forearms on the desk, "white folks gambling, white folks business. Our deal was that I'd keep you informed about happenings in the Line."

"So Mayhew would set up the location and invite all the right people."

"Uh huh, and from what I hear, some of those people were holding heavy money."

"What was Mayhew's end of the action?"

"Probably ten percent of every pot. That's the going rate."

"And he was doing this recently?"

"Yep, only more so."

"More so?"

The big club owner gave Walker a meditative look. "As you know, I've been wanting to sell my gambling interests, Captain. Well, guess who'd just took over all my poker games?"

"Edwin Mayhew?"

"Edwin Mayhew."

Walker sighed. "So now Edwin's dead and there's nobody in charge."

"Right! Of course that's okay up in Big Medford. The boys will probably get together and come up with some sort of gentleman's agreement."

"And down here?"

"Well, as you know, Billy," said Gilbey, "there ain't a lot of gentlemen in the Line."

"Somebody has to be in control."

"Totally in control."

"A tough man. I never knew Mayhew was that tough."

Uh Oh shrugged. "He was. And as bad as he needed to be."

"Bad as you," asked Billy with a grim smile."

"Modesty forbids, Captain, but Mayhew kept things in hand."

"So where do you stand in all this, Earl?"

"You mean, am I gonna be the man again?" Gilbey leaned back and crossed both hands behind his head. The cigar rested in an ashtray on the desk, curling rich smoke. "No, I'm not. Oh, I thought about it. Money's good. No question about that. I think I can still count on the understanding you and I have. But all the rest is different now. I got the club. It's making more than the games did and I don't have to worry so much about my physical well being, if you know what I mean. Also, when I took over gambling in the Line, it was my 'thang.' I created it and I didn't have to fight anybody for it. When I got out, I sold it to Edwin Mayhew, nice and businesslike. No problems. Now, Mayhew gets killed and there's a vacuum. The sharks are circling, so I'm gonna pass. It's all gotten . . . well, just a little more dangerous."

"Who are the sharks, Earl?" Walker was getting down to essentials.

Uh Oh didn't hesitate. "There's three. Nat Thomas, he owns and rents houses, the Line's slumlord. Wants it bad, but you can forget him. He'll either back out or get sent to the hospital. Not enough of a threat to get killed. The other two are Sleep Edwards and Eddie Partee. Edwards is a bad dude. Been in and out of prison a few times. I expect you've had some dealings with him."

"Yes, I believe I recall the gentleman. What about Eddie Partee?"

Earl nodded and said, "Most likely to succeed. Meanest of the three and a helluva lot smarter. He's flexible. Done everything from run whores to bootlegging. His problem is he can't keep a low profile. Believes in advertising."

Billy suddenly smiled and the club owner grinned back at him. "Yep, that's the one," he said.

Some time back, Eddie Partee had busted out in one of Earl's poker games to the tune of six hundred dollars. Evidently doubting the legalities of the game, he'd screamed something about "cheatin' motherfuckers" and swung on the dealer. This was bad judgment in two parts. First, the game happened to be on the up and up, and secondly, the dealer happened to be Slim. This same dealer also acted as Uh Oh's enforcer and sometime bodyguard. A slight, quiet man, Slim was unfailingly polite and soft spoken. He could also be as quick and deadly as a striking rattlesnake. None of the players saw Slim move. He certainly never got up from his chair, but suddenly Eddie Partee was flying backward from the table with bright blood spraying from a broken nose.

A few days later, this same gambler stood drinking in one of the bars, his nose covered by a large bandage. Eddie habitually wore a white windbreaker with the words *I'm Eddie Partee. Don't Fuck With Me* sewn across the back. Additional wording now appeared that further defined the legend. In a handwritten magic marker scrawl, he had added: *Please, Slim.*

"Well, he proved he's got a sense of humor," Billy chuckled.

"Yeah, and that's also a sign of intelligence," Gilbey warned. "Eddie's older now, and wiser. Probably, he's meaner. I wouldn't underestimate him."

"Oh course, we still have to consider you."

"Told you, Captain. I'm out of it."

"Yes, but the trouble is you're having a communication problem, aren't you Earl? You know you're out of it, and now I know it, but the circling sharks don't know it. They won't listen to you either, will they? They think you're sandbagging them."

Gilbey picked up his cigar and relit it. He tilted his chair back and blew smoke at the ceiling.

"And you're expecting trouble," Billy continued. "You're not encouraging customers this morning and you've slipped the leash on Slim."

"I know that everything they say about you is true," acknowledged Earl. "Still, it's always a pleasure to watch that brain in action. By the way, I'd have told you about Mayhew's purchase, and all the rest of it, before the day was out."

Walker nodded and stood up. "Well, you need to be watchful, Earl."

"Always am, Billy. Always am. Speaking of being watchful, you can call in your lookout now."

"Let's go join her. I'm finished."

Both men walked out of the office and Cordelia peered at them as they approached the bar. Slim glided back into the room and leaned up against the front wall. He stuck a cigarette between his lips and was about to light it when the window beside him crashed inward. A spray of glass filled the air and a quart whiskey bottle came flying through the midst of it, a flaming rag hanging from the neck. The bottle spun over and over and crashed to the wooden floor in an explosion of fire and smoke. There was a loud whooshing sound and Billy could feel a blast of heat across his face. He leapt for the doorway, but Slim was already there and disappearing through it. Billy heard a car engine rev and then die, and when he reached the doorway he saw a red Ford Bronco parked across the street. Slim was beside it and leaning into the driver's window. He straightened and flipped something shiny over his shoulder. Car keys glinted in the sunlight and landed with a clink on the sidewalk. Slim placed a small foot on the side of the Bronco and gave a heave to whatever he was holding. All of a sudden, the driver came flying through the open window, and Slim, stepping sideways like a bullfighter, watched him thud against the asphalt. Walker drew his revolver and covered him as he struggled to his knees and tried to rise. The man reached under his sports jacket, and suddenly the gun became very steady in Billy's hands. It was then that Slim saved his victim's life. The same foot that had been placed on the Bronco for leverage now blurred through the air and thudded against the driver's head. Billy watched him slump back to the street and then he stared at Slim. The small, dark fighter, outlined against the gleaming Bronco, still held his right foot suspended. He lowered it gently, while his body remained fixed and still. Then, Slim's head pivoted slowly around, and Walker observed the smile of satisfaction, spreading across his face.

Thirteen

Back inside the Hawaiian Club, Earl, with the help of Sheila, had managed to put out the fire. A huge burned and blackened circle appeared on the floor and dark smoke drifted above it. Earl had turned on the ceiling fans and their blades revolved slowly, eddying the smoke around and pushing it back downward. A smell of burnt kerosene and oil filled the building. Earl stood before the burned patch with a fire extinguisher dangling from one huge paw. His face held a sad and almost resigned look but the eyes signaled a different message. They were narrowed to slits and red sparks seemed to glint from them. He heard footsteps and turned to see Billy coming back in the door. Cordelia walked behind him. She had been behind him out on the street, too. His assistant was only just now putting the little Chief's Special back in her handbag. They stopped at the bar and surveyed the damage.

"Got the fire out, huh," said Walker. Cordelia wrinkled her nose and gave a small cough.

"Yep," Earl's voice was very soft. "Good thing it didn't land up against a wall or near any curtains. You get Mister Molotov?"

"I've got him now. He's locked inside our car. Slim had him first."

"Where's Slim now, Captain?"

"Out by the car."

"Probably wasn't any need to lock it, then. I doubt if your

man wants to get out."

Walker gave a thin smile. "Probably, you're right," he said.

Gilbey placed the extinguisher next to the bar and they all sat down at a nearby table. Sheila brought three ice-filled glasses over and filled them with Coke from a large plastic bottle.

"Okay," said Earl, "I'm gonna make a guess. The guy in the car is either Sleep Edwards or somebody who works for him."

"What makes you think that?" asked Billy.

"Because, what just happened here is too dangerous for Nat Thomas and too stupid for Eddie Partee."

"Well, it's Sleep himself," said Billy.

"What's going to happen now?" asked Earl.

"We're going to take him uptown and book him for arson and assault with a deadly weapon."

"Assault with a Molotov cocktail, or something else?"

"Both," said Walker, taking Sleep's .38 revolver out of his pocket and laying it on the table.

"Do I need to come with you?"

"No, they're Class A felonies. You don't have to charge him, Earl. You'll be subpoenaed when the trial comes up and you can testify to what you saw."

"It'll be my pleasure." A rumbling chuckle came from deep in his chest. "You know, Sleep is not only stupid, he's some kinda unlucky, pulling something like this with you two inside."

"I'd say he was even more unlucky that Slim was inside," said Cordelia. She had seen what her boss had seen, out by the Bronco.

Heading back to the station, neither policeman did much talking, and their prisoner didn't speak at all. A large bump swelled from the side of his head. He slumped in the back seat and gazed at his captors through the wire partition. Sleep's hands were manacled behind him and he leaned forward in the seat to take some of the strain off. Cordelia glanced back as the prisoner shifted around. This was one rule she knew the captain was almost fanatical about. You always, always handcuffed your prisoners. No matter how weak or ineffectual they seemed to be, no matter how trivial the crime. If Walker saw you with them, they'd better be handcuffed. Even Bob Claggert had never broken that rule and Hull reflected that it was a good rule not to break.

Walker pulled into the station parking lot and stopped next to the building. Cordelia went ahead to open the door, while Billy brought Edwards along, his hand grasping the prisoner's elbow. They entered and went upstairs to the CID room. There, Cordelia brought some forms out of her desk and called up Sleep's record on the nearest computer. Edwards's given name was what she noticed first . . . Murfred Edwards. Murfred? No wonder he had a nickname. Probably latched onto it as soon as he could. She glanced up to see the Captain lead Edwards into the interrogation room and close the door behind them. Hull got up and walked over to the two-way mirror. Walker and Edwards were seated across the table from one another. She reached over and flipped a switch beside the mirror. The machine inside was now recording, but the suspect wouldn't be aware of it. Cordelia knew they were now on sticky legal ground. Everything had to be done according to the letter of the law. So far, Edwards's rights hadn't been violated. When two people were being recorded, only one of them had to know about it, and of course, Walker knew. Just then, the Captain looked over at the mirror and gave a minute shake of his head. Hull knew what that meant. She reached over and turned the recorder back off. After watching the two men for a moment longer, she returned to her desk.

"Sleep, I'm going to give you a 'rights' form to fill out," said Billy. He reached in a drawer under the table and withdrew a sheet containing a list of questions. It was the old familiar litany.

"Do you understand that you have the right to remain silent? Do you understand that anything you say can be used against you in a court of law . . ." Underneath each question a space appeared for the suspect's response. A waiver statement showed at the bottom of the page, along with spaces for the suspect's and the interviewer's signature. If the suspect signed, he gave up the rights he'd just read about. The suspect's immediate inclination was, of course, to tell his questioner to stuff it.

The Captain held the form in his hand and continued, "Now Sleep, we've been through all this before and you know as well as I do that you can tell me to go to hell and not say a word. That's your right."

"Go to hell, then," said Sleep in a loud voice.

The prisoner slumped down lower in his chair and glared at Walker. His slacks and jacket were torn and bore black marks from the asphalt in front of Earl's place. The knot on his shaved head looked shiny in the bright light.

Walker walked around the table and stood behind the prisoner. He reached down, removed the handcuffs from Edwards's wrists, and tucked them in his pocket. He remained behind Sleep and spoke in an almost bored tone. "Well, that's about what I expected you to say. Given a choice between smart and stupid, you're always going to choose stupid, aren't you, Sleep? I've got you cold. You know that. Even you aren't that stupid. You tried to burn Uh Oh's place in front of two cops, for Christ's sake. Then you try to pull a gun on them. That's arson and assault with a deadly weapon and that's assault on a police officer. You know, this state has a special provision for that. It's right up there with attempted murder."

Walker came back around the table and sat down in front of his prisoner. Edwards rubbed his wrists and eyed his captor warily.

"Was it attempted murder, Sleep?" the Captain softly asked.

"Were you going to use that pistol on me? Because, if you were, this conversation is over." Billy tossed the 'rights' form in front of Edwards. "I really won't give a damn whether you sign that or not, and I won't be interested in anything you've got to tell me. You know who I am and what I can do. If I decide that gun was for me, your ass is headed for prison and you'll die there."

"This don't call for no lifetime sentence," exclaimed Edwards, but his voice held a slight quaver.

"For you it does. You know, Sleep, there are lots of inmates up at Tucker Penitentiary who'd love to have me put in a good word next time their parole comes up. Real hard cases, some of them. We understand each other, because sometimes I can be a hard case, too. They might decide to make you their 'joy boy' for awhile, that is until they get the word to slit your stomach open."

"I never meant to shoot you," mumbled Edwards. "I was jist tryin' to git loose from Slim."

Walker stared at him, then shrugged and said, "Okay, I'm going to believe you. Now here's the deal. You sign the form and answer my questions. If you do, and if they're truthful answers, I'll drop the assault thing. You're going up on the arson charge, but you'll do a lot less time and the time won't be so bad. I can handle that sort of thing also."

"I got to think about it. I ain't had my phone call yet. I might need to talk to my lawyer."

"Up to you, Murfred. I'll be in the next room for a few minutes." Billy took a chrome Cross pen out of his shirt pocket and laid it on top of the form. "If this is signed when I come back, I'll know we have a deal. If you ask for your lawyer, I'll know we don't."

Sleep Edwards stared down at the form, then leaned back and crossed his arms. After a moment, he gave a sigh and tenderly stroked the bump on his head. Billy got up and left the room.

He stepped over to Hull's desk and handed her a handkerchief. "Cordelia, do something for me. Dampen this and take it in to Sleep. Go straight up to him and hold it against his head. Just hold it there for a moment and don't say anything to him. Then come back out."

The captain watched through the two-way mirror as Cordelia followed his instructions. Her left hand held the cloth against Edwards's head and her right hand rested lightly on his shoulder. She took the cloth away and came back through the door. Sleep Edwards followed her with his moisture-laden eyes.

Billy waited a few minutes more, then reentered the interrogation room. The "rights" form now lay on his side of the table and he picked it up. Murfred Edwards's signature appeared on the bottom.

FOURTEEN

"Prior to this interrogation, I need to tell you that our entire conversation is being recorded and the recording will be used in evidence against you."

Billy spoke in a monotone. Cordelia had walked back to her desk after flipping the switch again. She began typing a confession form for Sleep to sign. The Captain had told her to keep it confined to arson.

"Do you understand what I've just told you?"

"Yeah."

"Please state your full name?"

"Murfred Edwards."

"What's your middle name?"

"Ain't got one. Everybody calls me 'Sleep.' "

"Where were you arrested?"

"Out in front of Earl's Hawaiian Club."

"And this arrest occurred at approximately ten a.m. Would you agree with that?"

"Uh huh."

"Let the record show that the arresting officers were Captain William R. Walker, head of the Criminal Investigations Division of the Medford Police Department, and Sergeant Cordelia Hull, investigator for the CID. I am Captain Walker and I'll conduct this interrogation. Now Sleep, tell us in your own words what you did to cause your arrest."

Edwards rolled his eyes around at the Captain, but said nothing. Walker fixed him with a stare and remained silent. The seconds ticked away.

"Mister Edwards, I will repeat the question. What had you done to cause your arrest?"

"I threw a bottle through a window."

"What kind of bottle and whose window?" The Captain's voice bore a trace of impatience.

"It was a whiskey bottle and the window belonged to Earl Gilbey. It was at his Hawaiian Club."

"What was in the whiskey bottle?"

"Gasoline and oil."

"And the neck was stuffed with a burning piece of cloth, isn't that right?"

"Yeah."

"A device commonly known as a Molotov cocktail."

"I guess so." Earl spoke in a resigned voice.

"That concludes this interrogation," said Billy. He got up, went outside, and turned the recorder off. Then he walked over and sat down across from Cordelia.

"How's it going?" he asked.

"Almost finished. Think he'll sign it?"

"I think so. Bring it inside as soon as you're finished." The Captain got up and returned to his prisoner. He pulled out his pack of Winstons and offered one to Edwards. Sleep took a cigarette, brought a box of matches from his coat pocket, and lit up. Walker leaned back in his chair and lit his own. The air between them moved with the smoke.

"Something else I want to ask you, Sleep."

"What's that?" The dark face took on a defensive look.

"Why did you throw that bottle?"

"How come you didn't ask that before?"

Billy blew out smoke and regarded Edwards for a moment. "Because, as far as the arson charge is concerned, it didn't actually matter. You did it. You admit doing it, so the motive wasn't a factor."

"Then, why you askin' me now?"

"No reason, really," the Captain replied. "Especially since I already know the answer. You thought Gilbey was going to resume control of the gambling. You want to be in control. You were trying to scare Gilbey off."

"If you say so." Sleep took the cigarette from his mouth and tapped it on the edge of the table. His hand trembled slightly.

"I do say so," said Billy, "because it's the truth. And here's another truth for you. The idea of someone like you trying to frighten Uh Oh Earl is like Michael Jackson trying to scare Mike Tyson. What the hell is wrong with you, anyway?"

Walker looked up to see Cordelia standing with the typed confession in her hand. He hadn't heard the door open.

"Well, in a way you're lucky. You got one of the charges dropped and the other one will put you away just long enough for Earl to stop thinking about killing you."

Cordelia leaned over and placed the papers in front of Edwards. A pen lay on the top.

"Sign it," demanded the Captain. Or else, Cordelia finished in her thoughts.

Sleep thumbed to the second sheet and signed at the bottom. He didn't bother to read them. Cordelia checked the signature, then handed the sheet to her boss. Billy signed it, and without looking up said, "Why did you kill Edwin Mayhew?"

Edwards stared at Walker for a moment with a puzzled look on his face. Then the eyes went wide and a strangling sound emerged from his throat. "Oh hell no," he yelled, half rising from his chair. "Naw! Fuck! Naw! You ain't laying that on me. Don't start that shit with me." Cordelia pressed down on the prisoner's shoulder and he slowly sat back down, still glaring at Walker. There was fear and hatred in the look.

"Why not start that shit with you, Edwards?" Billy's voice was calm. "You wanted Earl out of the way so you firebombed his nightclub. Prior to that, you wanted Mayhew out of the way so you shot him. Both for the same reason, so you could have the gambling. Looks like a pattern to me."

"Throwing a firebomb through a window and killing somebody is two different things," said Sleep. "I ain't never killed nobody."

"Well, just so I'll start to believe you," said Walker, "where were you last night between midnight and one o'clock?"

"I was home in bed."

"Who was with you?"

"Nobody. I live alone."

"Not much of an alibi, is it Sleep?"

Edwards mashed his cigarette out in the ashtray and placed both hands, palms down, on the table. His voice took on a plaintive tone. "Now you got to believe me, Cap'n. I heard about Mayhew this morning, down in the Line. We all did. I don't know nothing about it. Sure, I want the gambling. There's lots of money in it. A dude named Eddie Partee wants it too. Did you know that? Maybe you ought to talk to him. Eddie wants it bad and that sumbitch is crazy."

"Let me ask you something, Sleep. What makes you think I'd let you or Eddie run gambling in the Line?"

"Well, I didn't know. I sure was aiming to ask you first. I know that's what Uh Oh did."

Billy regarded his man with a thoughtful stare, seeing subtlety in Edwards where none had been evident before. "Officer Hull," he called through the door. Cordelia opened it. "Please take Mister Edwards downstairs to the holding cell."

Sleep stood up and Cordelia attached the handcuffs. She was guiding him toward the door when the prisoner turned back to Walker. "I never done it," he said. "Get Partee. That motherfucker done it."

"Oh I'm sure Mister Partee and I will be talking," said Billy. "By the way, who told you about Mayhew?"

"June Bug Jackson," replied Edwards. "You know him?"

Billy turned away without answering.

Going down the stairs, Sleep asked again, "Does he know who I'm talking about?"

"Sure," said Cordelia. "Last time I busted June Bug was a month ago. He was selling bits of chalk to the uneducated down in the Line. Told them it was crack. Two customers were in the process of cracking his head when I made the arrest."

"Yeah, but did the Captain meet him?"

"Not that time." Cordelia ushered Sleep into the holding cell and slammed the metal door behind him. She knew what he was trying to do. The more people for Walker to consider, the less heat on Sleep Edwards.

"When did he meet him?" asked Sleep as she walked away.

Cordelia glanced over her shoulder and said, "Oh, didn't I mention it. They were in the Jaycees together."

Night was drawing near and Billy drove slower than usual, only partly conscious of the familiar streets leading home. The overcast sky had turned to charcoal and a slow rain continued to fall. The windshield wipers in front of him moved back and forth, sweeping right and left before the empty, rainy street. He could hear the ticking sound as they hit their stops and started back again. It reminded him of something he had heard much earlier in this long, long day. Tick. Tick. And then he remembered what it was. It sounded like Mayhew's clock, the pendulum clock that sat in Mayhew's hallway and measured Mayhew's life.

The remainder of the day had been pretty much routine. He and his assistant had chuckled over Edwards's mention of June

Bug Jackson. June Bug of the chalk bits, who slept in dark alleys and prowled the Line like a homeless cat. But June Bug heard things and saw things and Walker made a mental note to look him up.

Claggert had come in later from interviewing Mayhew's neighbors. Billy read his deputy's notes but they didn't reveal much. Mayhew was murdered late. Most of the people were asleep. And, Billy thought, Bob was not a very good interrogator. Give him his due, he was probably no worse than most cops. They asked, but they didn't really listen, and if they listened, they heard only the words. Sometimes a witness's silences could tell you a lot, or the tone of their voices, or the way they moved their eyes. And they must sometimes be led to remember, to recall what had become lost to their consciousness. Walker was a consummate interrogator.

Cordelia opened the door to her apartment and flipped on the wall switch. It was comforting to see the familiar possessions. Her bed was unmade but everything else looked neat and orderly. She sat down on the couch and slipped off her boots. Stretching both long legs out in front of her, she gave a soft sigh and wiggled her toes. What a day! It had ended quietly enough. Claggert had come in and the Captain had sent him home early. She and the Captain had gone over some other cases, then left together. Cordelia had watched her boss drive out of the lot, reflecting on how little insight she had into this reserved and self-contained man. The doorbell sounded and Hull went to answer it.

"Cordelia! It's yo great big Cadillac in de parkin' lot ah love."

Bubba Henson stood there with a single rose in one hand and a bottle of wine in the other. His dark face glowed from the lamplight and an irrepressible good humor. Cordelia fondly gazed at her fiancée and stepped back to let him enter. "You're a mass of contradictions, you know that? Successful black attorneys do not quote lines from *Amos 'n' Andy,* and they are not, repeat not, nicknamed 'Bubba.' "

Detecting a note of tiredness in her voice, Bubba took her in his arms. "Just get off work?"

"Yeah, I was about to take a shower."

"Good idea," he said. "Tell you an even better idea. Why don't *we* take a shower?"

"Umm hmm," murmured Cordelia, as thoughts of this day faded from her mind.

Bob Claggert sat in front of Mayhew's liquor store. He rolled his car window down and stared at the darkened front. Who did it? Who killed the old man? Nobody on Mayhew's block was any help. They were mostly older people and they went to bed early. Edwin Mayhew had been just like them, a poor old guy who minded his own business and never hurt anybody. Bob thought about the times he'd spent with Mayhew inside this building and he felt his throat tighten up. Then he felt a surge of anger, because he knew, in general, who the killer was. Everybody did. It was some nigger from the Line, maybe more than one nigger. They'd shot Edwin for the hell of it and left him to die. Probably every nigger in the Line knew who it was, too. Then, Bob remembered that one of them was in jail tonight. Being in jail might make this one more likely to talk. Claggert suddenly grinned and started his car. He made a sweeping turn and headed back toward the police station. Sleep Edwards just might have something to tell him.

FIFTEEN

Walker had instituted a procedure for weekend duty in the CID. One investigator came in and worked cases. The other two took off. However, those two remained on call, and if an emergency arose, they were summoned in. Walker had told them, "Arrange it so we can reach you quickly." How quickly, he didn't say, but over a period of time, it became accepted that the department better have you on the phone within thirty minutes. Cordelia remembered that once a dispatcher had tried for over three hours to reach her. She'd left word where she'd be on her answering machine, but the damn thing had broken down. No matter. She didn't even want to remember her subsequent time with the Captain. He didn't say much, but after a while, she felt like she was bleeding.

Weekend duty was of course rotated, and this Saturday morning Billy manned the post. He sat at his desk, and for a moment considered calling Cordelia in. After all, Mayhew's murder was only thirty-three hours old. Then he thought better of it. Yesterday had been a full one for them all, and just now things seemed quiet. Walker knew it was the lull before the storm. He lifted a cup of coffee to his lips and frowned. Lavonia's reward notice would come out in the paper this morning. God knew what that would bring.

Right now, everything was blowing in the wind. True, he had an arrested suspect, but Walker knew the arson charge, now pending against him, would be the only charge. Edwards wasn't the type, of that he was positive. Not in a million years could Sleep have done that murder.

He heard footsteps coming up the metal stairs, and in a moment Bob Claggert came through the door. Billy wasn't surprised to see him. Claggert often came by the office on his off days, and Walker knew these visits always occurred when the boss was on duty.

"Hello, Bob." Billy glanced up at Claggert and saw instantly that his man was bursting with news. Bob's grinning face was flushed pink and the pale blue eyes shown mistily.

"Hi Captain," he said in a tight voice. "I got something to tell you. I know who killed old man Mayhew."

Walker gave him a level stare and said nothing. Bob jammed both hands in his pants pockets and leaned forward.

"I came by here last night to check up on a few things. Then I remembered we had Sleep Edwards in jail, so I talked to him for a few minutes." Claggert saw the Captain frown, so he hurried on. "Sleep told me Eddie Partee did the shooting, and when I asked him how he knew, he said because he saw him. He was afraid to tell you yesterday because he was scared of what Eddie might do to him. He was also afraid you'd think that he and Eddie were in it together."

"Did Sleep tell you that, too?"

"Almost word for word, Captain."

"Well," said Walker, coming from around his desk. "I guess I'd better have another talk with Mister Edwards."

Sleep Edwards lay on his bunk, staring up at the ceiling. One hand rested on his stomach. A cigarette, held between the fingers, sent a thin stream of smoke upward into the dead air. He heard footsteps approaching and turned his head to see Captain Walker and his assistant come up to the bars. The radio dispatcher walked over and opened the door. Billy and Claggert entered and sat on an empty bunk across the way. Sleep swung his feet around and sat facing the two men. His eyes darted back and forth between them. The Captain gave his prisoner a stern look.

"Forget to tell me something yesterday?"

"Well, I caint say as how I forgot, Cap'n. I guess I was just scared to."

"Tell me now," demanded Walker.

"I wasn't home all night, like I said. For awhile, I was parked out on Plaza Street, just down from Edwin Mayhew's house."

"What were you doing there?"

"Waiting to talk to Mayhew. See Cap'n, it looked like Edwin was gonna control the gambling now. Word was that Uh Oh had sold out to him and I'd already seen him around the games, giving everybody that hard look of his. The dealers were taking orders from him, too. Something about that old man, cold motherfucker, ain't no doubt. Anyway, like I told you before, I still wanted the play and I wasn't sure Mayhew was top dog. Maybe Earl was just using him for a front. If he was, I might still stand a chance. If not, I figured maybe Edwin could use a right-hand man. Somebody to deal at the rough games and sorta keep things in line. Also, Edwin might need a little protection now and then."

A faint look of amusement crossed the Captain's face. "You wanted to be another Slim."

Sleep glanced up, caught the look, and smiled. "Naw, ain't nobody can be another Slim, but I could have made myself useful. Anyway, I had to know what was going on, and I figured that if I got Mayhew alone, he might tell me."

"Why didn't you just ask Earl."

"Shit, Captain, you know what Uh Oh would say. 'Aw naw, I ain't got nothing to do with that now. Mayhew bought it all.' And all that time the motherfucker be in it up to his eyeballs.

Earl Gilbey ain't never told the straight about nothing."

"So you were waiting for Edwin to come home."

"Yessir. I knew what time he locked up, and a little after midnight, here he come. I watched him make a U-turn and park in front of his house. He got out and started across his yard. I started to get out, too, when I saw somebody come around the corner of the house. He was carrying a rifle and he walked up to Mayhew and let fly, four shots right in the chest. I sunk back down in my car, 'cause I recognized who it was and I knew he'd recognize me." Edwards paused and looked expectantly at the Captain.

"I imagine you're going to tell me who it was," said Walker.

"Eddie Partee, Captain. Eddie Partee, standing there with the street light full on his face. He looked over at my car, but he couldn't see inside."

"What did he do then?"

"Now, that's the funniest thing," Edwards said, placing both hands on his knees. "Eddie took a swig from a whiskey bottle and started pouring some of it on Mayhew. Then he stuck the bottle in his pocket and ran back around behind the house."

Billy's face had remained expressionless during the interview, but suddenly his head lifted and Sleep found himself staring into dark and depthless eyes.

"Why do you think he did that?" came the soft voice.

" 'Cause he's a mean bastard, that's why," exclaimed Sleep. "Got no respect for the living or the dead."

"Ain't nobody gonna argue with you on that one," said Claggert.

Walker glanced at his deputy, then turned his gaze back to Edwards.

"What did you do after Eddie left?" he asked.

"I left, too, just as fast as I could."

"Why didn't you call the police?"

"Come on, Captain. Here I am, a black man on a white man's street, where a murder's just been done, and besides that, you know I'm on parole. The PO-lice would have throwed me in jail."

"So why are you telling me now?"

" 'Cause now I'm in jail, and no offense, Captain, but it's always easier to pin an extra charge on somebody you already got than to go out and find somebody new to slap it on. Besides, you already accused me once. I'm fessing up now, so you won't start thinkin' about that again. Eddie Partee done it. I seen him do it, and I might be scared of him, but I'm more scared of settin' in the electric chair."

"You were in jail yesterday. Why didn't you speak out then?" Billy asked, surprised by the anger in his voice.

Sleep lowered his voice and mumbled, "I needed to think about it."

Walker looked over at Claggert, who wore a self-satisfied smile. He turned back to Edwards. None of this rings true, he thought. It's just not solid.

In the Captain's singular brain, a tale told to him was either wispy or solid. If solid, you could grasp it in both hands and turn it around and it wouldn't change. Squeeze it, it would remain the same, unalterable and solid. This was a wispy story, the kind you could stick you hand in and stir it around and the story would swirl into anything you wanted it to be. This wasn't to say that Sleep didn't sound convincing. He did. He knew about the rifle and how many shots were fired. He knew about the time and place, but all this he could have heard about by the time Claggert talked to him. Lots of people knew the details. Policemen knew. The medics knew some of them, and all these people were prone to talk. Hell, the newspaper probably printed all that information this morning.

But Edwards knew the "holdback."

81

In every murder, Walker always held back one bit of information that only the killer would know: the type of weapon used, or location of the wound, or maybe something left at the scene of the crime. A holdback weeded out the vindictive witnesses and the false confessions. In this case, the holdback was the pouring of whiskey on Mayhew's body. Only three people should know about that: he, Cordelia, and the murderer. Even Bob Claggert hadn't been told. Of course, an eyewitness to the murder would know.

Edwards was lying. Walker, with a perception that seldom failed him, knew that Edwards was lying. And tangible discrepancies in Edwards's story bore this out. Sleep said he'd held back out of fear, but he was talking now and nothing had changed since his arrest to make him less afraid. And why was he waiting at midnight on "a white man's street" when he could have walked into Mayhew's liquor store anytime before closing and talked to him.

But Edwards knew the holdback.

How did he know? Walker remembered talking to Cordelia last night and telling her what it would be. Telling it to Cordelia was like telling it to a corpse. Cordelia wouldn't talk. Walker knew he was missing something. He needed to color outside the lines. That was the example he used in his classes, held for the state, on investigative procedure. "When you were in grammar school," he'd tell the students, "your teacher would tell you to always color within the lines. You'd do it and the picture would be nice and neat and your teacher would be pleased. That started you on the road to restrictive thinking. As investigators, you've got to let your mind run free. Go outside the lines. Human behavior is not nice and neat. It's random and unpredictable and sloppy, especially if it's violent behavior." A grim smile touched the Captain's lips as he studied the man before him.

All that was very fine, he thought. But one basic fact

remained. The man before him knew about the holdback.

"Officer Claggert," Walker said as he rose from the bunk. "Go upstairs and get Eddie Partee's address from the files."

"Yes sir," Bob responded and called for the dispatcher. She came and unlocked the door.

"We'll need a uniform," Billy said to her as they exited the cell. "Tell him to meet us out front."

"Ten four, Captain," said the dispatcher in the radio jargon they habitually used. "It'll be Officer Simpson."

Billy looked down into the pretty upturned face. "How are things going, Sally?"

"Not bad, Captain. Hanging in there."

"I keep hearing good things about you," he said.

Sally Harris watched Walker and Claggert go out the door. She started back to her desk and caught a glimpse of herself in the hallway mirror. "What the hell," she exclaimed to the grinning face. "One pat on the back from Walker and you turn into a schoolgirl. Get real." Nevertheless her grin stayed in place.

SIXTEEN

"Bitch," screamed Eddie Partee. "Motherfucking bitch," he screamed once more and hurled the nylon gym bag at Ladonna's head. A bundle of twenties, neatly bound in banker's binder, flew out and bounced along the floor. The other bundles, totaling forty thousand dollars, remained inside, so the bag made a satisfying whump when it hit Ladonna's face. She held a hand to her cheek and backed toward the kitchen doorway.

"Eddie, baby, don't," she whined. "I swear I don't know nothing about it. I didn't even know what was in the bag till just now. You got to believe me, baby."

Eddie started toward her with his right hand raised. "Uh uh," he grunted. "You got to believe me. You got to believe that I'm gonna kill your motherfucking ass." Coming up to Ladonna, he cracked her across the face with his open palm and she fell shrieking to the floor. Partee watched her lying there, then slowly pulled a massive Browning .45 from the waistband of his pants. He pointed it at her and said, "There's just one thing I want to know before I blow your goddamn head off. Where's my nine thousand dollars?"

Ladonna Smith looked up at her lover and knew that unless she did some fast thinking and then some fast talking, she was a dead woman. How the hell had she gotten herself into this mess? It all began when she'd noticed Eddie's gym bag on the closet shelf and decided to see what was inside. That had been two days ago and the sight of all that cash had taken her breath away. Must have taken her brain away, too, she thought, because she'd started planning, right then, on how to make it hers. How much money was there? Ladonna didn't know. All she knew was the bag contained bundles and bundles of twenties, thousands of dollars, and all she had to do was scoop it up and get out of town. That was pretty much her plan, just grab it and run. But then, Ladonna remembered, she'd started doing stupid shit. She should have jumped on the first Greyhound bus. Instead, she decided she had to have a car, a good secondhand car, that could be bought in a hurry. She took a double handful of bundles from the bag, stuffed them in her purse, and caught a cab to Lacey's Used Cars on Sebastian Street. Old Man Lacey himself had sold her a 1994 Buick Century and she'd counted out eight thousand dollars to him. Only then did she realize how much must be in Eddie's bag. Each bundle of twenties held a thousand dollars and there were lots of bundles still there. It was dope money, of course. She'd known that right away. People came to the house at all hours, and after following Eddie into the bedroom, they'd come out walking fast and looking nervous. Eddie never said anything to her about it and she knew better than to ask. Ladonna wasn't lacking in survival instincts. Or hadn't been, until she decided to steal Eddie's money. Right now, one question kept running through her brain. Why did she come back to the house? What she should have done was took the bag, bought the car, and kept on going. But for some reason, she figured she'd buy the car, come back and pack her clothes, then head out with the money safely stowed in the trunk. Chicago seemed like a good destination. Besides, Eddie wasn't even in town. He'd gone to Memphis for the weekend.

The hardwood floor pressed into Ladonna's side. She drew her legs up and wrapped her thin arms around them. Looking up at the dark figure above her, she felt the same sinking, sick sensation she'd felt when she walked through the front door and seen Eddie, seated in a straight-backed chair and facing her with the open gym bag on the floor beside him. He appeared calmer now, after the initial rage, but the dark eyes glittered and his face had hardened to stone. Eddie Partee was ready to kill.

"Baby, I caint do nothing but tell you the truth," Ladonna whispered. "I took . . . no, I mean I borrowed a little of the money, but I would've had it back in the bag by Monday. That's when you was supposed to come back."

Partee stared down at the woman and nothing changed in his face. He might as well have been looking at an insect.

"How was you going to do that?" he asked. "Nine thousand dollars comes to a lot of money. About nine thousand times more than you worth."

He ratcheted a shell into the pistol chamber, as Ladonna watched, and she realized that it was all over. She couldn't think of anything more to say or anything to do and somehow she didn't even want to. A great tiredness swept through her and she thought about the toad.

Her daddy used to take her to the field with him sometimes when she was a little girl. She'd walk across the cotton rows, further and further away, until she could barely hear the pop-popping sound of his old John Deere tractor. Once, she'd spied a toad, hopping down a middle, and she ran after it, causing it to hop faster and faster. She saw the snake before the toad did, his head raised and his forked tongue running in and out. He was staring at the toad. She stopped dead still, but the toad didn't see the snake until it was within a foot of him. Then it stopped hopping and slowly turned sideways between the rows of cotton. Ladonna remembered that she began to holler, "Hop! Hop!" But instead of hopping, the toad just turned back with little jerky motions and faced the snake again. It sat frozen before him. The king snake regarded his victim for a moment, then lunged forward. He drew back with the toad's head and half its body in his mouth. The last thing Ladonna saw, before turning to run, was the toad's hind legs, flexing forward and back, as if trying to propel itself further down the snake's throat.

Partee's victim looked up at him and watched as he centered the pistol on her. She twisted around so that she was more square to him. If she gave him a good target, maybe it would end quicker and not hurt so much.

"Get up off the floor," came Eddie's voice.

A great relief swept through Ladonna and her bladder emptied. She stiffly clambered to her feet and leaned against the wall behind her.

"Shit," said Eddie, as he watched the wetness spread between her legs. "Gimme your purse."

Ladonna could only stare stupidly at him as he snatched it from her arm. "Now, you only eight thousand light," he murmured, withdrawing the bundle and dropping her handbag to the floor. "What'd you spend it on?"

"The car." Ladonna croaked out the words.

"Car? What fucking car?" Eddie was screaming again as he craned his head around to look out the front window. The blue Buick sat gleaming at the curb.

Partee didn't even look at Ladonna as he swung the pistol in a quick, vicious arc. Her jawbone shattered when the heavy metal barrel slammed against it. She collapsed with a startled grunt and her mouth filled with blood. A red film obscured her vision and she felt herself being hauled upright. It seemed her scalp was being ripped away and she realized Eddie was holding her up by the hair. Her vision cleared and she was staring into his distorted face.

"Don't fall again, Ladonna. If you do, I swear I'll kick you to death."

Ladonna leaned once more against the wall and stared at her

tormentor with shock-filled eyes.

"Now here's what gonna happen," he said. "We're gonna walk out to that car you bought with my money and we're gonna take a little drive. And Ladonna, I hope you call out for help 'cause then I won't have to wait to do what I want to do so bad right now. You understand me?"

The young woman jerked her head up and down once. She understood that Eddie was taking her to a place where the gunshot wouldn't be heard. Partee opened the door and motioned for her to go out in front of him. He placed the Browning's muzzle in the small of her back, pressed up close behind her, and followed her out onto the rickety front porch. They went down the steps and headed across the yard toward the Buick.

They were halfway there when Eddie saw the police car coming up the street.

SEVENTEEN

Patrolman Leonard Simpson cruised slowly down Mulberry Street on this lazy Saturday morning and listened to his stomach rumble. He owned a fairly generous stomach, large enough to press against the steering wheel, and the growl it gave off sounded like two cats fighting. Simpson glanced at his watch. Eleven o'clock, still an hour before his regular lunchtime. Well, I guess I'll move it up an hour today, he thought. Caint stand this noise much longer. Leonard was a simple man with simple tastes and it didn't take much to satisfy him and make him happy. A good wife and kids, which he had, a good job, which he thought this one was, and plenty of good food, which he was about to get on the outside of real soon. Right away, he started thinking about Pete's Rib Shack. "Pete" was Peter Moldavi, a second-generation Italian, but this paisan wasn't interested in pasta or pizza. His specialty was pork barbecue and he cooked the best in the state. Leonard would argue that fact with anybody. And the smell of that meat roasting would make you hungry if you'd eaten five minutes ago. Simpson's mouth started to water as he remembered all the times he'd sat in Pete's place and breathed in that wonderful aroma of tangy barbecue sauce and smoking pork. With something of a start, Leonard realized that Pete's place was just up ahead. He must have headed there without even thinking about it. He pulled into the parking lot, cut the motor, and reached for the radio mike. He was just about to announce a "ten seven" for out of service when the radio came alive and he heard Sally Harris's voice.

"Medford PD to Unit Seventy-five."

Simpson thumbed the mike button. "Go ahead, Medford."

"Unit Seventy-five, you need to ten nineteen for a ten twelve."

"Ten four, Medford," the patrolman replied, and replaced the mike in its cradle. "Crap," he said out loud, and pulled away from Pete's place. He cast a remorseful glance into his rearview mirror as the restaurant disappeared behind him.

Ten nineteen and then ten twelve meant return to the station house for a visitor or an official. When Leonard pulled into the police parking lot he saw who the official was and his stomach quit growling and tightened up a notch. Simpson had only served on the force for six months but he'd learned a few things. One of them was that if Captain Walker wanted a uniformed policeman to carry him somewhere, it meant he expected trouble when he got there. Then he noticed that Walker had one of his assistants with him and Leonard's stomach tightened even more. The Captain must figure three people would be needed on this one.

Simpson stopped beside the two men and they both got in. Claggert slid in beside him and the Captain sat in back.

"How've you been, Leonard?" the kindly voice came from behind him.

"Just great, Captain," the plump officer replied, and looked back over his shoulder.

Walker was smiling at him. "Little Leonard doing okay?"

"Yes sir, rowdy as ever." Leonard began to feel a little calmer in the gut. He smiled back at the Captain, surprised that the man remembered his young son. He'd only mentioned him to Walker once and that was four months ago. Then, the other man started to move around and Leonard glanced over at him. Claggert had pulled a .38 revolver from its holster and was checking the rounds. The man's face looked flushed and the hand holding the pistol shook slightly.

"Hopefully, you won't need that, Bob," said Walker. "Didn't you check it when you put it on?"

"Yessir," Claggert replied, and his face grew a little pinker.

Leonard Simpson, in his few short months on the force, had only met Claggert once or twice and he didn't really care about meeting him again. Something about the guy, like maybe he watched too many cop shows. Stuff like pulling out your pistol and checking it in front of two other cops. One thing for sure, the man was jittery and that worried Simpson. With a start, he realized the Captain was speaking to him again.

"Leonard, we need you to take us down to the Line. The address is four thirty-two Jimpson. If a gentleman named Eddie Partee is there, we'll pick him up and bring him back uptown. Do you know Eddie?"

"Nossir, I don't believe I do."

"Well, he shouldn't cause any trouble. We've brought him in before and he's always come willingly. Of course, this time he's suspected of something a bit more serious and Eddie does have a problem with his temper. Just be on your guard."

"Ain't we gonna need a warrant, Captain?" Bob's voice came out tight and high.

"No, we'll bring him in and I'll interrogate him." Walker leaned forward in his seat. "If I nod to you during the questioning, go out and type up the warrant and affidavit. Then, get it over to Judge Harrison for his signature. He'll be at home."

Walker leaned back, lit a cigarette, and studied his assistant. Claggert knew better than to ask a question like that. They didn't have enough evidence for a formal arrest. And he's nervous about something. What's wrong? Well, no time to think about it now. He felt the car start forward and reached up to place a hand on the patrolman's shoulder. "You heard what I said to Bob. This isn't an arrest. We'll park in front and knock on the door, but I want you to go around back. If anybody comes out, you stop them. If you hear anything inside that makes you think we're in trouble, come in quick."

"Just like at the academy, right."

Billy glanced at the policeman and saw that no irony was intended. Smiling, he said, "That's right, Leonard. Just like that."

Unit 75 lurched over the railroad tracks and rolled down Crescent Street. The Line's main thoroughfare held a good many parked cars and the Hawaiian Club's parking lot was almost full. Billy noticed that Uh Oh had already replaced the broken window. On both sides of the street, black faces turned to watch the cruiser and its three occupants pass by. A break appeared in the overcast sky, and for a brief moment, weak sunlight shone down, glinting off the rain-filled potholes, the water briefly rippling under a gust of winter wind. Simpson turned left off Crescent and stopped at the next intersection. The street sign had disappeared but he knew it was Jimpson. He paused for a moment. Would number 432 be left or right? Concluding it would be the latter, he turned right and began checking out the house numbers. Four twenty-eight, four thirty, and the next one should be . . .

"Jesus," yelled Claggert.

Simpson glanced at the man beside him, took in the bug-eyed expression, and without thinking, jammed on the car brakes. He looked back to the front and for a moment couldn't understand what had startled Bob. A young black couple stood in the next yard. The man held the girl in his left arm, and they remained there like lovers, watching the police car. Leonard turned back to Claggert and was going to ask what was wrong when all he had seen flooded into his brain and his eyes snapped back to the couple. A sheen of blood covered the woman's lower face and the dark hole of her mouth gaped in the middle. She wore a cheap pantsuit and the front looked splotched and darkened, as if someone had dashed a pail of dirty water on her. The woman's knees buckled, as Leonard watched, and the man beside her jerked her back upright. He appeared thin, like the woman, but Leonard figured he must be strong to hold her up with his left arm that way. Then the right arm flew out and pointed straight at the car and Leonard saw the gun. The windshield shattered in front of his face and he thought the sun must be coming out again, because the fractured glass shone brighter and brighter and blinded him with its brightness and he had to close his eyes against the light.

Patrolman Leonard Simpson's eyes stayed closed forever as Eddie's bullet tore through his brain and exploded from the back of his head. Claggert saw what happened to Leonard, and he felt himself sliding helplessly down the seat and onto the floor of the car. He just couldn't help it. A red mist filled the air and Bob felt it on his cheek. He placed his fingers there and they came away smeared with blood. Terror gripped him and a low moan issued from his lips. He managed to crane his head back and look up at the passenger window. His neck felt like hardened leather. It was so stiff with fear he could almost hear it creak and he knew that, in a moment, Eddie Partee's face would appear in that window and then he'd see Eddie's gun and that would be the last thing he'd ever see.

Suddenly, the left rear door opened and slammed closed. Bob quivered and cried out, and then he remembered Billy Walker. The Captain had gone through that door. The Captain was outside and taking care of business.

Oh, God bless you, Captain Walker. God bless you for the man you are, Captain Walker. God bless you, God bless you, and help you kill this son of a bitch before he kills us all.

The words ran through Bob's mind, and he might have even said some of them aloud. Then he heard the Captain's voice.

"Eddie, drop the gun and let the woman go."

"Fuck you, Captain!" Partee's voice was a hoarse screech, ragged and hysterical, filled with rage and terror. Claggert lay and listened to it and knew he was listening to madness.

"Bob, are you all right?"

It took a moment for Claggert to realize that Walker was speaking to him. "Yessir," he blurted out, and his own voice sounded like a stranger's.

"Stay down. Don't move."

Bob just nodded his head and drew himself into a ball.

"Eddie, don't make me kill you. I don't want to do that." Billy spoke in a normal tone, but Partee screamed his answer.

"You got to kill this bitch first. She's staying right here in front of me."

"No, I don't, Eddie," came the even voice. "I can hit you anywhere, and she can't cover all of you. Believe it. I'll hit a part I can see and more of you will show and then I'll kill you. It's something I can do."

Bob heard another scream from Eddie and the blast of his huge handgun. The bullet crashed through what was left of the windshield and exploded out the side window. A rain of glass fell on Claggert's head. He heard the Captain's revolver bark twice and the woman's shrill shriek, and suddenly she was beside the car and clambering into the back seat. She lay there, giving off blubbery moans, and Bob raised up and peered outside. Eddie Partee lay crumpled on the dead grass, his face turned toward the sky. The Captain was walking across the yard, and Bob, with shame flooding through him, stumbled after him, gun dangling from his hand. They knelt beside the body and Claggert saw the bullet wounds, one in the right arm and the other just above the right eye. Bob knew which wound came first, the one to Eddie's gun arm. The Captain had hit a part that he could see, and then more of Eddie had showed and the Captain had killed him. It was just something he could do.

Hours later, Billy stood beneath a group of pine trees in front of the Medford Hospital. The trees grew across a slight rise of ground, dividing the hospital from its parking lot. The setting sun washed a pale, orange luminance across the grove and lit up the dead pine needles at Billy's feet. He listened to an early night wind whisper through the living needles above his head and felt the touch of its chill breath on his cheek.

The sun touched the horizon and began to sink beneath it and the shadows it had cast became one caliginous covering beneath the trees. Billy heard a cheeping sound, followed by a rush of wings, and wondered what kind of bird would inhabit such a place at such a time. He took a long breath and watched the sun sink into the earth.

Leonard Simpson dead. Eddie Partee dead.

He'd killed Eddie Partee, but Billy felt little remorse and certainly no guilt. He knew that he'd acted sensibly and correctly, and anyway, there'd been no choice. Actually, he would have been justified in shooting Partee without trying to reason with him first. Billy knew why he'd held off. He wanted Eddie alive. He wanted Eddie to confront his accuser and tell his side of the story. Now, he was left only with Eddie's lover and the scant hope that she might have something valuable to say. Ladonna had lain in the hospital emergency room most of the afternoon while her jaw was being set. They'd moved her into the ward a couple of hours ago and Billy was waiting for her to regain consciousness. Just down the hall, Eddie Partee and Leonard Simpson rested side by side in the Cold Room.

Earlier in the afternoon, Billy had visited Simpson's widow. She didn't know she was a widow and stood smiling expectantly at the Captain. He gently informed her of her husband's death. She never uttered a word, just stared at the Captain with a white and stricken face. Then she'd folded her hands together and walked over to the fireplace, staring down into the cold ashes, a normally plump and pleasant woman, looking with dead eyes at her new reality of pain and loss.

Cordelia had left him a short time ago. She'd been waiting for him at the hospital and they'd wandered over to the pine grove to talk. Finally, she asked if he was all right. He told her that he was, and as Cordelia regarded that calm, dark figure, her eyes filled with tears. She abruptly turned and headed back to her car.

"Captain Walker. Captain Walker, are you out there?"

Billy looked up to see a small woman in white, walking with clasped arms toward the stand of trees.

"Yes, I'm here," he called.

"She's awake, Captain, but she can't talk."

"Is she able to write?"

"Indeed she is," answered the nurse. "A few minutes ago, she pointed toward a pad and pencil and we gave them to her."

"What did she write?"

"She asked how she was supposed to eat and I told her she'd have to sip liquids through a straw."

"What did she say to that?"

The nurse smiled up at him. "She ordered a scotch and soda."

Eighteen

He stood beside Ladonna Smith's bed and slowly unbuttoned his jacket. Other beds stretched away on either side. They held mostly elderly people and a couple of children. One small boy's arm was secured in a sling, and Walker with his policeman's mind, wondered if somebody was responsible. None of the patients showed any interest in Ladonna or her visitor. The nurse brought a straight-backed chair and Billy placed it beside Ladonna's head and sat down. He looked at the young woman and was struck by her thinness. The frail figure seemed barely outlined under the hospital sheet. Her gaunt face was turned toward him and she stared at him with wide, watchful eyes. A cloth bandage, wrapped tightly around her face, seemed lucent against the dark skin. She'd refused to give the pad and pencil back to the nurse and was holding them tight to her breast, like a little girl holding her favorite dolls.

"Hello, Ladonna," said Billy, looking into her eyes and giving her a smile.

Ladonna nodded her head and made a small noise in her throat.

"Do you know who I am?"

The head nodded again.

"I know you can't talk, but I need to ask you a few questions. I hope you'll be able to write down the answers for me." Billy's eyes widened slightly as he realized Ladonna had already started to write. She finished and showed him the pad. The writing was scrawled and spidery but Billy could make it out.

You killed Eddie.

"Yes," he told her.

Good. He taking to kill me. You save life.

"Why did Eddie want to kill you?"

I took money. He come back. Caught me.

"Came back from where?"

Memphis.

The single word stared up at Walker and he leaned back in his chair. He reached for a cigarette, remembered where he was, and let the pack slide back into his shirt pocket. "What was Eddie doing in Memphis?" he asked, and watched Ladonna turn to a fresh page.

Don't know. Then, after a short pause, Know where he stay.

"Where was that?"

Riverside Hotel. He love place.

Ladonna sighed as her hand moved across the page. Come back early. Sposed to be there till Monday.

"Is that what he told you, that he'd be there till Monday?"

Yes

"When did you last speak to him?"

Thursday. Ladonna was writing more slowly. Her fingers barely gripped the pencil. Jus fore midnite. I call.

"You called the Riverside Hotel and talked to Eddie at midnight, Thursday night."

Ladonna nodded and her head dropped back on the pillow. Her eyelids fluttered and finally closed and she began to breath deeply. The pad and pencil dropped from her fingers. Billy reached over, plucked them off the bed, and tucked them in his jacket pocket. He stared at Ladonna and thought about Eddie Partee. Eddie Partee sitting in a Memphis hotel room and talking on the phone to Ladonna, while at the same time Edwin Mayhew was in Medford, taking four bullets in the chest.

The Captain drove out of the hospital parking lot and headed north on Seventh Street. His headlights reflected off the wet pavement and lit up the street sign in front of him. He was about to cross Court, but decided to turn left instead. Mayhew's house lay just up ahead. One of the side windows glowed with yellow light and Billy took it to be Lavonia's bedroom. He drove past the unlit front then abruptly pulled to the curb and stopped. Sleep Edwards's voice sounded in his ear. Sleep might as well have been sitting beside him.

"Eddie Partee, Captain. Eddie Partee, standing there with the street light full on his face."

Billy climbed out of his car and stood looking at Mayhew's house. With the exception of Lavonia's window, the house lay in utter darkness, as did the front yard. There was no street light. There never had been.

Walker pulled into his private parking space at the police station and got out. The dispatcher, seated in his glass-enclosed cubicle, saw the Captain coming down the hallway and rose from his chair. Two patrolmen came around a corner, halted, and stood against the wall. They watched silently as the Captain approached. Billy stood amongst the three men and looked at each in turn.

"I'm sorry about Leonard Simpson," he said. The voice came out low and tired.

Both patrolmen shifted nervously and the taller one cleared his throat. "Captain Walker, everything you did was righteous. Leonard was a uniform. He was supposed to protect you, not the other way around." The tall patrolman looked embarrassed and straightened back up against the wall.

Billy turned to the dispatcher. "Lucas, you worked this shift yesterday, didn't you?"

"Yessir, four to twelve." The young black man had not taken his eyes off the Captain. None of them had.

"Did anybody talk to Sleep Edwards while you were on duty?"

"Yessir, Officer Claggert came by. He talked to Sleep."

"How long did they talk?"

" 'Bout a half hour, Captain."

"Anybody else? It's important, Lucas."

"No sir. The only time I left this desk was to go to the john and I leave the door open so I can hear the phone ring. I'd of heard anybody if they'd come in. Officer Claggert was the only one. I never even spoke to Sleep myself."

"Okay, thanks." Walker started on down the hall. "Goodnight, gentlemen," he said over his shoulder.

"Goodnight, Captain," they called in unison and then grinned at how ludicrous that sounded. Their eyes followed Walker until he disappeared up the stairway.

Billy unlocked the CID room door, flicked the light on, and sat down behind his desk. He dug a Winston out of its pack, noticed it was the last one, and threw the crumpled pack away. All was silent. No sound, not even from downstairs, and when Billy struck a match, he could hear the sulfur burning. The policeman leaned back in his chair and quietly smoked the cigarette.

The doubts he'd had this morning had all been confirmed, but Billy took no pleasure in that. He thought about the lie Sleep had told and all that lie had cost and his face hardened into a dark mask. But to hell with that kind of thinking. Edwards didn't know what the consequences were going to be. He'd only done what all his fellow felons did. They lied to help themselves or to get even or simply because lying came so naturally. Might as well get angry at the wind for blowing your hat off. But here we come to it, he thought. Sleep's lie was believable and significant for one reason only. He knew the goddamn holdback.

Walker stubbed his cigarette out, leaned further back in the chair, and folded both hands over his stomach. He breathed a tired sigh. Sleep lied, but someone had to tell him about the holdback. Me, Cordelia, and the killer, he thought. The only ones to know about the whiskey were me, Cordelia, and the killer. Billy's thin lips moved in the ghost of a smile. I must be tired, he thought. I'm not part of the equation, for God's sake. I know I didn't tell him. Also, he knew that he had to make two assumptions and treat them as hard facts. First, Cordelia didn't tell anyone either. The core of his perception told him this was so. And secondly, it told him that the man in the cell did not commit this murder. Sleep simply was not capable of such an act. That left the killer. The killer could have told Edwards, and thrown in the part about the whiskey. "God, I am tired," the policeman said out loud. The killer obviously would want to throw the blame on someone else, and might tell somebody that he saw Eddie do it. But would he mention the whiskey? The killer wouldn't know that he and Cordelia were using that as a holdback. And if the killer told Sleep, why would Sleep say that he was the witness. He'd just repeat to Walker what he'd been told and name the informant. Being Sleep Edwards, he wouldn't have wasted any time doing it either. No, no. Don't spend any more time on that. Whoever told Sleep about the whiskey, knew it was the holdback. That person knew it would make Sleep's story believable.

Walker took a deep breath and let the air out slowly. Three people knew that whiskey was poured over Mayhew, but only he and Cordelia knew it was the holdback. Wrong. Somebody else knew. They had, somehow, found out and told it to Sleep Edwards for what it was, and Walker knew that Sleep had been told in his jail cell. He'd known it all along, really, and after talking to Lucas, he'd known who the person was.

Yessir, Officer Claggert came by. He talked to Sleep. Officer Claggert was the only one.

The hard, dark mask came down over Billy's face once more, but this time it remained. He stepped on his anger, subdued it, and allowed himself only one line of thought. How did Claggert find out? Walker remained motionless and let Bob Claggert materialize in his mind. Claggert the inept, Claggert the jealous and ambitious, and yes, Claggert the coward. Bob was unable to function after the shooting and had to be driven home by a patrolman. The eager Bob, who wasn't much on hard work, but went for show or the easy way to impress. Like making it a point to be in the office first, not to work, but simply to be there when the Captain walked in. Waiting in the office for him and Cordelia. Waiting in the office alone . . .

Almost without thinking, Billy reached his hand under the desk. He felt the wires first, then let his fingers follow them to the small microphone, secured with tape beneath the desk's front edge. Walker pulled the wires, the mike, and a small recording device loose and placed them in front of him. He didn't play the tape. There was really no need. There was really only one more thing he needed to do today. Billy pulled the desk phone over to him and dialed a number.

"Bob, it's Captain Walker. I'm at the office and I want to see you right away."

NINETEEN

The metal stairway outside sounded someone's footsteps. They halted just outside the door. Billy waited. Finally, the door opened and his assistant shuffled in, his head lowered and the shoulders slumped. This day had taken its toll on Bob Claggert. He saw the small mound of recording equipment on the desk and the remaining color fled from his face. He sank into a chair and stared helplessly at the Captain, at the dark eyes that seemed to soak up the light, at the fixed face that would not move, could not move, because it had turned to stone.

To look good, Billy thought. All this day has cost and all the loss, so that you could look good. But it wasn't really that simple. Claggert's actions had been stupid and self-serving and even criminal, but he had not known what the consequences of his acts would be. He had not foreseen the coming deaths, nor his own destruction. And worst of all, for Claggert, he had not known that he would be forced to see himself as he truly was.

"Bob, I see you have your service revolver. Give it to me. I want your ID and badge also."

Claggert stiffly pulled out the items and laid them on the desk. He tugged his coat tighter across his chest and shivered slightly.

"As of now, you're no longer a policeman." The voice was measured and firm. "I expect you to leave town tonight and—"

"Captain, I—"

Walker raised his hand and the implacable voice resumed. "I

expect you to leave town tonight and not come back. If I see you again, I'll arrest you. Right now, I can think of at least two felonies to charge you with, so leave quickly before I change my mind. When you get to wherever you're going, call a dispatcher and let him know where to send your final check. That's all I have to say. That's all I want to say."

Claggert nodded, shuffled over to the door, and slowly closed it behind him. The Captain heard him going down the stairs. Bob's steps were irregular and barely audible. Billy knew that he was holding on to the metal railing as he descended.

He sighed, picked up the phone, and dialed Cordelia's number. She answered on the third ring and he briefly told her what had happened. She asked if he needed her tonight and he said no. Her voice sounded strangely formal. Billy had hung up and started out of the office before realizing that what he'd heard wasn't formality at all. It was anger. Cordelia Hull was mad as hell.

TWENTY

Walker sat up in bed and watched morning light illuminate the Venetian blinds. The bedside clock read a couple of minutes till six. Billy had awakened just before the alarm. He wasn't surprised. All his life he'd usually been able to awaken precisely when he wanted to. The alarm was for insurance. Swinging his feet to the carpet, Walker reached over and flipped off the alarm button. A soft sigh sounded behind him and he looked around at his sleeping wife. Sammy would sleep a while longer, usually getting up about seven thirty and opening her flower shop at nine. Neither ate breakfast on a weekday. Billy touched her face and smoothed a lock of red hair from her eyes. Their twenty-five years of marriage had produced two daughters, both red-haired like their mother, and both married and living in other states. They loved their mother and let her know it. They adored their father and constantly made inadequate attempts to conceal that adulation, like treating him as a pal. Walker, of course, understood all this and was secretly amused by it, since he himself was a master at concealing emotions. However, the most fundamental one, that of fear, he never had to worry about, for fear dwelled in him not at all. In that, he was a man apart.

The Captain rose and went into the kitchen. As he brewed coffee, he banished all thoughts connected to this Monday and thought about yesterday. Each Sunday, Sammy drove to Memphis in her van and picked up flowers and plants for the shop.

She'd begged him to go with her and he had reluctantly agreed. Cordelia had the duty and he'd briefly talked with her before leaving. She had nothing important to relate and he told her where he'd be. The ride to and from Memphis was a restful diversion and he was glad he'd made the trip. Once, Sammy had pulled to the side of the highway and stopped. They'd rolled the windows down, breathed in the frosty air, and watched blackbirds swarm and swoop over the barren cotton fields. It was nice to get out of town.

Walker parked in front of the station, climbed out of his car, and squinted up into bright sunlight, a welcome change from the last few days. A cruiser pulled away from the entrance door and its driver leaned forward and waved. He heard the short beep of a siren and turned to see another cruiser passing on the street. The patrolman inside saluted as he drove by. Billy wondered about this display and then he understood. It was tribute. They had lost one of their own, but the Captain had killed the asshole responsible. And what's more, he had done it right then. In their street-cop world this was nothing but justice. And it was absolutely "righteous."

Pruitt came out of his glass cubicle and met Walker in the hallway. The dispatcher had just finished his shift. A slight, dark, and intense man, he greeted Walker with a quick smile. Billy remembered that the patrolmen called him "Speedo." He had no idea why. Pruitt had done well on the night of Mayhew's murder and Billy had marked him for his intelligence, the trait that always caught his attention first.

"Good morning, Roger. Have a quiet night?"

"Not too bad, Captain. Processed two drunk-and-disorderlies, and Lieutenant Pollard served another warrant on Bad Paper Bob."

Billy nodded. Jake Pollard was the graveyard shift commander, and Bob, well Bob had floated enough worthless checks

to wallpaper the CID room. This practice had netted him several arrests and even a short stretch in prison. But old habits died hard. Once, Bob had temporarily drifted into car theft and stolen a Plymouth off Lacey's used car lot. His old nemesis, Jake Pollard, went straight to Bob's house and hauled him off to jail. How did he know who did it? Jake told everybody he'd found Bob's personal check laying in the missing car's parking space. Billy figured that at least that part of the story was apocryphal.

"Who were the drunks?" he asked. This had nothing to do with CID, but sometimes a routine arrest would shed light on a current investigation.

"Guy named Luther Hollings and our old pal Wingate," replied Pruitt, giving Walker a grin. Just the last name was sufficient. The latter was a perpetual drunk.

Whenever a policeman returned to his car, he'd always tell the dispatcher "ten eight," meaning "back in service." If he'd just placed Walter Wingate in the car, the transmission would be "ten eight with Wingate," and the dispatcher would go turn on the alcohol testing machine.

"Thing about this Hollings," continued Pruitt, "he could become another Wingate. We got him on Thursday night for the same thing. He was harassing customers over at Seventh Street Liquors, threatening to do them harm."

"Thursday night?"

"Ten four, Captain, but they locked him up about nine o'clock. Mayhew was still selling booze at that time."

"Okay, thanks Roger," said Walker, thinking that the dispatcher continued to show evidence of his quickness. He'd be keeping an eye on him. "By the way, don't you go off to Camden next week?"

"Yes sir. This'll be my last week in dispatch."

"How do you like police work so far?"

"Well, I think it's ruined me, Captain."

"Ruined you?"

"Yeah, for a regular job, I mean."

Walker smiled at the young man as he moved past him. "Well, don't worry about it, Pruitt. It happens to most of us."

Billy entered the CID room and sat down behind his desk. He gave a small sigh and began sorting through a stack of police reports. Cordelia walked in, holding a cup of steaming coffee in each hand.

"Thanks, Cordelia," he murmured, taking one and lifting it to his lips.

Sitting on the corner of her desk, she said, "I went by Bob's apartment this morning, talked to his landlady."

Billy stared at her over his cup.

"The landlady said Claggert moved out sometime Saturday night. One of the other tenants told her about it the next morning." She sipped her coffee in silence. "You know, I kept wondering why he would do that, rig the recorder, I mean. Then I realized he was just being Bob. Trying to find out what we were saying about him when he wasn't around, or about anything he could use to his benefit."

"Yes," murmured Walker, "that would be his perspective."

Hull gave her boss a grim look. "You should have prosecuted the bastard."

"It wasn't necessary," he replied, and Cordelia knew it was true. One glance at his face told her as much, and she didn't even want to think about what had occurred in this room on Saturday night.

"Which reminds me," Billy said, picking up the phone receiver and pressing a button. "Good morning, Chief."

Cordelia watched him pause to listen. "Yes," he said. "It was a bad business. There's a full report on your desk. Have you read it?"

Fat chance, thought Hull. The Captain had placed it on Chief Wheaton's desk on Saturday night. Wheaton never came in during the weekend. It was unusual for him to be here this early on Monday. The man had it made, she thought, and he should split his paycheck each month and give half of it to the Captain. Walker's CID operation was inviolate and self-contained, but Billy's influence radiated out from this room and strengthened the whole department. Wheaton had good clerks and shift commanders, so administration and operations ran smoothly, and everyone knew who the real authority figure was, the CID captain.

"Yes, Roland," Billy continued. "No, I'm not busy right now." Her boss hung up the phone and gave her a wry glance. "He's coming up," he said.

Cordelia rolled her eyes toward the ceiling, but said nothing. Walker would never have permitted any disparaging remarks about the Chief.

"Hey, Billy!" The Chief came through the door and looked around the room. Lowering himself down on a wooden chair, he gave a grunt as he swung one leg over the other. Wheaton was a short man, going to fat, and his belly flowed over his belt buckle.

The face, a trifle bloated, was veined and red from too much bourbon. He smiled at Hull and said, "Keeping him straight, Cordelia?" Cordelia returned the smile, but made no answer. Roland turned back to the Captain. "Helluva deal last Saturday. If you hadn't been on the case, I would've come in."

"That wasn't necessary," said Walker. "And besides, it ended quickly."

"So I heard," said Wheaton, giving him an appraising look. "I see you haven't lost your gun eye since Camden."

A slight frown touched Walker's face and Roland hurriedly asked, "This have anything to do with the Mayhew murder?"

"Yes, but it turned out to be a false lead."

"That's too bad."

"Yes, it is," said Billy, "considering what it cost."

"Yeah," stated the Chief. He hesitated, then said, "There was nothing critical in the report about Officer Claggert, but I saw some paperwork on his termination."

"Yes, Bob left town Saturday night. I don't think he'll be back."

"I see," said Roland, unwilling to take it any further. "Well, if there's anything I can do, let me know."

"As a matter of fact there is. The patrolman who was killed . . ."

"Leonard Simmons," murmured the Chief.

"Simpson!" Cordelia spoke for the first time. "His name was Leonard Simpson."

Roland flushed and the Captain continued. "Leonard had a wife and two children. They'll get the insurance and pension, but I thought perhaps the department could take up a collection."

"Say no more," said Wheaton, holding up a hand. He was in his element. "I'll start one today. I'm even gonna arrange to have contribution jars set up in all the main stores, banks, too."

"I'm sure his family would appreciate it," said Walker, and looked down at his paperwork.

"Well, lemme see what the hell is going on downstairs," said the Chief. He got up and hurried out the door.

The telephone on Billy's desk buzzed. He picked it up, listened for a moment, and said, "Okay Sally, send him up." Cordelia looked over and he said, "First of the reward seekers."

"Anybody I know?"

Billy smiled. "Why yes, I believe you do. It's the ever-interesting June Bug."

Cordelia emitted a groan and sank into her desk chair.

"Cap'n Walker." The voice on the other side of the door sounded high and anxious.

"Just open the door," Cordelia responded.

The door opened about a quarter of the way. June Bug entered sideways and stood in front of Cordelia's desk. He glanced over at Billy as the Captain slowly looked him up and down. Small, and skinny, almost to the point of emaciation, June Bug could have been a poster person for the homeless. His shoes looked a couple of sizes too large and were run down at the heels. His pants, on the other hand, were tight and much too short. They ended about four inches above the shoe tops. A faded gray shirt hung outside the pants and was covered by a moth-eaten wool coat. June Bug wore a tattered felt hat with a hole in the crown. His frizzled hair stuck up through the hole and twisted from under the hat brim. He smiled down at Cordelia, and Cordelia, staring at the rotten teeth, wished he'd kept his mouth shut.

"Mornin' Miss Hull," June Bug mumbled. "Should I talk to you or the Captain?"

"Well," Cordelia answered, "since you're standing in front of me and the Captain is right at your elbow, why don't you talk to both of us?"

"Yes'm," he replied, and glanced down at the chair by her desk.

"Sit down, June Bug," she said. "Now what did you want to tell us?"

June Bug Jackson sat, leaned back in the chair, and looked once more at Walker. The small black face bore a quizzical, knowing look. "Captain," he said, "look like, once again, I be in the right place at the right time." Cordelia grinned and turned her face away.

"And what place and time was this, Mr. Jackson?" The Captain was grave.

"The place was out in front of my church, and the time was twelve noon on Sunday, which was yesterday."

Cordelia muttered something under her breath. June Bug glanced quickly over at her and then looked back at the Captain. "It was at that time and place that I heard a conversation."

"Go on," said Billy.

June Bug drew himself up straight and rubbed his lips with the back of his hand. "The conversation was betwixt my preacher and the Deacon Wilbanks. The deacon was talkin' quiet, but I could hear every word. He told the preacher that something lay heavy on his mind and that he had to come clean with it."

Jackson paused and looked at the two policemen, but received no response. He cleared his throat and continued: "The deacon said he'd gone to see Edwin Mayhew at his house."

"When was that?" asked Walker.

"Last Thursday night about midnight."

"And what was the reason for this visit?"

"Well sir, Wilbanks told my preacher that he just couldn't stand to see Mayhew takin' the brothers' money at poker games down in the Line. Said he went to tell that to Mayhew." Jackson paused and glanced sideways at Cordelia.

"Go on."

"Well, Brother Wilbanks said that he'd only just got started talkin' when Edwin pulled a pistol on him. The deacon grabbed it, and while they were rasslin' around, it went off and plugged old Edwin right in the chest. It was an accident but the deacon is scared to come in." Jackson cast another sly look at Cordelia. "And if you bring him in, I'll bet he denies it."

Cordelia took a sip of her coffee and peered at Jackson. "What church do you belong to," she asked.

"Sinai Baptist," answered June Bug, smoothing the front of his coat.

112

"John Gilbey's church," she said to Walker.

Strangely enough, the pastor was a brother to Uh Oh Earl. Billy knew this and nodded as he picked up the phone.

"Well," he said, "I guess we'd better get the Reverend Gilbey in here."

"Oh no, Captain." June Bug half stood and was shaking his head back and forth. "The Reverend won't do that. He caint do that."

"Oh?"

"Naw sir. What the deacon done told him was in confession, and a preacher caint never talk about none of that."

Cordelia, in the middle of a sip, emitted a small choking sound and covered her lips with a napkin. Billy looked over and swept his hand from her to June Bug, as if to say, he's all yours.

Cordelia set her cup down and leaned toward Jackson. "June Bug, you dumbass. Baptists don't have confession, and you'd know that if you'd ever seen the inside of a church. Oh, you've been outside the Sinai every Sunday. How do I know? Because that deacon you're accusing called the station and complained about you. Said you were panhandling out front and pestering the members. He ran you off, too, didn't he?"

June Bug dropped his head and rolled his eyes at Hull. Billy got up and walked into the interrogation room. Cordelia tapped Jackson across the chest with the back of her hand. "Listen stupid, you picked a bad day to be bringing the Captain more false information. Now get your shagnasty ass out of here, and next time you tell us something, it had better be gospel."

A moment later, the Captain reentered and saw only Cordelia, working quietly at her desk.

TWENTY-ONE

"You have a visitor, Susan. It's someone you'll want to see."
Maude unlocked the metal door and swung it back. The room
beyond looked like a jail cell. A chair and table stood on the left
side, with all legs fastened to the floor. A Bible lay on the table,
along with some dried-out roses in a paper cup. On the right
was a commode and a sink. A mirror, fashioned from shiny tin,
was secured above the sink. Cold sunlight shone through a
window, its radiance defused by the wire mesh outside. The girl
lay underneath the window on a narrow bed. She had turned
on her side and the knees were drawn up to her stomach. She
clinched both hands under her chin and regarded the doorway
with wide, watchful, eyes.

"It's all right, Susan," said the matron, giving her a bright
smile. She moved into the room and turned back to the figure
in the doorway. "Look who I brought. It's your father."

The tall, gaunt figure remained in the doorway for a moment, and then came up beside Maude. He removed a felt,
broad-brimmed hat and clutched it over his stomach. "Hello
Susie," he said in a low voice. "How are ye, honey?"

The young girl remained motionless but a quick smile
touched her lips. Just as quickly, it was gone.

"She still caint keep any makeup stuff or toothbrush or
anything?" he asked.

"No Reverend," the nurse replied. But quickly added, "Oh
she uses some of that stuff. No problem there. She can brush

her teeth and comb her hair and care for herself. It's just we can't leave the items with her." Glancing at the visitor's face, she added. "At least, not yet."

The man nodded and looked back down at the girl. This was his second visit and Maude was, once again, struck by the man's quiet dignity and impressive looks. The long, dark hair, combed straight back, the black searching eyes, the prominent blade-like nose, all made for a striking appearance. He's got a little vanity, too, she thought. He's aware of his impression on people. Ah, but not right now. Not while he's here face to face with his daughter. On the lined, dark countenance, placid and still, she read only infinite sorrow. "I'll leave you with her now," she whispered, and quickly left the room.

The old man walked stiffly over to Susan's bunk. As he approached, she swung her feet to the floor and sat with both hands folded in her lap. She looked up at her father and shifted sideways on the cot.

"Why thank you, baby. I believe I will set a spell."

He slowly lowered himself and placed large, bony hands on his knees. The girl stared ahead, and when the father turned to her, he realized she had retreated back into that place which permitted no visitors. Placing an arm around her shoulders, he drew her against him and lightly kissed her on the temple. They sat quietly together, and after a while, Maude came and reopened the door. The preacher looked up at her, before rising and replacing his hat. Then, without a backward glance, he walked past the nurse and left her alone with Susan.

TWENTY-TWO

"Edwin Mayhew died because someone grew obsessed with killing him. The killer thought about that coming death for a long time and then he made it real. He planned it and did it methodically, almost ritually."

"And the pouring on of whiskey was a part of that ritual?"

"I believe that it was."

"You never believed anything else, did you?"

Walker stared over his desk at the wall beyond and into some private space beyond that. "No, but I couldn't disregard the regular paths."

"And are we done with the regular paths?"

"The murder was done out of loathing. The murderer had given it a lot of thought. We concentrate on that."

Cordelia let out a long sigh and placed both hands, palms down, on her desktop. Now they could move ahead in a straight and determined line. She stared at Walker and said, "It was a revenge killing, wasn't it?"

"Yes."

"Shades of Bob Claggert. No chance it could have been anything else?"

"No."

A sardonic look over Cordelia's face and she said, "My Captain, how is it you know these things?" It was an old quip. Their "in" joke.

Walker gave her a grim smile. "It was personal, Cordelia, very personal. At first the killer was enraged at Mayhew. Then that rage solidified into a great and terrible hatred. Mayhew was hateful in his eyes, constantly hateful in all his waking thoughts, and Mayhew had to die.

"The killer carefully planned it all. He would make a liturgy out of it, a rite. He waited for Mayhew on that dark street and when Mayhew arrived the ceremony began."

Billy's face bore no expression and his voice droned away in an otherwise silent room. "He didn't run up to Mayhew, he walked. He carefully placed the muzzle against the old man's chest and squeezed the trigger. He did it three more times and there was never any hurry. Then, the shooter pulled a full bottle of whiskey from his pocket. He slowly unscrewed the cap and poured all the whiskey over his victim's body. Mayhew probably felt it burning into his open wounds."

Cordelia stared transfixed at her boss. "I guess being slow and deliberate was part of his ceremony," she said.

"Yes," he murmured, "the killer wanted to draw it out. He wanted to make it last."

Cordelia wondered how Walker thought he could know what was in the killer's mind, but then she dismissed the thought. Wondering how Walker came to know certain things could lead to a very superstitious frame of mind. Finally, she stirred herself and asked, "So what's our starting point?"

The Captain turned in his chair and regarded his assistant. "We start where we started before," he answered, "with Edwin Mayhew's murder. Only this time, instead of moving forward, we're going to go back."

★ ★ ★ ★ ★

BOOK TWO: THE KILLER

★ ★ ★ ★ ★

TWENTY-THREE

The old man sat in his rocking chair and stared at the turbulent river, coursing southward beyond his back yard. The Mississippi current had been brown a short time ago. Now, beneath the setting sun, it had turned to liquid brick. Strange, he thought. It's been cloudy all day, but as soon as I came outside, the sun appeared. Maybe, it's a sign.

The old man believed that a "sign" was one of God's ways of communicating with man. Few men could interpret them, and most times he couldn't either, but sometimes God whispered the meaning, and once He had spoken with a thunderous voice.

Sign or not, the old man acknowledged the sinking sun by lifting his face toward it and delivering a reverent utterance: "As thou hast commanded, so it has been done."

It was finished. The whiskey seller, the fornicator, the corrupter of young souls, was dead. Killed by my own hand, he thought, and accomplished through God's power and strength. A grim smile appeared on the old man's face. He was remembering the words of Job:

> The womb shall forget him,
> The worm shall feed sweetly on him.
> He shall be no more remembered,
> And wickedness shall be broken as a tree.

TWENTY-FOUR

Billy and Cordelia sat at a table in Pete's Rib Shack and munched on barbecue sandwiches. Cordelia peered through the window at a pallid sun, slipping behind the trees. As she watched, the day grew darker and a chill wind sprang up, whipping part of a newspaper across Pete's parking lot. Pete's place countered all this with warmth and light and the fragrance of spicy pork. The owner came out of the kitchen and walked over to their table.

"How are the sandwiches, folks?"

"Real good, Pete," said Cordelia, looking up at the round, smiling face.

"How about yours, Captain?"

"It's fine, Pete. How's business?"

"Oh I can't complain. Listen, I can't tell you how sorry I am to hear about Officer Simpson. Terrible thing."

"Yes, it was," replied Billy. "Did you know him?"

"Oh yeah. He was one of my best customers. Loved my barbecue. Fine man. Fine man. I've got his collection jar on the counter. Gonna make sure it gets filled up."

"Mrs. Simpson will appreciate that," said Billy. He stared at his sandwich.

"Well, enjoy your meal," said Pete, returning to his kitchen.

They ate in silence for a moment. Cordelia swallowed and said, "Boy, Mayhew's sister sure brought the weirdos out with that reward."

Walker chewed and nodded his head. After June Bug's visit, they'd seen three more informers. All were obvious fakes, and as soon as this became evident, the Captain would leave the room and let Cordelia dismiss them. This she did with unfailing rough glee. She watched her boss finish his sandwich and said, "So what's our first step on this backward journey?"

Question answered, she thought. Our first step begins with Edwin's last one. They were standing, once again, in Edwin Mayhew's front yard. The wind lifted a few dead leaves and blew them toward her face. She ducked her head and followed Walker toward the front porch.

Lavonia answered after the first few knocks and ushered them inside. Billy began unbuttoning his jacket and nodded toward Cordelia. "Lavonia, this is my assistant, Cordelia Hull."

"Please to meet you, Cordelia," responded the old woman. "It's too warm in here for them coats. Take 'em off and make yourselves at home."

Cordelia gratefully shed her coat. The room was uncomfortably warm and she reflected that this was usually true of old people's houses in the wintertime. A faint smell of cat, hanging in the air, was also part of the pattern. They sat down on the couch as the old woman lowered herself into her rocking chair.

"I expect you've got some more questions for me. That right, Billy?"

"No, not at the moment. But I do need to ask you a favor."

"What's that?"

"I want to go through Edwin's personal effects. All his papers, correspondence, anything that might help us with the case."

Lavonia frowned, and Cordelia thought for a moment that she was going to refuse. It occurred to her that the old lady was angry about something, had been since they'd first entered the room.

"Well, it's all right with me," she finally said, "but you won't find any of that stuff here. Edwin kept all that down at the liquor store. Half his personal belongings are down there, too."

"May we have a key to the store? Or maybe you'd prefer to go down with us."

Suddenly the anger that Cordelia had sensed became apparent on Lavonia's face and she actually emitted a snarling sound. The Captain showed no change of expression. He'd been aware, thought Cordelia. Of course, he had.

"Guess you haven't been out that way today, have you Billy?"

"You mean by the liquor store? Why no."

"Well, it so happens that the store is open, open and operating."

"Who's running it?"

"Why, Edwin's ex-wife, that's who." Lavonia leaned forward in the rocking chair, both hands gripping the armrests. "She came by this morning to pick up the key. Had a lawyer with her and he was holding a contract between her and Edwin. Seems she owns one third of the business and a right to operate it during Edwin's absence." Lavonia leaned back in the chair and a wry smile touched her lips. "Since this absence is permanent, I don't know what's goin' to happen. My lawyer came over and said I've got to let her operate it till we can work it out. I'm supposed to get two thirds, less my share of the operating expenses, and that's where she stands."

Cordelia glanced over at her boss and said, "Miss Mayhew, we do need to look over Edwin's belongings, especially his papers."

"Oh, it's okay with me, and his ex won't give you any problem. In his will, Edwin left all his personal property to me."

"What did his will say about the liquor store?" Billy asked.

Lavonia's thin lips pressed together and the old eyes narrowed. "Said I inherited his business interests at One-oh-one

Court Street. Wasn't till this morning I learned that his 'interest' would only be two thirds."

Walker stood up and Cordelia walked over to her coat. The Captain gave Lavonia a long look. "Her name is Josephine, isn't it? That's the name I recall."

"Uh huh! They call her 'Jo' for short. Oh hell, Billy. She's all right, I guess. And it's the way Edwin wanted it. The only thing I'm hoping right now is that she's honest."

TWENTY-FIVE

The neon sign shone red and bright in the twilight and proclaimed "Mayhew's Liquor" to the passing traffic. An electrician's panel truck was drawn up next to a floodlight pole and the worker was busily replacing a burnt out lamp. Ground floodlights, directed at the store, had also been serviced and the old brick building gleamed like hearthstone in their glow. Several cars waited in the parking lot while their owners made purchases against the coming night. Billy and Cordelia both noticed a white Cadillac, resting in quiet splendor in a far corner. Additional chrome strips had been added to its side and the license plate, encased in more gleaming chrome, read ALOHA.

"Sole proprietor of the Hawaiian Club," said Cordelia. "What's he doing here? There's plenty of booze at his place."

"Mayhew's Liquor is his supplier," answered Walker. "Nightclubs in Arkansas can't buy direct from a whiskey salesman. Their liquor has to come through a wholesaler and Mayhew was also a wholesaler. He serviced most of Medford's party places."

"Well, well," she murmured.

The Captain lit a cigarette. Blowing a puff of smoke against the windshield, he said, "Uh Oh tells me that Edwin also extended them credit and even made loans to them. I don't imagine the loans were at regular bank rates. Mayhew wound up with part ownership in at least two clubs that I know about."

"Curiouser and curiouser," said Cordelia, stretching her legs out. "Liquor store owner, liquor wholesaler, nightclub owner, loan shark, and he ran a gambling operation. Old Edwin stayed busy."

"He was more than most people thought," replied the Captain. "He was probably more than we think."

Both policemen climbed out of Walker's sedan. He flipped his cigarette butt onto the concrete and they moved toward what was now Lavonia and Josephine's store.

Josephine Harvey stood behind a long counter on the right and slipped a customer's quart of Jack Daniel's into a brown paper bag. She glanced up as the detectives entered, staring at the Captain for a moment before ringing up her sale. Tall and willowy, with honey blonde hair brushed straight back, she looked younger than her fifty-four years.

She'd been twenty years younger than Mayhew on the day they married, and even then she'd known about Edwin's penchant for young girls. Josephine wasn't worried. With twenty years going for her, plus her own good looks and intelligence, she figured she could control Mayhew. That proved to be about as easy as controlling the wind, and a pretty fierce wind at that. The news of Mayhew's murder had stunned her, numbed her, and she was still amazed that this could be so.

Captain Walker knew her from chance meetings in the past. Once, they'd met at a party and he remembered how the men were drawn to her, not from any overt actions of her own, but from a sort of sensual essence emanating from her like scent from a flower, the soft smile and slow languorous movements promising an experience of overpowering sexual pleasure. Her walk was still smooth and flowing as she came around the counter to greet him.

"Evening Captain," she murmured. Her gaze moved briefly to Cordelia and returned to rest on Walker's face. The wide set eyes were cobalt, still and steady. "This a duty call?"

"I'm afraid so. Could we talk in your office?"

"Sure." Turning to a short, red-headed man who was lining up vodka bottles on a shelf, she called, "We'll be in the back, Robert." Robert nodded his head once without turning around.

They passed, single file, through Chinese bead curtains hanging at the rear of the store, and walked along a dark aisle, piled high on each side with cases of liquor. The office door was ajar and soft lighting shone through the opening. Leaning against the wall, to the right of the door, was Slim, arms folded and a sleepy expression on his face. He nodded at Walker and Cordelia as they passed through the doorway.

Both stared in surprise at the office's interior. Cordelia gave a soft whistle. The room was larger than she expected and was decorated in a style that could only be described as lavish. Dark oak paneling covered all four walls, lending a somber tone. A couple of oil paintings, featuring female nudes, hung behind the desk, and an oriental rug stretched across the floor. A couch and two plush chairs stood at the room's center. Mayhew had built a wet bar in one corner and next to it rested an antique slot machine. Cordelia wondered if it still worked. Several free-standing lamps with ornate shades cast a muted glow throughout the room. A wooden file cabinet, holding four drawers, rested against the right wall. Earl Gilbey was leaning against the cabinet, studying an invoice. He glanced up at them, placed the invoice in an inside coat pocket, and withdrew a pen and checkbook. Filling out the check, he murmured: "I'm sorry I had to bring the law into this, Miss Harvey, but the prices you're charging has become a matter for the authorities."

"Now Earl, with your keen eye for detail, I'm sure you noticed a ten percent discount at the bottom of your bill, in addition to your regular 'club' prices. That's something you never got from Edwin and he had a helluva lot more money coming in than I do."

Gilbey looked at Josephine and grinned. He turned to the Captain and his expression sobered. "I heard about the trouble, Billy. Good to see you're still standing."

Walker gave a slow nod and said, "I need to drop by your place tomorrow, Earl. Say early afternoon?"

"Sure thing, Cap'n, and bring that assistant with you. I got some sweet nothings to whisper in her ear."

"In you dreams, Uh Oh," Cordelia muttered as the huge black man walked past her. He winked and went out. Slim's small, dark hand appeared and softly closed the door behind them.

"Well, what can I do for you folks?" asked Josephine as she walked behind the desk. Her silk dress clung in all the right places and undulated with her movement. She lowered herself into the leather desk chair and motioned toward the couch. The two detectives sat down. Seeing Josephine light up a cigarette, Billy did the same.

"We need to see Edwin's papers, Miss Harvey, and anything else that might shed some light on the case."

"Oh call me Jo, Captain. Everybody else does." She made an outward gesture with her cigarette hand, leaving a swirl of gray smoke. "Everything in this office and the next room belonged to Edwin. All his business papers are in that filing cabinet. I keep my records out by the cash register. Look at anything you want. If it's okay with Lavonia, it's okay with me. The only thing I have control of is one third of the store's revenue."

"Next room?" inquired Cordelia.

"Yes, through there," replied Jo, pointing to a door on her left. "I thought that door was to a closet until I opened it. Edwin's little hideaway. Go ahead, take a look."

Cordelia got up, walked across the floor, and opened the door. The Captain followed. Most of the room was taken up by a four-poster bed and a massive cedar chest standing at the foot. To their left, a half-opened door led to a small but complete bathroom. Near the doorway, a stereo system sat on a glass table. Lavonia heard a tinkling sound and glanced up at the ceiling. She began to smile as she stared at the crystal chandelier. Then the smile faded and her mouth gaped open. She could watch her mouth gape open, because there above her, just beyond the chandelier and covering most of the ceiling, was a huge, all-reflecting mirror.

TWENTY-SIX

On Tuesday morning, Billy and Cordelia came in late. The day before had been a long one and the Captain decreed that work would not begin until ten o'clock. A few minutes before that hour, the door to the CID office opened and Walker entered. He'd just removed his leather jacket when he heard Cordelia's footsteps on the metal stairs.

"Oh yeah," she exclaimed as she came in. "I loved that extra shut-eye."

"I know what you mean," murmured Walker. He sat down behind his desk and began sifting through papers. "Let's get some of our other work cleared away. Then, we'll go through the boxes."

Five cardboard boxes sat in front of Walker's desk. Four of them displayed images of Wild Turkey and Jim Beam bourbon and contained everything they'd taken from Mayhew's filing cabinet. Cordelia placed both hands at the small of her back and massaged gently as she recalled helping lug them up the stairs.

"Fine with me," she replied, unbuttoning her long, wool topcoat and hanging it on the wall. Underneath she wore tight stone-washed jeans and a black silk blouse.

"By the way," said Walker, "how well do you know Roger Pruitt?"

"Not very well. He seems to be doing okay. I think he goes to the academy next week."

"Have you ever talked with him?"

"Sure, couple of times. Why?"

"What's your impression of him? How did he strike you?"

A light came on in Cordelia's head. He's looking for Bob's replacement.

She thought for a moment before answering. "He's sharp. Seems to be the serious type . . . but not Bob Claggert serious," she quickly added.

As an afterthought, she said, "I like him."

Walker went back to his paperwork.

"So when do we bring him upstairs?"

The Captain smiled and laid a sheet in the OUT box. "Let's see how he does at the academy," he said.

Billy and Cordelia often kept a conversation going as they pursued their deskwork. After a certain period of time, the ordinary paperwork required little concentration.

"You know, I always wondered about something when I was at the academy," she said. "Most of your time is spent in classrooms, in the field, or on the exercise yard. Maybe a fifth of your time is spent on the firing range. Yet, when final tests come up, your marksmanship counts for one half your grade."

"Well, there's always an instructor on the range. They encourage you to practice at every opportunity."

"Yeah," said Cordelia, thinking "encourage" was too weak a word. "But, come on, half your total grade?"

"Maybe," mused the Captain, "they figure all that classroom and field knowledge, plus a sound body, won't mean much if you allow yourself to get shot."

"Guess so," Cordelia replied. She went over to a filing cabinet and fished out a folder. Taking it to Walker, she asked about something inside. It was time to change the subject. Eddie Partee's ghost had begun to shimmer in the air.

They worked at their desks for a couple of hours and then

broke for lunch. Returning to the CID room, they pulled their chairs up beside the boxes. Billy opened one and took out a document. He scanned it, then handed it to Cordelia. She looked it over and laid it beside her. The process continued. For a long time, they were looking at nothing but invoices, invoices for liquor, invoices for repair work, invoices for supplies. These filled two boxes and accounted for the top two drawers in Edwin's filing cabinet. The next two boxes, representing the two bottom drawers, contained bank statements, canceled checks, and twelve ledgers, a ledger for each of the dozen nightclubs that Mayhew sold liquor to. The policemen examined these thoroughly, but noticed nothing of special interest. They saw, not surprisingly, that the Hawaiian Club was Edwin's best customer.

The fifth box had not come from the wooden filing cabinet and wasn't really a box. It was more like a cardboard filing drawer with a top that lifted off. Walker had discovered it under Edwin's four-poster bed.

Cordelia removed the lid. She noticed there was a divider in the middle, separating the drawer into two compartments. Both front and back compartments were full of ledgers. Cordelia pulled one from the front. Its cover read DOTY'S PLACE. Cordelia recalled a small bar, located on Medford's north side. She looked at the first page. It listed a record of loans and payments continuing on to the next page. When she passed it to the Captain, a paper fell out and Walker picked it up. It was a deed. Edwin Walker owned one fourth of Doty's Place. The other ledgers also showed loan transactions of varying amounts. Cordelia was looking at one for two hundred dollars. Another was for four thousand. Not all the ledgers were for nightclubs. One had JAKE'S GARAGE printed on the cover and another one bore the words LACEY'S USED AUTOS. Billy noticed that only loan amounts were entered in the journals, no record of interest charges or total sums.

"Arkansas has a usury law," he said. "You can't charge over ten percent interest."

"Yeah, I know," said Cordelia. She traced payment on the four-thousand-dollar loan and did some quick arithmetic. Interest on four thousand should not be more than four hundred dollars, for a total of forty-four hundred. The borrower had already paid back close to five thousand. It appeared he was still paying.

Billy and Cordelia turned to the drawer's back section. These ledgers showed nothing but addresses on their covers. Billy recognized some of them as locations for nightclubs. Others appeared to be residences, and exclusive ones at that. Cordelia checked out a couple of the numbers in the police reverse directory and found that they were motels.

"The gambling files," Billy murmured.

Cordelia glanced at some of the pages and saw that this was so. Dates and amounts. Dates and amounts. On and on for page after page. Mayhew had penned a name beside each entry. Cordelia gave her boss a questioning look.

"His dealers," said Walker.

They found that Mayhew always rotated his dealers from place to place. It was obvious Edwin didn't want any of them getting too friendly with the clientele. Their honesty could also be checked. If four successive dealers each turned in three hundred dollars a night from a certain place and the fifth dealer only turned in two hundred, and this went on for a period of time . . . well, Old Edwin would probably start looking at that fifth dealer with a cold eye.

Cordelia wondered who would be the worst man to have pissed off at you, Edwin or Earl. Against all practical considerations, her gut feeling was it had to be Edwin. Uh Oh was a brute force, something to be feared and avoided. But Edwin?

Edwin was just . . . scary.

Finally, all the papers had been examined and put back in the containers. Walker and Hull dragged them into the evidence room and stacked them in a corner. They returned to their desks and Walker lit a cigarette. Each stared at the other through the smoke.

"Not too productive, was it?" remarked Cordelia. "Really, those papers just verified what we already suspected."

"Yes, but it helped, Cordelia. We suspected in general. Now we know in specifics. For instance, we know who obtained the biggest loans from Mayhew, who struggled the hardest to repay him, and who lost part of their business to him."

"How do we know who was struggling?"

"The payment dates. You can tell who started to miss them and was trying to catch up."

Cordelia nodded. "And we know a lot more about the gambling, don't we?"

"Indeed we do. We know where they were held and who the dealers were. And with that information we're going to find out who the players were. Maybe one of the big losers figured the game was rigged."

"So what happened to the revenge motive?"

"Well, financial ruin can be a pretty good reason for revenge." Walker stubbed his cigarette out and stretched both arms over his head. "Anyway, we've got lots of interviewing to do. These records have shown us a bunch of contacts and that's the most enticing thing about them."

Odd word to use, though Cordelia. Enticing. What the hell did he mean by that? She cast a dubious look at her boss. "Everything you say is true. Now what is it you're not saying. I'm a little slow today. Must be too much sleep."

"There's something . . . something . . ." said Walker in a dying voice. "Edwin wouldn't just . . ." The Captain's eyes held that black, faraway look. He gazed past her shoulder and Cordelia felt, for a crazy moment, that he was looking at Edwin Mayhew. Walker fumbled at his shirt pocket, fumbling for the pack of cigarettes. Suddenly, the hand became still and his gaze regained its focus. The pack remained in his pocket. Turning to Cordelia, he asked: "What kind of records have we looked at?"

"Invoices," she replied, "canceled checks, statements, bills, plus all the account ledgers."

"What kind of accounts?"

"Well," said his assistant, "there were his records showing liquor sales to the nightclubs. Then, his personal drawer under the bed. That one held the gambling and loan ledgers."

"And the loans were to various businesses around town," replied Walker. "Businesses that, for one reason or another, couldn't get a regular bank loan."

"Yes."

"Mayhew was a hustler, Cordelia, and he didn't let many opportunities pass him by. Liquor, gambling, loan sharking, and part ownerships. He exploited everything to the hilt. That was his nature. And he was meticulous about bookkeeping. We've seen that."

"Captain, I . . ." Cordelia was lost completely.

"What did you call the box under his bed, Cordelia? Didn't you say it was his 'personal' drawer? Since it contained records outside regular business, not to mention outside the law, it could be called personal, but the loans and the gambling were just more of his professional enterprises. Now, think about his loan-sharking. The records show that all the loans were made to businesses, Cordelia, businesses. Remember, Edwin was a hustler. He exploited everything and took it to the limit."

For the second time that day, the light came on in Cordelia's head. "There were also personal loans," she said. "There had to be. Edwin wouldn't have ignored such a large market." She remembered the Captain's words. Mayhew would have to exploit it, she thought. And he was meticulous about records. She looked up to see the Captain watching her.

"Yes," he said, "there's another drawer, the most personal drawer of all, containing names of people who could have a very personal reason for hating Mayhew."

"But it's not at the liquor store," she replied. "We searched everywhere."

Billy smiled. "And we found that 'personal' drawer under his bed. That is, under one of his beds."

Lavonia opened the door, in answer to their knock, and stood staring at the two policemen. She smiled and said, "Well, you're too early for supper."

"That's a shame," said Cordelia. "It sure smells good."

"Well honey, you're welcome anytime." The old lady cast a questioning look at the Captain.

"Lavonia," he said. "We need to look in Edwin's room."

"Sure," she replied. "Not much to look at, though. Come on inside."

Lavonia returned to her kitchen and the policemen walked into Mayhew's bedroom. Cordelia switched on the lamp and Billy got down on his hands and knees and peered beneath the bed.

He immediately saw the box. It was shaped like a drawer and had a lift-off top and it waited under Mayhew's bed like all the ancient debts of the world.

TWENTY-SEVEN

By ten o'clock on Wednesday morning, the Captain and Cordelia had looked at all the ledgers in Mayhew's last box. There were twenty thin volumes. They contained names and addresses and phone numbers. Like the business loan files, the amounts were listed but no interest figures were entered. Edwin kept a careful record of payment. Other documents were inserted in some of the ledgers: motel bills, arrest records. A couple contained explicit sexual pictures. No doubt Edwin used this additional information to keep his borrowers honest.

The policemen emerged onto the station parking lot under a heavy overcast. Snow began to fall, flakes tumbling straight down through the still air. The fall increased, as they watched, and one cold crystal touched Cordelia's cheek. She laughed and performed a quick little dance step. The Captain gave her a quizzical look.

Cordelia carried five of the twenty ledgers. In their estimation, these were the important ones, the people most likely to strike out against Mayhew. The old man played rough, she thought, very rough indeed.

These five people they would call on together. The remainder would be divided up and handled individually. The ledgers for the gambling and the business loans would be looked into later. It seemed to Cordelia that the Captain was placing all the emphasis on these personal loans.

They pulled out of the parking lot and headed up Court

Street, into the thickening snow. Cordelia looked at the top ledger.

"Three-twenty North Seventh Street," she said. "Edward Wheeler."

Walker picked up the radio mike. "CID One, Medford."

"Go ahead, CID One."

"One and Two will be out for most of the day. I'll check back for messages."

"Ten four, CID One." Sally Harris had the duty.

"And Sally, call the Aloha Club. Tell Earl Gilbey we'll have to postpone our business till tomorrow."

"Ten four, Captain. Oh, the Chief wants to see you when you get time."

"Ten four." Walker replaced the microphone.

Cordelia couldn't resist. "He must have just come to work, huh?"

No answer. She didn't expect one. "Uh, you can make a U-turn right up here Captain, take you right back to the station." She heard her boss chuckle. First time this week.

Wheeler's dilapidated frame house sat well back from the street. Peeling paint curled from the cheap siding. The front porch sagged. A pane was missing from one of the windows and a piece of dirty blanket had been stuffed into the opening. The detectives stepped carefully across the front porch and knocked on the door.

Ed Wheeler seemed very cordial. He invited them in and offered them seats on a worn, lumpy sofa. Walker made the introductions. Wheeler sat down in an armchair, carefully balancing his coffee cup. The fragrance emanating from the cup explained Ed's diligence, and perhaps his cordiality.

Booze, thought Cordelia, one of the more economical brands. As Ed lifted the whiskey to his lips, she noticed that two of his fingers were missing.

"Thanks for seeing us, Mr. Wheeler," the Captain began in his ever polite tone. "We'd have called first, but couldn't find your phone number. Glad we caught you at home."

"Ain't got no phone and I'm generally at home," grinned Wheeler.

Cordelia noted that some teeth, as well as the fingers, were missing. Ed kept staring at her legs.

"Retired from the Fausco Sawmill last year," he continued. He sat the cup down and held up both hands. "Figured it was about time."

Cordelia saw, with dismay, that two fingers were also missing from the left hand.

Wheeler grasped the liquor-filled cup and thrust it toward the Captain. "Likely this had something to do with it."

Walker gave a quick nod.

"Booze and sawmill work don't mix," declared Ed. "I was drinkin' when I lost these, and drinkin' when I lost these." Each mutilated hand held up in turn. "Sawmill work's all I know. Worked at Fausco for twenty-four years, but I seen right quick I'se goin' to have to quit one or the other. That or git whittled down to nothin'. Cah! Cah! Cah!" A harsh cackle issued forth. "So I hung on to the one I enjoy. Cah! Cah!" A drop of spittle oozed down Wheeler's chin. Cordelia turned her head.

"So you retired," declared Walker.

"Yep. Money ain't much, but my Social and what little I git from Fausco keep me goin'."

Billy glanced at Cordelia and she leaned forward. "Mr. Wheeler, when was the last time you had to get a loan?"

The old man studied her as he took a sip from the cup. "You mean, the one from Edwin Mayhew," he stated.

"Why would I mean that one?" she asked.

"You know why, Cordelia, if I can call you that," said Wheeler. "Edwin's been murdered, and you've been going through his records. I may be a drunk, but I ain't a criminal, so why else would you be visiting me."

"When did you get the loan?" asked Walker.

"Well, let's see. It was about a month after I quit my job. The Social Security hadn't kicked in and Fausco was late with my first retirement check. Things were gettin' a little lean. I didn't really want to float a loan from the bank. Bastards want to know your life history and the last time you went to the toilet. Besides, with my rep, they probably wouldn't have give it to me anyway." Wheeler lifted his cup and drained it.

"So I went to Edwin. Word was he'd loan you money, but the interest was high. And the word was you'd damn sure better pay him back. Well, Mayhew asked how much I needed. I told him five hundred. He reached down beneath his cash register and brought out five one-hundred-dollar bills. Then he made a note in his little ledger and that was it. I paid him back in full."

"Ever late with a payment?" asked the Captain.

Wheeler lowered his head and cast a furtive glance at Cordelia. "Well yeah, once. I went on a drunk and kinda let one slip."

Walker gazed at Wheeler. The silence lengthened. "Did Mayhew pay you a visit, Ed."

"Yeah, he come out. I'se drunk at the time." The old man gave a feeble grin. "Think I mouthed off a little. Told him I'd bought enough whiskey from him to make up for a dozen loans."

Walker reached out his hand and Cordelia placed the ledger in it. He opened the cover. The first page gave the total history of Wheeler's loan. A notation appeared in the middle: "paid visit/whacked mutt."

"Did Edwin do anything, get violent," he asked, looking up.

"Naw, he just said I'd better be on time from now on and left. I paid the loan off. The book will show that."

Billy handed the open ledger to Ed Wheeler. The old man

pulled a pair of half glasses from his shirt pocket and looked down at the entries. Suddenly, his eyes opened wide and he glared up at Walker.

"The rotten son of a bitch," he muttered. "The dirty, rotten son of a bitch." He got up and lurched into the kitchen. He returned and sank back down in his chair. The cup was full again.

All three sat silently and Cordelia noticed that the old man's eyes had tears in them.

"You had a dog, didn't you Ed?" Walker's voice was thoughtful.

Wheeler took a deep swallow from the cup and cleared his throat. "Yes sir. Wasn't much. Jist an old hound." He stared into his whiskey.

"What was his name?" asked Billy.

"Jeff, jist Jeff. My brother, the one who give him to me, his name was Jeff, too."

"What happened, Ed?"

Wheeler shook his head in wonder. "Mayhew had a baseball bat. I was settin' in this same chair and Jeff was stretched out on the floor. Mayhew walked over to him and old Jeff raised his head and Mayhew clubbed him, jist clubbed him on the head, and then hit him again for good measure."

"Go on," said Billy.

"Then he stood over me with that bloody bat and said, 'This time it was the dog, Wheeler. Next time it's gonna be you.' Then he turned around and left."

A tear trickled down the old man's cheek. Cordelia walked over to the window and stared out at the falling snow.

"Mr. Wheeler." Billy asked the question quietly. "Did you kill Edwin Mayhew?"

"Naw, Captain, though I wanted to. Mayhew was a killer. I never was."

"What did you do after Mayhew left?"

Ed wiped his eyes with a stained handkerchief. "The only thing I could do," he replied. "I paid Mayhew his money. And then I buried Jeff."

TWENTY-EIGHT

The police car turned back south on Court Street and lost traction, for a moment, in the accumulated snow. Cordelia turned and placed Ed Wheeler's ledger on the rear seat.

"I think we can keep looking," she said. "Ed's not the one who killed him."

"Are you sure?" asked the Captain.

Cordelia smiled and nodded her head. "Yeah. He would never have wasted that whiskey." She heard her boss chuckle. Second time that day.

"Of course, that's mainly it, isn't it?" he said. "Ed would sit and drink and think about it, but that's all it would amount to."

"Yep. Of course, if old Edwin had been brained with a baseball bat, we might think differently. We could also call it justifiable homicide." Glancing at Walker, she murmured, "The unbelievable bastard."

Billy nodded his head and asked, "Who's next?"

Hull scanned the next ledger in her lap. "Gloria Reisner, One-fourteen Zenith. This is the one with the restaurant. Loan's not paid off yet."

They were approaching the station house. Walker slowed down and turned into the parking lot. They entered the building and Cordelia went to the bathroom. Billy walked back to Chief Roland Wheaton's office. He stood in the open doorway and stared at a display, which had no doubt been set up for his benefit.

Ten mason jars were stacked in a pyramid on Roland's desk. Each jar displayed the smiling face of Leonard Simpson and each was filled with coins, plus a good amount of paper money. Roland sat behind the jars. He rose and grinned at Billy.

"Yesterday was pick-up day," he exclaimed. "Whaddaya think?"

"This is very impressive, Roland," Walker commented, as he walked from side to side. "I had no idea you'd get this much. Have you counted it yet?"

"No, but I'm thinking it's got to be two or three thousand."

Walker didn't think it was quite that much, but he wasn't about to say so. "Well, it's a wonderful thing you've done. The Simpsons will sure be surprised."

"Yeah, well I've been known to have a good idea occasionally," said Roland. His face looked redder than usual.

"More than occasionally, Chief, and this was one of them." He knew Roland had honestly forgotten that the idea had not been his own and that, in his own way, Roland *had* done a wonderful thing. "When does Leonard's family get this?" he asked.

"I'm taking it over right now."

"As it is?"

"Sure. Why not?"

"Well, it's none of my business, Chief, but all those coins. That's going to mean a lot of work for Mrs. Simpson. Separating them, rolling them, cashing them in. Maybe you should let the bank handle it."

"Yeah, maybe you're right," said Roland, scratching his chin. "But hell, Billy, I wanted her to see it still in the jars."

"Hold on, Roland. I think I've got the solution."

Walker went to his office. A moment later, he reappeared with a self-developing camera. A beaming Roland Wheaton stood beside the display and Billy snapped the picture. He left the Chief content.

Back in the car, Cordelia gave him a questioning look.

"The Chief wanted to show me the collection for Leonard."

"Oh," she said. "By the way, did you know his family is moving back to Mississippi?"

"Yes," answered Walker. "They're going to live with Leonard's parents."

"What about Leonard?"

"He's going with them," said Walker. "He'll be buried in the family plot."

They turned right on Zenith Street and drove northward into the wind. The snow had lessened and only a few flakes swept against the windshield. The bright glow of a strip shopping center lightened the gloom ahead. Billy pulled into the parking lot. In front of them appeared a Piggly Wiggly Supermarket, Dottie's Hair Salon, and the Opening Night Video Store. Just to the right of Opening Night, stood Gloria Reisner's restaurant. A neon sign, in the shape of an antlered deer head, hung over the door. To the right of it, were large block letters, spelling out THE HUNGRY HUNTER. The policemen went inside.

A checkout counter, complete with extra menus, a cash register, and a gum-chewing teenager, stood on their left. Polished dining tables stretched in front of them.

Cordelia began taking off her overcoat while she stared at the walls. She kept staring at all four of them, turning around in a complete circle. She'd never seen so many deer heads. Mounted side by side, they ran down every side. More heads appeared on the wall in back, looking out with blank, glassy eyes.

"Just pick a table," stated the cashier, "the waitress will be with you in a minute." Somehow, she'd managed to keep chewing the gum throughout her message. Cordelia hung her coat on a free-standing rack. She and Billy took a table next to the wall. Above them, a six-point buck gazed in serene indifference at his friends across the way.

"Are we eating?" she asked.

"Are you hungry?"

Menus were already laid out on the table. "Um hm," she responded, picking one up.

A waitress came over, carrying two glasses of water and the silverware. She was slightly stooped with lines of fatigue about her mouth. Nevertheless, she produced a quick smile. "You folks ready to order," she asked. "The 'special' goes on till one o'clock. Choice of two meats and you get two vegetables, plus dessert."

"Is one of the meats venison?" asked Cordelia.

"Why no," came the surprised answer. "One is meat loaf, the other is chicken." Then another smile crossed her face. "Oh, I get it," she said. "No, the rest of those deer are someplace else."

"I'll just have a cheeseburger and Coke," stated the Captain. Cordelia ordered the same.

"Is the owner in?" he asked.

"No sir. Gone to the bank. She should be back shortly."

Their order came and the detectives ate quietly. As they were finishing, a tall, spare woman came through the door and walked toward the back. A few moments later, she reappeared and came over to their table.

"You wanted to see me?" she said. The green eyes rested on Walker. He returned her look, for a moment, before answering. An attractive woman, just shy of being beautiful.

"Are you Gloria Reisner?" he asked.

"Yes." The voice was flat.

"I'm Captain Walker, Ms. Reisner. Medford Police. This is Sergeant Hull."

"Yes, I recognized you, Captain." She nodded at Cordelia. "My office is in the back, if you want to go there."

"Yes, thank you," said Billy.

The office was cramped and unadorned. A battered desk occupied one corner. A folding metal chair sat in front of it. Cardboard boxes lined the walls. Cordelia noticed a faded sofa and took a seat. The Captain sat down beside her. Gloria stared at them and continued standing. Finally, she sat down on the metal chair.

Billy took the ledger from Cordelia and opened it. The loan to Gloria had been twelve thousand dollars, given in January. She'd made regular payments since then. About three thousand dollars had been repaid. As usual, the amount of interest was not shown.

Walker continued to scan the amounts, while Cordelia stared at the restaurant owner. Gloria's face remained impassive. The silence lengthened. Finally, the Captain looked up.

"You've got a nice place here, Ms. Reisner. When did you buy it?"

A slight pause, then, "Last January."

Walker raised the ledger slightly. "And that's when you received this loan from Edwin Mayhew."

"You mean the guy that got killed? The liquor store owner? You're way off base, Captain. I never even met the man. The only loan I got was from my husband. He helped me with the down payment."

"No, you obtained a loan from Mayhew." The Captain's voice was firm. "It amounted to twelve thousand dollars. Edwin made a ledger for it. This one. You've made ten payments so far. Since the loan was illegal, he probably made you pay in cash."

Gloria pointed at the ledger. "Is my signature in there anywhere? Since you think I paid in cash, I guess you didn't find any checks."

"No," Billy replied. "No signature. No checks."

Gloria leaned back in her chair and lit a cigarette. "Well, I'm sorry, Captain, but I don't know what you're talking about."

Cordelia stared at her. The green eyes didn't blink and her high-cheekboned face remained immobile. She's a cool one, thought the detective . . . tough nut. The Captain had a hole card though. It lay between the pages of the ledger. She knew her boss. He wouldn't use it unless he had to.

Walker let out a soft sigh. "Ms. Reisner, if you're worried about the loan's illegality, let me tell you that you won't be held accountable. Edwin would be the only one charged with usury."

"And Edwin is dead," she said.

"Yes, which also means you can tell me the truth without having to worry about paying off the loan. It was illegal and only Edwin could collect."

Gloria pulled on the cigarette and blew smoke out through her nose. "No," she said, "Mr. Mayhew could never collect any money from me, because he never loaned me any." Studying the Captain, she added, "And I'm starting to wonder if I should call my lawyer."

Billy lowered his eyes to the ledger. He turned the first page and studied the black and white photograph. It had been enlarged to five-by-seven size and the clarity was excellent.

Gloria Reisner lay on her back in the four-poster bed. She had raised one knee and the leg was slightly spread. Her naked body shone in tawny splendor under the chandelier lights, the pubic thatch making a dark contrast. One arm reached out to the man above her. He stood at the foot of the bed and his left hand rested on a camera, laying face up on the cedar chest. His figure was not as distinct as Gloria's, but there was no mistaking who it was.

The policemen had studied the picture earlier. They knew how Mayhew did it. He'd carefully arranged the camera so it would photograph their reflection in the ceiling mirror. As soon as Cordelia saw the picture, she somehow knew that the woman on the bed didn't know about the camera. She was relaxed, unworried, with eyes only for her lover.

And Mayhew, in that picture, was all the vile connivers of the world.

Without another word, Walker walked over and placed the snapshot in Gloria Reisner's hands.

Cordelia watched a terrible change come over the restaurant owner's face. The blood drained away. The prominent cheekbones seemed almost visible under the skin. Then, the blood rushed back and her face swelled and turned crimson. Her hand trembled as she returned the picture to Walker. She turned in her chair and faced away from them.

"Did you know about this picture?" asked the Captain.

"No," she whispered.

He returned to the couch and sat facing her. Softly, he said, "Ms. Reisner, I've no wish to embarrass you. You don't know me, but people who do will tell you that I know how to keep a confidence. My associate is the same. If you're honest with us, and if you're innocent in the matter of Mayhew's murder, I promise there's nothing to worry about."

"Innocent in Mayhew's murder? My God, you don't think that I had anything to do with . . ." Gloria turned her wide eyes toward Cordelia.

Hull glanced at the Captain and said, "Gloria, we don't know what to think. You haven't been very cooperative."

"What was the percentage rate on the loan?" asked Billy.

Reisner hesitated a moment before answering. "Twenty percent. He said that was five percent cheaper than what he usually charged."

"And why would he let you have a loan at cheaper rates?" The Captain's voice gave away nothing.

Gloria blushed again and dropped her head. "I don't know. That was before we became . . . involved. But I guess he had that on his mind from the first." She straightened and leaned toward Billy.

"Captain, this restaurant came up for sale the first of the year. I came over to look at it, and I knew, soon as I saw it, that I wanted this place more than I've ever wanted anything in my life. It was like I woke up and finally realized what I was meant for . . . to own my own business, to be my own boss. And this was the place I had to have.

"I knew I could make a go of it. Trouble was, the down payment was twenty thousand dollars. The owner would finance the rest, but he had to have twenty thousand up front. I borrowed six thousand from the bank and my husband gave me two thousand." Gloria lowered her eyes. "It was all he had. The owner told me about Edwin Mayhew, so I went to see him. The rest you know."

"Did Mayhew mention any collateral," asked Cordelia.

"No. I expected him to, but it never came up. I just couldn't believe he was actually going to lend me all that money. He gave me six thousand right then and told me to come back the next day for the rest of it. When I saw him the following day, he only gave me three and told me he'd have the remaining three by the weekend. That Saturday, I got the rest of it."

"Why do you think he made you return twice more?" asked Cordelia.

"I kind of think he just wanted to see me again. I guess he wanted the extra time to work on me. He knew how to work on people. At the end of that week, he didn't have to work on me any more."

Cordelia spread both hands, palms up, in front of her. "What did he do, Gloria? What did he say to persuade you."

Gloria Reisner turned to the Captain.

"It might be helpful to know," he said.

The young woman spread both hands, as if imitating Cordelia. "I honest to God don't know. I had never been unfaithful to Earl. Edwin was an old man, but there was something about him. Of course, I was grateful for the money, but that wasn't it. I'm not a whore. He was interesting, and I could tell, just by talking to him, that he'd never needed anybody. Oh, I think I knew he was a bad man, but he was his own man. He fascinated me, and he finally convinced me that going into that back bedroom with him was the only thing to do."

"How long did it go on," asked Cordelia.

"About a month. I got busy here and stopped calling or going by, except to make a payment. Edwin never tried to force anything and the only thing I'd come to feel was shame."

"Gloria, during that time, perhaps in an intimate moment, did Mayhew mention anyone he thought might be a danger to him, someone he feared?"

A sad smile crossed Gloria's face. "No, Captain Walker. I don't think Edwin ever had an intimate moment with anyone, or ever met a person he feared."

The Captain rose from the couch. "Is there anything else you can tell us? Anything that might help?"

"I honestly can't," she replied. "Although, there's one thing I wasn't accurate about."

"What was that?"

"I said that Mayhew didn't get any collateral, but he did, didn't he? He snapped it from the foot of that bed."

"Yes," said the Captain. "I think that was his intention."

Gloria's face sank into her hands, her shoulders began to shake, and the detectives could hear her muffled sobs.

Cordelia rose and went out the office door. The Captain walked over to the weeping woman and again took the photograph from Mayhew's ledger. Gently, he placed it on the desk beside her and followed Cordelia from the room.

They drove back to the station house in silence. The Captain hadn't ventured anything, but Cordelia figured they were in agreement. The first two interviews had produced no suspects. They had produced only victims.

The remainder of the day was spent in the CID room, pursuing other cases, making calls, talking to a few informants. At five o'clock, Cordelia left for home, and a few minutes later, the Captain followed.

He drove northeast along Florence Avenue. Medford Cemetery lay off to the right, vast, misty, and nebulous in the darkening air. The ashen tombstones seemed to rise up out of nothingness. On an impulse, Walker turned right and passed under the graveyard's arched entrance way. He slowly drove to the top of a slight rise, stopped, and peered down the opposite slope.

Below him lay an open grave. Two women stood at the edge, staring into its dark depths, looking at the coffin there. A back-hoe was parked next to a mound of freshly turned earth and the operator slouched in its seat. An old Buick waited behind the women. They did not look up, but in that dying light, Walker recognized them both.

Slowly and carefully, he backed around and drove away.

Edwin Mayhew had returned from Little Rock, and only Josephine and Lavonia were there to see him lowered into the ground.

Twenty-Nine

By noon, Cordelia and the Captain had visited the addresses in two more of Mayhew's ledgers. They planned on doing the final one after seeing Earl Gilbey. That would complete the five most promising ones. The others could be divided up and handled one on one.

Their first call that day had been to the home of Nathaniel Briggs, which availed them nothing. Nathaniel had long since disappeared, and his house was in the process of doing the same thing. The asphalt shingled roof had collapsed in two places and a series of gaping holes looked down on the rooms below. The open front door hung crookedly on its hinges and the wooden porch leading to it was an obstacle course of ripped-up boards and exposed joists. A sign, almost hidden by tall weeds, stood in the front yard. It announced that the house was condemned, but that the lot was for sale. The name "Watson Realty" appeared at the bottom.

Billy and Cordelia had visited the real estate office and talked to Baker Watson. He informed them that Briggs had been the last tenant and had left two months ago. Baker hadn't been able to tell them much else. He mentioned that Briggs was a quiet man, living alone with his teenaged daughter, who seemed to have been a wild one.

"Of course, that would figure," he added.

The Captain wanted to know why.

"Why hell, you know what they say about preachers' kids,"

he laughed. "Oh yeah, Nathaniel Briggs was a preacher. He didn't have a church or anything, just preached at revivals or showed up as sort of a 'guest preacher' at various fundamentalist churches. Rest of the time, he did carpenter work."

Billy had pushed Watson to talk more about Nathaniel Briggs, to tell them anything he knew of a personal nature.

"Well," the realtor responded, "if you want to know what kind of man he was, I can tell you that he was a good man and an honest man. One thing for sure, he never missed a rent payment. You know, every once in a while, you meet somebody that you just know you can rely on, and that was Reverend Briggs. I liked him. Hell, once, when he was sort of hard up, I even offered to spot him a couple of months."

"You mean, not pay any rent?" asked Cordelia.

"Sure, and if you know me, you'd know I really have to like somebody to do that. But, like I say, Briggs was in a tight, and besides, he used to work on that old house a lot, nailing up shingles and so forth. Anyway, he refused to do it, take my offer I mean. He got the money from somewhere and paid me right on time."

Cordelia had asked about the daughter.

"Just kind of wild," said Watson. "She came by a couple of times, and well, I sensed she might be flirting with me. But I backed off in a hurry. She was only sixteen, if that."

Hull asked if Baker knew where Nathaniel might have gone.

"Nope. He came to me one day and said he'd be leaving in two weeks. Didn't say where. I wished him good luck and that was that. Maybe he wanted to get the daughter out of town and away from bad influences. Besides, that old house was getting pretty raggedy."

Watson had been curious as to why the police would be interested in a man like Nathaniel. Billy and Cordelia left him that way.

The other borrower was Robert Howell, an ex–Morton Rubber Company employee, who lay quietly dying of lung cancer. He'd help build thousands of auto tires for Morton in a factory full of smoke, dust, and rubber particles. His family thought the company was responsible and had hired lawyers. Robert was past caring. Earlier, the hospital had given up and sent him home. Billy and Cordelia looked down on a breathing corpse, eyes closed, lifeless hair plastered to the skull, withered chest rising and falling with each labored breath. His wife said he'd been like this for a month.

The loan to Howell had been a small one, made a year ago and paid off quickly. The wife hadn't known about it. The policeman didn't ask her any further questions. They left Robert undisturbed.

The squad car bumped over a set of railroad tracks and Cordelia looked up from the third ledger. The Line lay before them. Billy turned right, drove beside the railroad tracks for a ways, then turned left on Crescent.

He turned to Cordelia and said, "When we get back, I want you to do a complete rundown on Nathaniel Briggs. Check his name out through our computer base and then go national. You may have to see Baker Watson again for a Social Security number or whatever else he might have. The preacher is . . ." His voice died away.

Cordelia gave him a look. Yeah, he was definitely thinking about Nathaniel. "You want me to keep on going after the rundown?" she asked.

The Captain understood what she meant . . . follow the trail, talk to people, and if possible, track Briggs down to wherever he was? The question was necessary. It meant spending extra time.

"Yes."

"You didn't like what you saw in the ledger, did you?"

The Captain gave her a benevolent smile. "What makes you think so?"

"Briggs defaulted on the loan. And that's kinda strange, because he was meticulous in paying all his other debts, at least according to his landlord. He skipped town owing Mayhew, let's see," Cordelia perused the ledger, "at least two thousand. If we believe Watson, that was completely out of character."

"Yes," said Billy, "and Watson is a hard-nosed businessman. I know Baker Watson and I'd go a long way with his character assessment on anybody."

"I'll work on it," said Cordelia. The Captain didn't respond.

They continued down Crescent and passed its small commercial cluster. A few idlers stood on the sidewalks. Three young black men eyed the police car, then turned their backs to it. Billy stopped in front of the Hawaiian Club and picked up the radio mike.

"Medford, CID One."

"Go ahead, CID One."

"One and Two at the Hawaiian Club. Will inform you when we leave."

"Ten four, Number One."

The Captain gave a slight grimace. CID One was his regulation radio code. Lately, people on the force had started referring to him as "Number One." The term was beginning to replace "Captain" and even his name. A few daring souls had called him "Number One" to his face. They did not get a favorable response.

Cordelia listened to the familiar exchange and experienced deja vu. The vision of a flaming Molotov cocktail flickered through her mind. They got out of the car and heard, from inside, the discordant sounds of a band at practice. They also heard, as if keeping time, a rhythmic whacking sound. It came from behind Earl's place. They looked at each other and walked around back.

A group of children sat in a circle, watching a small, dark man in their center. He stood motionless, facing a post with a projecting arm. From the arm hung a long, leather punching bag. In spite of the cold, the man wore only a tee-shirt and some loose-fitting trousers. His feet were bare. As they watched, the man's right heel raised up a couple of inches. His left leg blurred around in a flat arc and his foot crashed into the bag. He lowered the leg and became motionless again, both feet flat on the ground. The man repeated the blow twice more and Cordelia would have sworn that the heel and leg were the only parts of his body that moved. The bag, in the meantime, swung wildly to and fro.

"Do it, Slim. Do it," shouted a small boy.

The fighter ignored him and stared at the bag.

"Aw, come on, Slim," the boy entreated.

A grin flashed across the ebony face and Slim floated into the air (that was the only word for it), slashing his foot once more into the leather bag. This time, the blow landed near the top and the bag twisted back and forth like a church bell in a tower. A whapping sound echoed across the yard and the children jumped to their feet, screaming in glee. The fighter lightly descended to his original position and looked over his shoulder. He gave the detectives a slight nod and watched them as they walked away.

Walker and Hull returned to the front entrance and went inside. They stood inside the doorway for a moment, while their eyes adjusted to the subdued lighting. A well-dressed man sat at the bar, nursing a vodka Collins and talking to the bartender. Two older men, one with white hair and the other wearing a broad-brimmed hat, played dominoes at a center table. A walking stick hung from the table's edge. Four musicians were on their platform practicing different approaches to "Dock of the

Bay." The piano player hit a sour note.

"God damned, man," shouted the white-haired domino player. "When y'all gonna git through with that shit? I caint think what I'm doin'."

The skinny guitar player looked up and called, "Hey Roscoe, you still work at that barber shop?"

"That's exactly right," returned white hair.

"Well motherfucker, when I come over to where you work and yell, 'when y'all gonna git through with that shit,' then you may do that to me."

The old man with the hat had been staring at the dominoes, but now he snatched his walking stick and shook it at the guitar player. "You best watch yo name callin'." he yelled.

"Hey, I didn't call you no motherfucker," the guitar player answered. "I called him a motherfucker, but if you want to be a motherfucker, why then, you can be a motherfucker, too."

"I aint gonna be many more motherfuckers," shouted the first old man. At this, everybody, including the domino players, broke up in laughter.

Billy and Cordelia walked across the wooden floor and knocked on Earl Gilbey's office door. Every eye in the place was on them. The door swung open and Uh Oh loomed before them.

"Hey Captain! Hey Cordelia! Come on in." Earl leaned past them out the doorway. "You gentlemen take a break," he said to the musicians.

They left the bandstand, walked over to the domino players, and stood watching the game. The white-haired one cut his eyes up at the guitar player and said, "Uh Oh Earl just saved you from gittin' a walkin' stick crost yo ass."

Earl went behind his desk and motioned for them to sit down. Cordelia took her coat off and caught Gilbey giving her an appraising look. He noticed and immediately went into his routine.

"Sorry old thing. It's just, oh how shall I put it? You are simply most awfully appealing, and I, after all, am not completely without a libido."

Cordelia started laughing. She couldn't help it. That high-timbre voice and the Etonian accent coming from Uh Oh broke her up every time.

Billy lit a cigarette and Earl picked up a cigar from the ashtray. The small office began to fill up with smoke and Cordelia tried to breath as shallowly as possible.

"Any management problems?" asked Billy, and Cordelia knew he wasn't talking about the nightclub. Gilbey had taken over the gambling again.

"Nope. At the moment, it's about like it used to be. Occasional problem here and there, but I think the control is back in place."

"Yeah, I saw part of it in the back yard," murmured Cordelia.

Uh Oh smiled at her. "Who Slim? Aw, he's just a pussy cat."

"Um hm," she said. "I saw a pussy cat like that at the Memphis Zoo. How does he do that stuff anyway?"

"He gives up years of his life learning how, and then more years getting better," answered Earl.

The bartender opened the door and Earl nodded. He returned in a moment carrying two frosted glasses of Coke.

"As you know," said Gilbey, returning to business, "I had three sharks circling. Now, as you also know, only one is still . . . active."

"That would be Nat Thomas," said Billy.

"Yep. Well, old Nat is now my number-one poker dealer."

"If you can't lick 'em, join 'em," said Hull.

"Exactly," he replied.

They were silent for a moment. Billy and Cordelia sipped from their glasses. Earl's cigar smoke swirled in front of them.

"When are you gonna get to Edwin Mayhew?" the big man asked.

A smile touched the Captain's lips. He leaned forward and said, "Very well, talk to me about him."

"What do you want to know?"

"Everything," said Walker. "Tell me the story of Edwin Mayhew."

Uh Oh ground out his cigar, leaned back in his chair, and placed both hands behind his neck. The huge biceps strained against the shirt cloth.

"Okay," he said. "Once upon a time there was a liquor store owner named Edwin Mayhew and he had no friends. He had customers and he had little girls for sex and he had people who hated him and a bunch of folks who feared him, but he had no friends. And here's what made Edwin different: he absolutely did not give a damn. He didn't even think about it, because Edwin never needed anything like that."

"When did you first meet him?" asked Cordelia.

"Oh, 'bout ten years ago. I dropped by one night to pick up a bottle. I'd been in several times before, but this time Edwin introduced himself. Said he'd heard about me down in the Line. I asked him what he'd heard and he said, you know, about how I handled the gambling. I told him somebody must be pulling his leg and he just smiled and kept on talking. Said he might organize some poker games around Big Medford. Said no way would they be near my games. Wanted to know if I had any advice to give him. I told him that if I were into that sort of thing, my advice would be to keep out of it. Bad hours and just a little dangerous. He said not from his gamblers. They'd mostly be Medford businessmen. I said that wasn't what I was talking about. In case he hadn't heard, gambling was illegal. That got a chuckle out of him."

He's remembering all the details and that was ten years ago, thought Cordelia. Edwin had even captivated Uh Oh Earl.

"I tell you honestly," said Gilbey, "I don't know that many hard facts about Mayhew. He didn't say any more about the poker games, but he went ahead and organized them, had them up and running in no time. I didn't see much more of him until I opened the Hawaiian Club. Then, of course, I had to buy my product from him. Did you know he was the only liquor wholesaler that sold to nightclubs?"

"I think he was the only one that could afford to carry them on his books," replied Billy.

"Well anyway, I'd pick up liquor from him once a week. The club was booming and I figured I must be his biggest customer. One night, he walked out to the car with me and we started talking about our gambling thing." Earl scratched the top of his head. "I don't remember exactly when, but it might have been that night that I mentioned wanting to get away from the games and go full-time into the club. Anyway, not long after, Mayhew made an offer to buy me out, and it was very serious money. I decided to take it."

"Just like that," stated Walker.

"Yep. Like I said, it was serious money and I wanted out."

"No other considerations?"

"None that I remember."

The Captain lit another cigarette, blew out smoke, and stared at the club owner. His lips twitched in a smile.

Earl grinned and placed both hands on his desk. "Well, I was thinking ahead. Edwin was paying the whole amount up front, so no matter what happened, I had my money. Edwin was Edwin, but when push came to shove, he'd still be just one old white man trying to control a gambling operation in the Line. He'd bust out, or someone would take him out, or he'd just get disgusted and fold. I'd wait, and when it happened, I could decide whether I wanted the games back or not."

"And then Mayhew got killed," stated Cordelia.

Earl took her meaning and gave her a long, hard look. She reflected it was the first time he'd ever looked at her in a serious way.

"Yes, he got killed, but I don't think it had anything to do with the gambling."

"Why not?"

Earl stared at her a moment longer, then relaxed back into his chair. "Because that old man took it over and ran it like a master. He was white, and he didn't have Slim, and he still had it operating like a McDonald's. See, my love, the operator is usually gonna get hurt at the game itself, spur of the moment thing, some hothead. It usually happens because of weak control. That wasn't the case with Mayhew." The big man sighed and glanced at the Captain. "Not a damn thing changed after I left."

He looked back at Cordelia. "Of course, I could have popped him to get the gambling back, but I think the Captain left that place a long time ago. And so did you."

Cordelia gave him a rueful grin. "Mayhew may have done other deals in the Line. Heard anything since the killing?"

"One thing," answered Earl, turning to the Captain. "Heard about it yesterday. Saved it for your visit."

Walker nodded.

"Arnold Hines just hit town. I happen to know he once got a loan from Mayhew. He told a few people he was going to turn that loan into a gift."

"Bubba Hines," mused Cordelia. "The Line's token white. Well Earl, you do stay current."

She reached into her leather handbag, withdrew a ledger, and handed it to the Captain. He passed it unopened to Earl Gilbey. The nightclub owner pulled a pair of reading glasses from his shirt pocket and perched them on his nose. He opened the ledger and stared at the first page. Mayhew had written Bubba's name large across the top. The date and loan amount followed.

Uh Oh gave a soft whistle. "Twenty thousand. Man, I wouldn't have loaned Bubba twenty cents."

"Look in the back," said Walker.

Gilbey removed two folded sheets from behind the ledger's last page. He spread them on his desk and whistled again. "Two more loans," he murmured. "Each for twenty thousand dollars. Bubba paid them both off in three monthly installments." He replaced the pages and handed the ledger back to Cordelia. "So that's where Bubba got it," he said.

"Yep," answered Cordelia. "I remember when you came to the Captain, what, about a year ago. Bubba was going into the marijuana business you told him. Small-time, but there he was. We all wondered where his investment money was coming from. We even guessed the amount, said he'd need about twenty thousand. Bubba didn't have diddly."

"Of course, Edwin bankrolled him," said the Captain, "and Bubba paid him back. That is, except for the last time."

Cordelia was looking at the ledger. "He got the loan in August and made a payment the same month."

"He left town in August, too," said Earl. "I told the Captain."

"When did he get back?" asked Billy.

"Last night. Of course, he could have paid Edwin an out-of-town visit the night he was killed."

The Captain glanced at Cordelia and nodded.

"No," she said, "he's clean on Mayhew. Last Thursday Bubba was behind bars in Memphis, finishing up time served for assault."

Walker cleared his throat. "One of his customers might be able to tell us something. Bubba served both sides of the track."

"So you figure your killer is white?"

Cordelia smiled at the black man. Old Uh Oh was still pretty swift. The Captain was rising from his chair and she got up too. She wasn't about to answer Earl's question, and for a moment, figured the Captain wouldn't either.

But Billy said, "Yes, I think he was, Earl. Edwin did business here, but his personal affairs were in his own world. Edwin's killing was a personal thing."

"Revenge," said Gilbey. "And you also think the killer was a man."

Earl was on a roll.

The Captain buttoned his jacket. "Revenge? Yes, I think so." He looked to see Earl and Cordelia staring at him. "As for it being a man, well, the odds point to that. Most violent crimes are committed by men. The weapon was a rifle, not generally used by women."

Earl was disregarding all that. "Can you see him yet, Billy?" he asked. "Can you see him out there in the distance?"

The Captain was going through the door. "Not nearly clear enough," he said.

THIRTY

The detectives headed up Jimpson Street through a cold drizzle of rain. Cordelia was driving. They'd stopped for lunch and the burrito from Taco Castle felt like wet sawdust in her stomach. She reached a hand into her purse for an antacid tablet, then snatched it away and placed it back on the steering wheel. It had just struck her where she was. Up ahead sat Eddie Partee's house. It slid by on the right and the Captain gave the yard a lazy look. He said nothing and neither did she.

How does it feel to take a life, she wondered. And how does it feel to visit the place where you took that life? You're there and the place is there, but the person you killed is gone, permanently gone, capital GONE, never to return. You have erased that person's existence from the earth. She glanced at the Captain. He was looking at a ledger.

"Anything new?" she asked.

"No, just something I noticed this morning."

"What's that?"

"While I was checking through the ledgers, I noticed that most of the borrowers paid their loans off in three months, just like Bubba. I looked further. It turns out Edwin was a much bigger usurer than we thought. His interest was compounded quarterly. The only way you could get away with twenty-five percent was to pay off within the first three months."

"Jesus," said Hull. "If you took a year, you were paying one hundred percent."

"Not if it was an Edwin Mayhew loan," replied the Captain. "According to the ledgers, interest was permanently affixed to the original loan. No matter how large the first-quarter payments were, if you went into the second quarter, you were charged fifty percent on the original amount."

"So, in old Bubba's case, if he'd gone into the final quarter owing, let's say, just one hundred dollars on the original twenty thousand, he'd still be owing twenty thousand one hundred, despite what he'd already paid."

"That's right," said Walker. "It was a big incentive to pay up the first quarter."

"I'll say," replied Cordelia. "Wasn't that Edwin Mayhew a wonderful human being?"

She turned left on Vincent and drove to where the street dead-ended by an abandoned warehouse. A barren dirt lot lay on the other side of the street. On it, sat a one-room, rusted-out house trailer. The trailer's hitch rested on a concrete block and its wheels had been drawn up on pine planks. The tires needed air. A worn, wooden picnic table with a bench attached stood in front of the trailer. Off to the right, in magnificent contrast to its shabby surroundings, a maroon Cadillac Eldorado gleamed in the winter light. Cordelia pulled over and parked beside the Cadillac.

A hand drew a curtain aside in one of trailer's windows and a bearded face peered out. A few moments later, the door opened and Bubba Hines stepped down to the ground. Standing with both hands on his hips, he watched the detectives walk toward him.

"Always bring your rolling home back to the same place, don't you, Bubba?" Cordelia glanced over at the Cadillac. Its bumper was rigged for towing.

"I own this property, paid for it years ago."

Bubba spoke in a singsong voice, starting out high, dropping to a lower tone, then rising again, all in a single sentence.

They both knew Hines was lying. Baker Watson owned this lot. Bubba leased it by the month. Cordelia looked him up and down and Hines stared defiantly at her, hands still resting on his hips and chin thrust forward. He wore tight, faded jeans and scuffed boots. A denim shirt, unbuttoned at the top, hung outside the jeans. An Arkansas Razorbacks cap covered his lank hair, which hung over his shoulders and mingled with the beard.

"When did you get back?" she asked.

"Couple of days ago. Mercy! Don't take long for the law to know I'm here."

Cordelia remembered that Bubba said "mercy" a lot. The man didn't know it but the Captain had been about to bust him on a narcotics charge. Bubba had skipped town in the nick of time. She nodded and said, "So where've you been?"

"Well, if it's any of your damn business, I been to Little Rock, takin' care of some things."

Bubba tilted his chin up and glanced at the Captain. He shifted slightly and moved his hand to the small of his back.

Cordelia saw the Captain's open leather jacket flutter and suddenly Walker's revolver was pointing rock steady at Bubba Hines's belly. Bubba gasped and jerked both arms straight over his head.

"Don't shoot," he screamed.

"Lean forward," said Walker in an even voice, "and place both hands on the table."

Cordelia looked back at Bubba and saw that his hands were already on the table top. The Captain, in that same low voice, was telling him to spread his legs. Jesus, he could have been discussing the Razorbacks' chances for a conference title.

Billy walked behind Hines and lifted his shirt tail up. He withdrew a shiny Colt Python and tossed it to Cordelia. She caught it and dropped it in her coat pocket.

"Wider, Bubba," said Billy. "Now hold completely still."

"Jesus Christ, Cap'n Walker," panted Hines. "You know me. I'd never pull a gun on you. I was just tryin' to figure how to get it out and give it to you."

Ludicrous as that sounded, Hull figured that Bubba was telling the truth. Giving it up was probably better than them finding it on him. Knowing Bubba, he probably planned to make a show of it, flashing the gun and enjoying the startled look on their faces before handing it over. Weak thinking when Walker was part of the game. Dangerous, too. Billy stood in back of Hines and holstered his revolver. He reached under his jacket and withdrew a set of handcuffs. "Bubba, leave your left hand on the table and put the right one behind your back."

Bubba did as he was told, staring wide-eyed at Cordelia.

"Now put the other behind your back."

Hines, docile now, allowed himself to be led to the police car. The Captain guided him into the back seat and climbed in beside him. Cordelia went around and got behind the wheel. She watched both men in the rearview mirror and listened to Walker deliver the familiar litany.

"You have the right to remain silent. Anything you say can be used against you in court. You have the right . . ."

She wondered if Bubba had seen Walker's hands move.

The Captain nodded to her in the mirror. She swung the car around and headed for the station.

THIRTY-ONE

Bubba Hines sat slumped in front of the Captain's desk. Billy had removed the cuffs and Bubba's hands lay clenched in his lap. He kept shaking his head and the long hair swung with the movement. He lifted his face and gazed at the Captain with sorrowful, hound dog eyes.

"Mercy," he said.

Cordelia walked over, laid Bubba's now empty Colt on the desk, and said, "Mercy, indeed."

"Now looky here, folks," the singsong voice pleaded. "I was gittin' ready to go out when you pulled up. I'd already stuck the gun in my pants. I had forgotten it was even there."

"But then you remembered," said Walker.

"Yeah, I remembered and I was worried that my shirttail wasn't covering it. Then I thought, what the hell. I might as well give it to you."

"And enjoy watching us jump when you pulled it out," said Hull.

"Mercy, no."

Walker picked the gun up and eyed it appreciatively. "Nice revolver," he said.

"Best Colt makes," replied Bubba. "Cost me seven hundred dollars and I got a discount."

Billy opened the desk drawer and placed the pistol inside. He closed the drawer and glanced up at Bubba.

"You won't be needing that again," he said. "Convicted felons can't own a handgun."

"Aw come on, Cap'n. You ain't seriously thinkin' 'bout bustin' me down about the gun."

Cordelia sat down on the edge of Billy's desk and smiled at Bubba. "You mean like assault on a police officer with a deadly weapon?" she asked. "That's serious business in Arkansas."

"Well, yeah. I mean no," exclaimed Hines. "There wasn't no assault." He cast a sly glance at the Captain. "I mean, hell, I'm still alive ain't I."

Walker sighed and leaned back in his chair. His hand moved in a small wave of dismissal, like shooing away a child.

"Forget about the gun, Bubba. I never intended to charge you on the gun."

"Then what?"

"Edwin Mayhew was murdered last Thursday. Did you hear about it?"

An expression of relief flashed across Hines's face. He studied his hands and tried to look noncommittal.

"Mercy! Naw, this is the first I've heard about it." The sly look was there again. "Last Thursday, you say?"

"That's right. How well did you know Edwin?"

"Not too well. I'd get a bottle from him now and again. I hope you don't think I had anything to do with that."

Cordelia walked back to her desk and sat down. She was helping her boss play out the game.

"Did you kill him?" she asked.

Bubba looked over his shoulder at her. No nigger, he thought, and when I finally tell you where I was last Thursday, old Bubba's gonna have the last laugh on you and the main man over there.

"No ma'am," he answered, "and that's the Lord's truth."

Cordelia shrugged and reached for her coffee cup. Bubba turned back around and found himself staring into black, cold, and implacable eyes.

"Let's come to an understanding, Bubba. You wouldn't know the truth if you were drowning in it. And don't try to get cute with me about Mayhew. I know you didn't kill him because you were in the jug at Memphis last Thursday. You didn't tell us that right away because you were hoping to make us look foolish."

Hines slumped deeper into the chair and shook his head, the long hair flopping.

"Straighten up and look at me," commanded Walker. "You're the only one looking foolish right now. You're going to prison and you don't even know why. Here, take a look at this."

Billy flipped a paper toward Bubba. Hines picked it up and scanned the contents. He straightened up and looked hard at the Captain.

"Yes, Bubba. Delivery and sale of a controlled substance, a Class Y felony. That warrant was issued the day you left town. Now, you don't seem to think I do my homework. Do you think I failed to do it before making this drug charge?"

Hines continued to stare, but did not respond.

"Deep down you know I did, don't you, Bubba? The charge is solid. I've got two dozen people who witnessed your drug transactions. I've got three dealers in jail, who've copped a plea and given you up." Billy glanced at his watch. "And oh yes, by now I've got your inventory. Your wholesaler took a fall this morning, ratted out a bunch of his customers. The Little Rock cops told me you brought back half a bale. Our cops just picked it up. That old warehouse across from your trailer was a good place to hide it, Bubba, but you used it once too often. Someone finally saw you. I've got them for witnesses, too."

Billy leaned forward and stared at his prisoner. "To sum it all up for you, Bubba. I've got you."

The Captain offered him a cigarette and Bubba took it. He exhaled smoke and said, "You expect me to cop a plea?"

"That's between you, the court, and your lawyer," said Walker. "I won't get involved in this one."

"I can name names," Hines said. "I can do you a lot of good."

"Maybe you can and I won't object to whatever deal is made. Marijuana is all you've ever dealt in. As long as that holds true, I won't stand in the way. But that's not what I want to talk about right now."

"You want to talk about the murder."

"Yes."

"I don't know who killed him, Cap'n."

"Then I won't ask you that."

"So what are you gonna ask me?"

"Just leave the questions to me, Bubba. All I want from you is a willingness to answer and be truthful."

"And what do I get in return?" asked Hines.

"My goodwill," said Billy.

"Done," said Bubba Hines.

THIRTY-TWO

Walker and Bubba went into the interrogation room and sat across from each other at the wooden table. Cordelia flipped the tape recorder on and went back to her computer. She was in contact with the Criminal Intelligence Center and had begun a rundown on Nathaniel Briggs. All she had to work with right now was his name. While the computer searched, she went over and looked in the one-way mirror again. The Captain had begun to talk so she flipped the recorder to audible and listened.

"What kind of business dealings did you have with Edwin Mayhew?" Walker asked.

She knew that if Hines lied on this first question, the interview would be over.

Bubba had seen the light. He answered promptly. "I got loans from him."

"The loans in this ledger?" Billy pushed the journal across the table.

Bubba picked it up and opened it. He read the first page. "That's one of them," he said.

"There are two loose pages in the back."

Hines studied them also. "Yep, that's the other two. Three loans is what I got."

"And you paid off the first two in three monthly payments?"

"Mercy, yes," said Bubba. "You took longer than three months to pay off a Mayhew loan, you might be payin' on it forever."

"You needed money to make a marijuana buy, twenty thousand for half a bale. How did you come to know about Mayhew?"

"Cap'n, I'm being honest with you. I don't rightly remember. Lots of people told stories about that old man. Somebody told me that Mayhew made loans. Probably it was one of my customers. I was gettin' more of them than I could handle and I needed to make a big buy."

"Somebody in the Line?"

"Naw, I don't think so. Likely it was somebody in Big Medford. Might have been a nightclub owner. They were my steady customers."

"Think about it, Bubba."

"Well, let's see. It could have been Mike Kelly. He was always talking about Edwin. Always ready with the latest Mayhew story."

"Owner of Mike's Place?"

"Yeah. I hear he also runs a liquor store at Medford Crossing."

"So you went to see Mayhew?"

"Yep, went to see him about midnight. Figured to talk to him after he closed. I thought it would be a good time. Turned out, it wasn't so good after all. While I was standin' there, gettin' ready to make my pitch, this young girl sticks her head out the back door and asks if he's closed up yet."

"Did you know the girl?"

"No," said Bubba, "and I remember thinkin' to myself that I was better off not knowing her."

"Why was that?"

"Well, young don't quite cover it, Cap'n. This girl wasn't much more than a kid. I'd heard Mayhew liked 'em young, but mercy."

"Go on," said the Captain.

"Well, Edwin tells the kid to get back in the office and gives me one of those 'I ought to be ashamed of myself, but I'm not' looks. Then he asks what he can do for me and I make my pitch."

"Which was?"

"Told him I needed twenty thousand for a major investment. Told him I wasn't sure what the return would be, but that it would be huge. Said I could pay it all back, including the interest, in less than a month.

"Well, Mayhew locked the door and led me back to his office. We sat down and he made us a drink . . . and you know what?"

"The girl wasn't there," said Billy.

Bubba stared at the Captain. "How'd you guess that?" he asked.

"Never mind," replied Walker, thinking about the adolescent girl, lying beneath Mayhew's mirror. "Go on."

"So Edwin is settin' behind his desk and he lifts his glass and says, 'To business.' That sounded promising so I toasted him back, and then Edwin made his little speech. He said the loan was mine and that I didn't even have to pay it back the first month. Then he explained his repayment plan which was fixed so that—"

"That's okay," Walker interrupted. "We know about the plan."

"Yeah," Bubba murmured wonderingly, "that fourth quarter's a bitch. Well anyway, Mayhew finally gets to the punch line."

"Which was a threat."

"Oh yeah," said Bubba, and the wonder returned to his voice. "And the way he put it let you know he was preachin' gospel."

"What did he say?"

"Said if I ever got to where I couldn't meet a payment, I had to see him in person and that it had better be within twenty-four hours. If that didn't happen, then I was a dead man. He said that I could run to him with a million dollars, but if it was after twenty-four hours, he'd kill me."

"And you believe he would have done it?"

"Captain, I believe he would have enjoyed doin' it."

Walker surveyed Hines across the desk. "But you skipped town after receiving the third loan."

Bubba eyed the Captain's pack of cigarettes and Billy offered him another one. Hines took it, pushed his chair back, and stretched his legs.

"Yeah, I took off. See, I'd made some heavy money on the first two buys and so did Edwin Mayhew. After all, he got his forty thousand back, plus ten thousand interest."

Cordelia spoke from the doorway. "But you still left him ten thousand in the hole."

"Yeah, well Edwin would have figured at least twenty-five thousand." Bubba grinned at Billy. "I figured I didn't owe the child molestin' bastard anything."

"I take it you planned on not seeing him again," said Hull.

"Mercy, it was worth my life not seeing him again." Bubba ran the fingers of both hands through his lank hair. "I headed for New York. I'd been there once before and I had me a contact. With the stash I held, I could go into business big-time. Hell, in five years, I could've retired to Long Island."

"But you stopped off in Memphis," said Walker.

Bubba mournfully shook his head. "Mercy," he said. "Big mistake. See, I had to collect some money from this nigger, uh, from this black dude named Little Guns." Bubba paused and turned to Cordelia. "Look Sergeant, I use that word, but hell, everybody I know uses it, white and black. It don't mean nothin'. At least not where I live."

Cordelia gave him a bleak smile. "Well," she said, "you stay in the Line and you're still alive. You could be telling the truth."

"Damn straight," said Bubba, and turned back to the Captain. "Anyway, Little Guns gets hostile. He pulls a pistol on me, and the next thing I know, we're blazing away at each other. I shot the son of a bitch in the shoulder. Then, the cops showed up and I wound up doin' time at the County Farm." Bubba shook his head. "And it was all over five hundred dollars. Hell, I tip that much. But it ain't good business lettin' somebody owe you."

"So you got out last Saturday," said Cordelia.

"Yeah, and I'm here to tell you I wasn't sure if I wanted to get out. I expected Mayhew to be waitin' at the gate. I called a friend of mine in Medford to see how the wind was blowin' and he told me Mayhew was dead."

"Who did you call?" asked the Captain.

"Nat Thomas, one of Uh Oh's dealers. Well, what he told me was sure welcome news. I decided to put New York on hold. I picked up the money I'd stashed and came back to do a little more business. I went to Little Rock, got another half bale, and here I am."

"Yes, here you are," murmured Walker.

"Oh mercy me, and in a world of hurt." Bubba gave Walker a quick look. "Have I got your goodwill?"

"You're getting there," said the Captain.

"What else do you want to know?"

Walker leaned forward. "I want to know who killed Edwin Mayhew."

"Captain, honest to God, I don't know. I can't even put you on to anyone who might know."

Billy leaned back in his chair and Bubba visibly relaxed. The Captain gave him a long look.

"Well Bubba, I'm going to give you some time to think and I want you to do just that. Think long and hard. I'll send a pencil and paper to your cell. When you think of a name that might interest us, write it down. Tomorrow or the next day, you and I will go over them and you can tell me about each one. I expect to see quite a few names."

"Just people who had some contact with Mayhew?"

"That's right," said Walker. "Don't think about whether their connection is important or not. I'll decide that."

"You got it, Cap'n. Anything else?"

"Yes, how did Mike Kelly come by all those Mayhew stories?"

"I dunno. Probably got some of them from bullshittin' with Mayhew. The old man supplied him with liquor, just like he did with all the other nightclubs. Edwin was closemouthed, but he could tell a cock story. Got a kick out of it. 'Course, Mike might've made some of them up himself. He liked to talk about the old man."

"Mayhew interested him?"

"Oh yeah." Bubba was starting to get the drift. "Anything he heard about Mayhew, he'd remember it."

The Captain stood up. Cordelia came over and placed her hand on Bubba's shoulder. He rose and she replaced the handcuffs.

The prisoner twisted his head around and gave her a wide grin. "Say, ain't your boyfriend called Bubba?"

Cordelia gave him a gentle push toward the office door. "I'm afraid so," she sighed.

The Captain sat back down and listened to Hines's cowboy boots, clumping down the metal stairs. People called him "Bad Bubba Hines" and only half in jest. A white Eddie Partee, but smarter and more controlled. And fear seldom touched Bad Bubba.

Walker logged him down as useful.

THIRTY-THREE

Billy went out to his desk and pulled a liter of Johnny Walker Red from a drawer. He sat down and placed the bottle in front of him. Cordelia came back in, saw the liquor, and gave a grateful sigh. She brought two glasses from her desk, placed them in front of Billy, and took a seat. He filled both glasses and Cordelia lifted hers in a toast.

"To Veteran's Day," she declared.

"What?"

"It's Veteran's Day, *mon capitaine,* and you're a veteran, so's here's to you."

"Why, so it is," said Billy, taking a sip of scotch. "I'd quite forgotten."

"So did I, till I ran into the Chief downstairs. He was going home early. Said he shouldn't have even come in since it was Veteran's Day. I never knew Wheaton was in the military."

"He served in the Arkansas National Guard for awhile," said Walker with a smile.

Cordelia chuckled and shook her head. "The computer didn't show anything on Briggs. Of course, all I could put in was the name."

"Well, start working on that tomorrow. Get data that the computer can use. You'll probably want to talk to Baker Watson again. Go wherever you have to. No need to come to the office first. I'll contact you sometime during the day."

"I take it you'll be visiting Mike Kelly."

"Yeah, he may know something useful."

The policemen sipped their scotch in silence. Billy gazed off into the distance, his face composed and impassive. Cordelia found herself watching him. She knew he was aware of it, but he gave no sign. Finally, he looked at her and smiled. Heat mounted to her face. She looked down at her glass and quickly drained it.

She cleared her throat and said, "Well, it's been a long day."

"Yes, let's call an end to it," said Billy.

Cordelia put on her coat and walked through the office doorway. She waited while Walker locked up, then preceded him down the stairs. Billy stopped at the dispatcher's office and she continued on out to her car.

A gust of wind blew around the old brick building and she felt its icy breath on her still-warm cheeks. Cordelia got into her car, started it up, and turned on the headlights. She sat motionless until she saw the Captain come out the station house door. He started toward his car and she watched the wind ruffle his hair and blow it across his forehead. She kept her gaze fixed on him until he was in his vehicle and heading off the parking lot. Then, Cordelia put her car into gear and drove into the night.

THIRTY-FOUR

Walker slept an extra hour this morning. After getting up, he and Sammy drank coffee and shared the morning newspaper. They left the house together and Sammy waved as she pulled out of the driveway and headed for her flower shop. His wife had wanted to know if he was working this weekend and he'd told her probably not.

He drove slowly down the quiet residential street. Overhead, the sun shone brightly from a cloudless, cerulean sky. Patches of snow dotted the yards and icicles hung, like crystal carrots, from the mailboxes.

Billy glanced at his watch. The hands indicated eight o'clock and the tiny window announced that today was Friday. It had been a week since someone had pumped four slugs into Edwin Mayhew's chest and anointed the wounds with whiskey. Anointed, he thought. Strange word to pop into my head. Billy reached forward and picked up the radio mike.

"Medford PD? CID One."

"Go ahead, Number One."

Walker sighed. "Sally, did you contact Mike Kelly?"

"Ten four, Captain. Said he'd be at his liquor store from eight thirty till noon."

"Ten four. Any messages for me?"

"No sir, not really. I made a cell check a few minutes ago. One of the prisoners said he had a list for you."

"Ten four," replied Billy, giving silent approval. Prisoners' names were never announced over the radio.

He turned south on Court Street and swept by the police station. A patrol car was heading toward the street and Billy heard its siren give a short beep. Billy grimaced and hoped that wasn't becoming a ritual. He neared Mayhew's store and noticed two women standing outside the front door. He turned into the parking lot and drew up beside them. Lavonia and Josephine smiled down at him. Jo fished a door key from her purse.

"Good morning, Captain," she murmured in that soft, slightly husky voice.

"Mornin' Billy," said Lavonia. "You come to pay us a call?"

Walker wasn't comfortable sitting in his car while two women stood outside in the cold. He got out and leaned against the car door. "No ma'am," he answered and looked from one to the other.

Lavonia glanced at Josephine and chuckled. "Looks like we're gonna be working partners," she said. "Jo's gonna handle the front, and I'll manage the inventory and keep the books."

Jo nodded. "Mayhew's Liquor is on its way up."

"I don't doubt it," said Billy, returning their smiles. "And you're starting at a good time of year."

"That's what Vonnie said. The holidays should bring us a lot of business. You want to come inside?" The question came out like some licentious invitation. Being Jo, she couldn't help it.

"No, I have to be going," he answered.

"Any progress, Billy?" asked Lavonia.

"Some, but we've still got a ways to go."

"Has my reward been any help?"

"Well, it's too soon to tell. In the end, it may be a great deal of help."

Billy turned to his car and opened the door. "Good luck, ladies," he said over his shoulder.

Their thanks followed him as he drove away. The Captain

shook his head and thought about the bonds that link women together, and about the utter myth that stated they could not be pragmatic. He turned left on Ridenour Street and followed it into Medford Crossing.

Medford, Arkansas, had originated in two places. The first was where it contacted the Mississippi River and began its life as a riverboat town. Later, the railroad passed through to the west and a railhead, calling itself Medford Crossing, was established. Both points grew toward each other, eventually merged, and all became Medford. Riverboats no longer docked at Medford and the railroad (the same one fronting the Line) had fallen into disuse, but the town had prospered and lived on. And old Medford Crossing, laying on the western city limits, still retained some of its original identity.

Walker pulled parallel to the rusty train rails and stopped. To his right, a gravel road led off through empty cotton fields and disappeared over a slight rise. He looked left, down the street he'd come in on, at drab, wooden houses, all in need of paint.

The Captain got out and stood staring at the structure in front of him. A wooden porch ran along its front with a roof projecting over it. A hanging sign, reading MIKE'S LIQUOR, swung gently in the breeze. Walker peered through one of the dirty windows and could just make out a man's figure in the store's dim interior. He opened the front door and stepped inside.

Mike Kelly came forward, carrying a case of whiskey. He sat it next to an empty shelf and stretched out his hand to Billy.

"Captain! Good mornin' to ye."

Walker heard the faint accent, and from some compartment of his memory extracted the information that Mike had come to this country from County Cork, albeit many years ago. His brogue had been diluted by southern drawl, a combination not unpleasant to the ear.

"Good morning, Mr. Kelly. How are you?"

"Ah, call me Mike, Captain. Mr. Kelly was my father's name."

Walker took his hand and returned the big man's smile. Kelly stood well over six feet with massive shoulders and powerful arms. Bright blue eyes peered out from a ruddy face, topped by short gray hair. A slight belly rise stretched the waist of his pants and all this presented the typical picture of a happy Irish brawler.

"Excuse me a minute, Captain, while I switch on the lights." Mike strode into the back room, and a moment later the ceiling fluorescents flickered into life. At the same time, canned music floated forth. Billy recognized the Irish tune.

Kathleen Mavourneen, the gray dawn is breaking,
The horn of the hunter is heard on the hill.

"So what can I do for you," said Kelly, returning from the back.

Walker glanced around and Mike took the cue. "There's a couple of chairs behind the counter, Captain. Come around and sit."

The two men sat down and Billy gazed at Kelly for a moment. "Mike, one of your competitors was murdered last week. Anything you can tell me about it?"

The blue eyes twinkled. "Well, it was the only way, Captain Walker. I tried to buy him out, but he just wouldn't sell."

Billy smiled in spite of himself and Mike Kelly laughed and leaned back in his chair.

"I wouldn't call Edwin Mayhew a competitor," he said. "If you competed with Mayhew, you usually wound up in a bad way."

"But you had dealings with him."

"Oh sure. Anybody who was involved in the nightlife, or liquor, or gambling had to deal with Mayhew."

"Did Edwin have an interest in your liquor store?"

"You mean did he own part of it?"

"Yes."

"Nope, but sometimes he acted like he did."

"What do you mean?"

"Well, here's what the bastard would do. It was kinda strange. He'd come in here every once in a while and pick out a bottle of something, something expensive, maybe a quart of Chivas Regal. Then the old man would just walk out without paying. It was supposed to be understood, you see, that Edwin Mayhew didn't pay for liquor in your store. It was like you owed him some sort of tariff. I talked to some other store owners and they all admitted that he did them the same way."

"Ever hear of anyone refusing to pay this tariff?" asked the Captain.

"No, not ever. I guess we all figured Mayhew's goodwill was worth the price of a bottle of booze." Mike grinned suddenly and the blue eyes twinkled again. "Tell you what I did do once. I dropped by his store when I knew Mayhew would be there. We bullshitted for awhile, and when I got ready to leave, I picked up a bottle of good champagne from a display case and headed on out. Mayhew never said a word. He just rapped three times on his countertop. I looked around at that face and reached for my wallet."

"Apparently," said Billy, "he viewed professional courtesy as a one-way street." He regarded the Irishman with a bemused look. He couldn't resist. "You know, of course, that Edwin never drank."

"He didn't?" Kelly's face grew even redder. "Why, the son of a bitch."

"How long did you know him, Mike?"

"Oh, about five years I guess. Known him almost as long as I've lived in this town. You know, I opened this liquor store first.

It never did set the woods on fire, but it's made me a livin' and a little more besides. A couple of years later, I took my savings, got a loan to go with it, and bought my nightclub."

"Where did the loan come from?"

"From the bank, where else?" Kelly cut his eyes up at the Captain and turned his face sideways. The look was pure Irish. "Oh, I know that Mayhew gave loans, but I wanted no part of that kettle of fish. All my dealings with Mayhew were strictly legit."

"What dealings were those?"

"Why my nightclub, of course. It's against the law for me to supply it out of my own liquor store. I'm sure you know that. I'm sure you also know that every nightclub in town got their liquor from Mayhew."

"Yes, I know. Why do you think that was?"

"Pure economics, Captain. Nothing crooked there, I can assure you. First, Mayhew had the largest stock of any licensed wholesaler in the county. Second, Mayhew was willing to bill you weekly and that tied a lot of store owners to him."

"Part of this week's sales paid last week's bills."

"Exactly," said Kelly. "Some guys never got back to the point where they could pay for the liquor at the same time they bought it."

"Lots of businesses operate that way," said Walker.

"Sure, nothing wrong with it. And here's something you may not know. Edwin's prices were fair. More than fair, because he gave all the nightclub owners a special rate. I tell you, Captain, I've owned clubs in other towns and none of my suppliers were as generous as Edwin Mayhew."

Walker nodded. "Sounds like good business to me."

"It was, Captain. Mayhew became the sole supplier in Medford and he was big in most of the surrounding towns. The man was on his way to sewing up the whole county."

"Do you think he made any of the competition mad?"

"Nah! Every liquor store owner around here is a mom-and-pop operation, just like me. They don't want the expense or the hassle of becoming a wholesaler."

"And the wholesalers out in the county?"

"Far as I know, they're all small-time and happy to stay that way."

Walker stood up, placed both hands on his hips, and arched his back. "Do you know Bubba Hines?" he asked.

"Bad Bubba? Yeah, I know him. I also know he's in the calaboose. Some of my customers were talking about it last night."

"He a friend of yours?"

"No, I wouldn't say that. I get along with Bubba okay, but I discouraged him coming into my club. I guess you know why."

"The dope?"

"Yeah. Of course, Bubba only dealt in marijuana. At least, as far as I know. I got no problems with him earning a living that way, but I don't want him earning it in my club. He don't pay me any rent, and last I heard, his business is against the law."

A bell over the front door tinkled and a dark-complected, middle-aged man entered. Mike stood up and placed both hands on the counter. The man flashed him a smile, teeth brilliant in the dusky face.

"How's it going, you crazy Mick?"

"It'd be all right if I could keep you damn Mexicans out."

Both men laughed and patted each other on the shoulder. The Mexican looked at Walker and raised his hand: *"Qué tal, Capitán?"*

"Bien, Manuel. *Como está?"*

"Así, así," said Manuel, wigwagging his hand in the air. "You here to arrest Mike?"

"No, just having a talk. How's Lupe?"

"She's fine. Pregnant again."

"Congratulations. Tell her I said hello."

"I'll do it. Give me a case of Corona, Mike."

Kelly brought the beer and placed it on the counter. Manuel paid him and shouldered the case.

"See you later, Irish," he grinned. "Don't take any wooden potatoes." Then turning to the Captain, he composed his face and straightened his body. *"Con su permiso?"* he asked.

Walker slowly nodded his head and the Mexican walked out the door.

"Did he say what I thought he said?" asked Mike.

"Yes, it's just an expression."

"I dunno. I think old Manuel Lorales was really asking."

Billy was becoming embarrassed. "Some locals were giving him a hard time once and I happened to come along. I was a patrolman then, just doing my job."

"Uh huh," said Mike. "Well sir, what else can I tell you?"

"Bubba Hines said you knew a lot of Mayhew stories."

"Oh a few. Just things I heard. Gossip and tall tales mostly. Hell, I've even . . . well, embellished some of them. All the usual stuff. The gambling, the loan sharking, the young girls."

"How about whiskey?"

"Whiskey?"

"Yes. Did you ever hear a Mayhew story where liquor played a part?"

"Well, I just told you one. And of course, there were the ones about him running bootleg across the river. Mayhew liked to tell those himself."

Walker stepped around the counter, took a card from his shirt pocket, and handed it to Kelly. "That's my office number," he said. "If you think of anything I might be interested in, give me a call."

He was halfway to the door when Kelly's "wait a minute"

brought him to a halt. He turned around.

"I just remembered something, Captain. What you said about the whiskey? There was something, something I heard."

"What was it?"

"There's a guy works for me named John Boles. He told me a story once about a friend of his. Seems this buddy had a girlfriend who somehow got tangled up with Mayhew. She was the age Mayhew liked, mid-teens I think. Anyway, the girl became a booze hound, then graduated to serious dope, eventually wound up in the asylum at Benton. At least, that's what John says. He also says that, according to his friend, Mayhew was the cause of it."

"I'd like to talk to Mr. Boles."

"Well, he won't be in today, Captain. It's his day off. You can catch him tomorrow."

"Do you have his home address?" asked Billy.

"Yessir, but you won't be able to find him there, either. He'll be busy with something else."

Walker stared at the liquor store owner and Kelly's face reddened again. "Ah hell," he said, "I guess I can tell you. John is an ex-alcoholic, a recovering alcoholic they like to say."

Mike began to straighten some pint gin bottles on the shelf behind him. "I know. I know. An alky working in a liquor store. But I tell you, John's been with me three years and there's never been a problem. Why the hell he wants to work around all this temptation, I don't know. Anyway, about a year ago he finally told me about the drinking. He kinda had to because he wanted Fridays off. He'd just taken some position with Alcoholics Anonymous that required him to be available on Fridays. Well, that's one of my busiest days, but I let him have it off anyway. He does that good a job for me, and besides I like the guy."

"I understand," said Billy. "My questions will keep till Saturday."

He started toward the door again. Mike Kelly followed him out onto the porch. They shook hands and Mike turned to go inside.

"By the way," said Billy. "When I talk to him, I don't plan on mentioning his past."

"Thanks, Captain. God be with ye."

Walker looked in his rearview mirror and watched Medford Crossing dwindle in the distance. He reached for the radio mike.

"CID Two. This is CID One."

"Go ahead, Number One . . . Er . . . CID One."

Walker could imagine the grin. "You in the middle of anything, Two?"

"Ten four, but I'll be finished in about an hour."

"Ten four. Please meet me at the station when you're through."

"Okay, CID One."

And the case goes on, thought the Captain. And how long before it ends? He remembered the old Irish ballad he'd heard in Mike Kelly's liquor store . . . "Kathleen Mavourneen." How did the last part go?

> It may be for years,
> And it may be forever.

Captain Walker knew better.

THIRTY-FIVE

Bubba Hines sat on his cell bunk and scanned the list. He'd written down ten names, and mercy, they were all the legitimate ones he could come up with. The Captain had said put down any that came to mind, but Bubba knew that any besides these ten would be bullshit names and he didn't want to piss Walker off with bullshit names. He was glad to be helping the Captain and he hoped to be helped by the Captain. Bubba Hines reflected that truly, honest to God, he'd rather have Walker on his side in a fight than J. Edgar Hoover, no lie. The dude was unreal. Bubba had done a stint at Cummings Penitentiary once, and when the cons found out he was from Medford, half of them asked the same question: did he know Billy Walker? Seems they believed that one "attaboy" from Walker to the parole board was as good as a free pass. Then Bubba thought of something and chuckled out loud. Once, while he was there, the fucking governor showed up for a tour, old Oscar Edmondson himself, and he's walking down the cell block and he stops just across from Bubba's cell. He's talking to a bro over there, who's also from Medford, and the governor goes, "Where you from, son?" And the guy says, "Medford, governor," and damn if Oscar don't go, "You ever heard of Captain Billy Walker?" If I'm lyin', I'm dyin', thought Bubba. He chuckled again when he remembered the jailbird's reply: "Yessuh, governor. Cap'n Walker's reviewin' mah case."

"What you laughin' at, white ass?" The stocky black prisoner had raised up on the opposite bunk, a menacing frown on his face.

Hines had been challenged before, in places just like this, and he knew exactly where to take it. He gave his antagonist a long, level stare.

"You want some trouble, motherfucker?" he asked. "I'll give you all the trouble you can handle."

The other prisoner eyed Bubba for a moment, then turned his face to the wall. Hines took another look at his list, shrugged, and placed it in his shirt pocket.

"Is that my list, Bubba?"

Hines looked up and saw the Captain standing outside his cell. He immediately wondered if Walker had heard the altercation.

"Yessir. Ten names is all I could come up with, but they may do you some good."

The police dispatcher, a pretty blonde, stood behind the Captain, a ring of keys in her hand.

"Sally," said Billy, "take Mr. Brownlee over to cell two, please, and let him remain there."

So he had heard, thought Bubba. He stood aside and watched the blonde escort the other prisoner out. She had a wonderful ass.

Walker came in and they sat facing each other. Billy pulled out a pack of Winstons and Bubba eyed it hungrily. Mercy, he was dying for a cigarette. The Captain offered him one. Bubba snatched it and passed his list to Billy. The policeman studied the names. "Greg Holcomb?"

"White boy. Worked for Edwin doing odd jobs. Helped load and unload trucks, cleaned up, stuff like that."

"Buddy Riggs?"

"Same description, same job."

Billy glanced up at Hines. Hines gave him a weak grin. Billy looked back down.

"Willy Stafford."

"Dealer for Mayhew, down in the Line. Edwin caught him stealing and ran him off."

"Is that all Edwin did?"

"I think so," said Bubba. "Nobody's seen Willy lately."

Billy continued down the list and Bubba filled him in. None of the people seemed promising. Walker came to the final name.

"Donald Jenkins."

"Saved the best till last," said Bubba. "Donald Jenkins had a big brother named Hal. Me and Hal did some things together. You know, worked a few deals. Hal's at Tucker Farm now. Anyway, the little brother was just the opposite. Straight arrow. Hard worker. Used to work for Medford Wholesale. He had a teenage romance going with this girl and she spun out on him, took to drink, and then went on to dope, the kind you need a needle for. The story goes that all this happened to her after she got tangled up with Mayhew. Hal told me that Donald took it hard. About a month ago, Donald ups and disappears. Nobody's seen him since."

Walker folded the list of names and placed it in his pocket. "This may be a help, Bubba. Let me know if you think of anyone else."

"Will do, Captain. Don't forget where I live."

Walker shook the cell door and the pretty dispatcher came back and opened it. "What's the weather like, Sally?" asked Hines, giving her his widest smile.

The young woman ignored him as she relocked the door and followed the Captain.

Bubba sighed, lay back on his bunk, and listened to Walker's footsteps, going up the stairs.

Billy opened the office door and found Cordelia already there.

She sat with her back to him, tapping the computer keys.

"How's it going?" he asked.

Cordelia swung around and Billy noticed with surprise that she was wearing a dress. Of course, Cordelia's was made of leather and ended eight inches above the knee, but still, it was a dress.

"Right now, it's not going at all," she said. "I can't get a line on this guy anywhere."

"I assume you talked to Baker Watson."

"Yep, and he couldn't add much to what he'd already told us."

"Did you get a Social Security number?"

"Nope, Watson didn't even have anything with the preacher's name on it."

"Didn't Briggs have to sign some sort of form when he rented the house?"

"No, he paid Watson in cash for a month's rent and just moved in. I'm sure that was okay with Watson. He was lucky to rent that rat trap under any circumstances." Cordelia switched the computer off and walked over to her desk. She picked up a pen and started tapping it against a flower vase. Irritation plainly showed on her face.

"Captain, the guy's a phantom. I checked the banks. He never opened any sort of account. I checked the credit bureau. No record. Seems he's never charged anything, at least not around here. He never bought a car, and as far as I know, he's never owned one. No chance of a license plate number. I just called the Social Security Administration, gave them our code number, and asked for data on Briggs. They came back with nothing. Zilch. No number. No nothing. Apparently, what we have here is an older man who never filed for a card and never in his entire life worked for a salary."

Walker sat down behind his desk and gave Cordelia a quizzical look.

"No sir," she said.

"No sir, what?"

"No sir, he's not using an alias. I also called the Bureau of Vital Statistics in Little Rock. They faxed me this."

Cordelia walked over and placed a form in front of the Captain. He stared down at Nathaniel Briggs's birth certificate.

His assistant recited from memory. "Nathaniel Franklin Briggs, born February ninth, nineteen thirty-nine, in Simpson County, City of Medford. White male. Born of Raymond and Allison Briggs."

Billy lifted his eyebrows toward Cordelia.

"Both dead," she responded. "Bureau of Stats has no record of any other relatives."

"Nothing on the wife and daughter?"

"No sir. The bureau has no record of Nathaniel being married and no birth certificate on the daughter."

Walker smoothed back a lock of hair and lit a cigarette. "Well," he said, "you don't have to be married to have a daughter, and if she was delivered without a doctor present, there might not be a record."

"I know, Captain," said Hull, "but there's no record of anything. Jesus, we know the preacher and his daughter were here, but it's like they only existed in people's minds."

Billy blew out a cloud of smoke and smiled at his assistant's gloomy face.

She gave a short laugh and stretched both arms out in front of her.

"You've had a busy morning," he stated.

"Yeah, been busy turning up almost nothing."

"It's not your fault, Cordelia. It was professional work."

Cordelia smiled and nodded. "By the way," she said, "I found a couple of churches where Briggs preached. Both of them Pentecost with small memberships. I've got the regular preachers' names."

"Good, we'll go see them this afternoon." Walker then proceeded to tell his assistant what he'd learned that morning.

Cordelia's face brightened. "Now that is very interesting. And we get a chance to deal with real people again."

Walker chuckled and said, "Oh, Briggs and his daughter are just as real. And," he added, "somewhere there's more documentation to prove it. You just can't exist today, Cordelia, and not leave records somewhere. We'll come across them eventually."

"After what you just told me, maybe we can forget about the Briggses."

Walker didn't answer and Cordelia was confirmed in her belief that the Captain had a thing about Nathaniel. He would not let go until the preacher was found, examined, and explained.

THIRTY-SIX

Cordelia wiped her lips and watched her boss take a sip of coffee. She took another bite of the barbeque sandwich and closed her eyes in enjoyment. Pete Moldavi had come through again. She formed an O with her thumb and forefinger and lifted it to the owner. Pete smiled an acknowledgement and went back to slicing a pork shoulder.

"So whaddaya think?" she asked after swallowing. "Mike Kelly and Bad Bubba were talking about the same girl?"

"We'll know that when we find out the name of John Boles's friend."

"Right, but it sure looks possible, doesn't it?" Cordelia pushed her plate away. "Both were young girls about the same age. Both were into drinking and dope. And both knew Edwin Mayhew, presumably in the biblical sense."

"Yes," replied Billy, "and from what we've learned about Mayhew, there's probably several more young women you could say the exact same thing about."

He went over to pay Pete and Cordelia put on her coat. They emerged into a gray day, heavy with overcast. Cordelia glanced upward and pulled up her coat collar.

"You want to go see the preachers now?" she asked.

"Yes, maybe they can make Nathaniel and his daughter seem a little more . . . substantial."

His assistant gave him a rueful grin and picked up the radio mike.

"CID Two, Medford?"

"Go ahead, CID Two."

"Any messages?"

"Affirmative, Two. Is the Captain with you?"

"Yes."

"Captain, I have some ten thirty-five for you. Please advise."

Walker took the mike. "We'll come by in a few minutes, Sally."

"Ten four, Captain."

Ten thirty-five was code for "confidential information."

"Probably some more reward seekers," stated Hull. "With five thousand up for grabs, I'm surprised we haven't had more of them."

Walker nodded but made no comment.

Cordelia swung into the station parking lot and parked beside the Captain's car. They entered the building and Sally stood up as they approached.

"You got a call from someone named John Boles, Captain. He said it was confidential." She handed the policeman a slip of paper. "Wants to know if you can come and see him at this address. Said he'd be there this afternoon and tonight. He also asked that you come alone."

"Thanks, Sally," said Walker, taking the paper and turning to his assistant. "Cordelia, why don't you go ahead and talk to the preachers. I'll be in touch a little later."

He headed up Court Street, turned right on Seventh, and then made a left on Bledsoe. At first, the houses were huge and prosperous, with well-kept lawns and expensive cars in the driveways. The street made a bend to the right and Billy followed it. Gradually, the view outside his windows changed. The houses were still large two-story affairs, but these showed signs of decay and hard use. All were in need of paint and the yards appeared untended. Finally, Walker saw the unequivocal indication of a once-proud neighborhood gone to seed; a ROOMS

FOR RENT sign was nailed to one of the porches. Billy was familiar with the address he'd been given—1140 Bledsoe lay just ahead. Built by a wealthy cotton planter, it had stood for many years as one of Medford's more imposing homes. Then, this end of Bledsoe had started to deteriorate and the house was sold to succeeding buyers for less and less money. The last resident sold it ten years ago, and the building became, of all things, a funeral home. After that, it operated as a boarding-house, and eventually its rooms were leased out as offices and meeting places. The federal food stamp program, along with of-fices for Head Start, occupied most of the downstairs. The remaining area was leased by a bail bondsman. His sign, MARVIN'S BAIL BONDS, stood in the front yard. Upstairs, Cohart's Detective Agency took up two rooms. The remaining two housed Alcoholics Anonymous.

Walker stood in front of an unadorned door and softly knocked. It was opened by a slim young man with wavy dark hair. He regarded the detective for a moment and stretched out his hand.

"Captain Walker? I'm John Boles. Please come in."

Billy stepped inside and looked around. He was standing in a small anteroom, which held a desk and two metal filing cabinets. A worn sofa, accompanied by a coffee table, sat across from the desk. A heavy glass ashtray on the table overflowed with cigarette butts. In one corner, a large, café-type coffeemaker burbled once and was silent.

"Take a seat, Captain," said Boles, waving toward the couch. "How about some coffee?"

"Yes, I'll have some. Thank you."

"How do you take it?"

"Black, please."

"The only way," replied Boles, coming over with two steam-ing mugs. The policeman noticed that he walked with a limp.

Walker took the coffee mug, set it down, and reached for his cigarettes. Boles picked up the full ashtray, walked over to a trash can, and emptied it. The specially built shoe on his right foot minimized the limp. He replaced the ashtray and sat beside Billy.

"Now you look like a regular," he said.

The Captain gave him a questioning look.

"Most of the members are chain-smokers and endless coffee drinkers."

"But you don't smoke," observed Billy.

"No, that's one bad habit I've managed to avoid."

"Sorry," said the Captain, "if the cigarette bothers you, I'll . . ."

"Are you kidding?" he laughed. "If I was bothered by cigarette smoke, I'd have to set up my own private AA. No, go ahead, Captain. Enjoy."

Billy felt drawn to this pale young man with the solemn face, yet ready laugh. Mike Kelly admired him. He could see why.

"Mike gave you a call," he stated.

"Yes sir, but don't hold it against him. He was on a guilt trip."

"Because he told me about this?"

"Right. I told him not to worry about it. This is a special case. I did have to get permission to ask you down. As the name implies, the organization is anonymous."

"That the reason we're alone?"

"Yes, I arranged that in advance. We only have one meeting a week, but people are always dropping by."

"And you're here every Friday?"

"Yeah, that's my day to make the coffee and man the phones. We don't want to miss any calls."

The Captain looked up from his coffee. "Calls for help?"

"Exactly," the young man stated.

Walker tapped ashes from his cigarette and leaned back on the couch. "What did Mike Kelly tell you?"

"Just that he'd mentioned the story about my friend and that he'd told you about me."

"At first he tried to shield you."

"I know."

Walker leaned forward. "What's your friend's name?"

Boles gazed at the Captain and made no attempt to answer.

"Is he an . . . ?"

"Alcoholic, Captain? The word's in common use around here. No, he's just a friend. We went to high school together."

The Captain waited.

Finally, Boles said, "I hesitate, because when I tell you all of it, you'll suspect him of Mayhew's murder."

The Captain waited.

John Boles let out a sigh and said, "His name is Donald Jenkins."

THIRTY-SEVEN

"He's a year younger than I am," said John, "but I was in a car crash. That's how I got the limp. Anyway, I had to repeat my junior year because of it, so Donald and I wound up in the same grade."

"Were you friends back then?"

"Oh yes, we ran around together. Double-dated. Hunted and fished together."

"What was Donald like?"

"Captain, Donald Jenkins was the salt of the earth. I'm not kidding. If you knew him, you'd have to agree with me. Sort of serious and quiet, but easy to be around. Always obliging and courteous. His parents own a grocery store, just a small place over on Fourth Street. Donald helped them out in the afternoons or on Saturdays. He'd help anybody that needed it. That's the way he was."

"Ever see him lose his temper."

"No sir. Never."

"Did he ever become violent?"

"Can you do the second without doing the first?"

Billy gave the young man an appraising look. "Yes, John, you can."

"Well, I saw old Donald get violent on one occasion and I'm glad he did, because he saved my ass."

"What happened?" asked Walker.

Boles held his mug in both hands and gazed at the contents.

"We were in our senior year. School had let out for the day and I was walking home. I could have rode, but my limp was much worse then and I was trying to build up the strength in my leg. I stopped off at Jay's Stop N Shop for a Coke, and when I came out, they were waiting for me."

"They?"

"A gang of hoodlums who hung around together. Stanley Reese, Butch Murdock, and a couple of other bums. They were all school dropouts. Stanley was kind of the leader. He'd been in a lot of fights. Word was, he'd pulled a knife on a couple of people. Anyway, they were all draped over an old Buick. As soon as I came out the door, they slid off the car and started toward me. It seemed Stanley had a score to settle.

" 'Where you goin', gimp?' was the first thing out of his mouth.

" 'I'm on my way home,' I said. I tried to make my voice neutral. I don't mind telling you, Captain, I was scared. I couldn't beat 'em all and I damn sure couldn't outrun them. Stanley put his face up close to mine.

" 'You ain't goin' nowhere yet, gimpy,' he said.

"I took a couple of steps to the rear and found my back pressed against a garbage bin. That was good. At least, they couldn't get behind me. Now old Stanley unburdened his mind.

" 'I'm gonna show you how dangerous it is to go sniffin' around one of my women,' he snarled.

" 'Which one is that,' I asked, and scared as I was, I could barely keep from grinning. Stanley had to be one of the ugliest bastards ever to come out of reform school. He was short and squat and he had this funny orange hair that stuck out in all directions. Serious acne covered his face, and most of the teeth in his head were rotten.

" 'Which one?' he shouted. 'I'll tell you which one, you little gimp faggot motherfucker. Jeanine, that's which one.'

"Well, then it came to me who he was talking about. This little fat gal named Jeanine had made a pass at me the day before and I'd brushed her off. Evidently, she and Reese liked the same insults. She'd also called me a 'gimp faggot motherfucker' and said she'd 'fix' me. And she did, because whatever lie she told Stanley, had 'fixed' me good and proper."

Billy sipped his coffee and nodded. Boles was obviously reliving the experience. The young man slowly shook his head and continued. "Next thing I know, Reese has pulled a knife and the blade is stuck up under my chin. I rose up on my toes and he brought the blade toward him a little and opened up a gash. Blood poured down over my Adam's apple and into my collar. Stanley pushed his face closer and I could smell his foul breath."

Boles paused and drank from his cup. "Well, you know what, Captain? Suddenly, I got mad, just plain mad, and for a moment, I wasn't scared anymore. I lashed out at Reese with my built-up shoe and he jumped back. I'd missed him, of course. He stood there a moment, and then he shifted the knife in his hand and started for me again. I think he meant to kill me. I was scared all over again, but not for long."

"Why not?" asked the Captain.

"Because just then I heard a quiet voice say, 'Stanley, why don't you turn around and take me on.' "

"Donald Jenkins."

"Yep. He'd come up behind the gang. I looked over and there he stood with a baseball bat laid over his shoulder. I remembered that sometimes he'd get a chance to play sandlot ball in the afternoon. He must have been on his way to a game."

"What happened then?"

"Nothing at first. Everybody froze and stared. I mean, it was like something out of a western movie, and old Donald was the sheriff. He just stood there, silent and calm. Then, he lifted the bat off his shoulder and started toward Reese. Stanley still held the knife, but he just stood there with his mouth hung open. He was as stupefied as the rest. Donald came up even with the gang and Butch Murdock reached out to grab him. Donald slammed the point of that bat right into Murdock's stomach. Murdock sank to his knees and started throwing up and Donald just kept on walking. He only had eyes for Reese. I don't think he even looked at Butch. Well, Stanley had seen all he needed to see. He started to back away, but by that time Donald was in bat range and he let fly. He swung like I'd seen him swing at batting practice, hard and flat. Reese threw up his left arm and the bat thunked into it and the arm sort of flopped sideways. You could see it was broken. The knife flew from his right hand and fell to the ground. Stanley screamed, grabbed his arm, and headed for the car."

Boles drained his coffee and smiled at the recollection. "Well, that did it. Suddenly, all of them were jerking at the car doors. Somebody was holding Butch Murdock up and someone else was trying to ease Reese into the back seat. Every time the guy touched him, Stanley would holler. His arm had swelled up like a sausage.

"Donald stood in front of me, tilted my chin up, and examined the cut. Then he hefted his bat and walked over to Reese. I thought he was going to hit the guy again, but instead, he actually helped place Reese in the car. Reese looked up at him and Donald leaned over and said, 'Stanley, John Boles is a friend of mine. You need to remember that.' "

The telephone rang and Boles got up to answer it. Billy rose and stretched. He walked over to an open doorway and peered into the next room. Rows of folding metal chairs faced a wooden podium. That was the extent of the furnishings. The room was without windows and no pictures hung from the walls. He heard the telephone receiver being replaced and turned around.

"Jenkins was a good friend to have," he said.

"The best, Captain."

"So you graduated together."

"Yessir. Donald went to work for Medford Wholesale and I bummed around for a bit and eventually became a drunk. I stayed that way for a couple of years."

"Did you still see your friend?"

"Only during the times I was drying out. He'd come by, offer encouragement, ask if there was anything he could do."

"When did he become involved with the girl?"

"Oh about a year and a half ago. Right after I got back on my feet. Donald met her at some youth function. He was a few years older than her but they hit it off right away. Pretty soon, when you saw one, you saw the other. They never lived together, though. She stayed with her father. I think he was a preacher. Anyhow, she brought it all home for Donald. Fun, romance, and I suppose sex. Those things had been in short supply."

"Do you think he loved her?"

John Boles stared at the Captain. He was constantly having to reappraise the man. Surprising question, coming from this quiet professional. Boles's alcoholism had not diminished his perceptions. They were quite good, and he sensed that beyond this policeman's thoroughly southern manners lay a cold danger and the capacity for unemotional violence. Yet, his warmth lay at the forefront and he had asked what any of John's women friends would have asked . . . Did Donald love her? Come to think of it, that was a very professional question. It was the one pertinent question when you knew what he was going to ask later. And John knew.

"Yes," said Boles, "he loved her."

Billy walked back to the sofa. John perched on the desk with both legs dangling. The reinforced shoe hung at an odd angle.

"No problems at first," stated Walker.

"No, but when they started, they got worse in a hurry."

"Go on."

"Well, Donald and Susan, that was the girl's name, would go to parties, but he seldom touched liquor and she didn't drink at all, at least not at first. Then, she acquired the habit. Donald continued to drink moderately, but Susan became a boozer. And I mean suddenly. Like she just woke up one morning and said to hell with it. She'd get drunk and cause scenes, pass out at parties, get in fights with other women. She was obsessive about Donald and jealous as hell."

"How did Donald handle all this?"

"He didn't handle it at all. He couldn't understand what was happening. He damn sure couldn't handle Susan or what Susan had become."

"A new experience for him."

"Exactly, Captain," said Boles, giving the detective another appraising glance. "Donald always knew exactly where he was heading and what he was going to do next. If something unexpected came up, he handled it and went on his way."

"Like he handled Stanley Reese."

"Yeah, but now he was powerless and that really worked on Donald."

"Susan couldn't be turned around?"

John lifted both hands, palms upward. "Didn't want to be. She went into a steep slide and kept on going. It got steeper when she discovered cocaine."

Boles slid off the desk, walked behind it, and sat down. He placed his chin in his hands and stared at the Captain. "I've always believed that girl encountered something awful, something far removed from Donald, and that it started her downfall."

"You may be right," answered Billy.

John Boles wasn't listening. He gazed across the room and said, "She lost her mind, you know. Went crazy. She's up at

Benton now."

"And Donald?"

"What?"

"What about Donald?"

"Gone. Disappeared. He left his job about a month ago and nobody's seen him since. I haven't seen him, and believe me, I've spent some time looking."

"He confided in you, didn't he, John, talked to you about his problem."

"Yes sir. I was his best friend. Still am. But honestly, he didn't tell me that much about Susan. Hell, he never even told me her last name. He just talked to me in general about her. Asked me for advice."

"Did you have any for him?"

"Only the obvious. Talk her into coming to an AA meeting. Maybe get into the program."

"Did she come to one?"

Boles grimaced and shook his head. "Yeah," he said, "she made one. Showed up drunk . . . and loud. I had to call Donald. He came and got her." The young man sighed and said, "I never saw a sadder or more hopeless look than the one on Donald's face. But you know, he never lost his patience or his temper with the girl. He would treat her like a child."

Billy stood up and walked over to Boles' desk. Three heavy books lay in a neat stack on top of it. The Captain glanced down at them. ALCOHOLICS ANONYMOUS appeared on the spine of each book.

"Must reading for all members," explained Boles. "Sort of the AA Bible. We call it the 'Big Book.' " He gave Walker a bemused look. "It was written by someone named Billy."

Walker smiled and said, "John, tell me everything that Donald had to say about Edwin Mayhew."

Boles leaned back in his chair. "He only talked about him

209

once. It was after they'd taken the girl away. Susan had finally lost it. I mean totally. She didn't even know Donald. I don't think she knew her own father. She was still staying with the old man when she went insane. Anyway, she'd finally reached the point where she didn't crave booze and drugs anymore. The preacher had her committed."

"And what did Jenkins say?"

"Huh? Oh sorry, Captain. Well, there's not much to tell. Donald came by my apartment one day and got to talking about his girl. He said that Mayhew had started Susan drinking, had provided her with dope, and that he had preyed upon her. That's the word he used, 'preyed.' Said Mayhew was responsible for everything that happened."

"Did Donald say how he knew this?"

"He said someone told him."

"Who?"

"Donald wouldn't give his name, but he said it was someone who wouldn't lie."

"What else did he say?" asked the Captain.

John Boles sighed and said, "This is the part I didn't want to tell you about. Donald said he was going to pay a little call on Mayhew."

"And then?"

"And then he was going to make Mayhew suffer."

"Did you ever see Jenkins again?"

"Nossir. Wasn't long after that he disappeared."

Walker studied Boles for a moment. "You knew him, John. What do you honestly think?"

"Captain," said the young man, "Donald Jenkins might swing a mean baseball bat, but he's no killer."

"Well thank you," said the Captain, handing over his card. "My number's on there. Please contact me if you think of anything else."

The phone rang again and Billy left John Boles engaged in earnest conversation with the caller, talking quietly, then pausing to listen.

Walker had started down the stairs when he heard a door open and someone calling his name. He turned and looked over the top step. A rumpled, bloated figure stood in the hallway. Burt Cohart beckoned to him. The Captain remained where he was and coolly eyed the fat man. Cohart shrugged and waddled forward. Billy climbed back up the few steps to meet him.

Burt Cohart had once served on the Medford Police Department and had not distinguished himself. In fact, he'd been such a misfit even Chief Wheaton had become fed up and fired him. All this was before Walker's time, but he'd heard the stories, including some about Cohart being too free with his nightstick. After his dismissal, Burt went to work driving a bulldozer at the city dump. Everybody said that was appropriate. However, Cohart remembered the good old days. He knew he could never return to them, but he managed the next best thing. One fine morning, he opened his present offices and was now a full-fledged private investigator. Folks wondered how he'd managed to get an Arkansas license, and their wondering pleased him no end. Cohart had passed a certain amount of money to a certain state official, and lo, his license arrived in the mail. Burt believed that he and the official were the only ones who knew about the bribe. He was wrong. Billy Walker knew, and when the time was right, he planned to do something about it.

"Captain, Captain. How're you doin'?" Cohart stuck out a doughy paw. A cold draft flowed down the hall, but sweat had popped out on the fat man's face and his hand felt damp.

"Fine, Burt," replied the Captain. "What can I do for you?"

"Oh nothing. Haven't seen you in a while. I read about your run-in with that nigger."

Walker stared at the PI and made no comment.

Cohart pulled a handkerchief from his hip pocket and ran it across his pudgy face. "You know. Eddie Partee. I'm glad you did the fucker. He was a bad 'un."

Still no response. Walker continued to stare at Burt and the big man started to fidget. Jerking his chin toward the AA entrance, he said: "Are the alkies turning criminal now, Cap'n?"

Billy regarded Burt a moment longer and said, "Cohart, I don't want to hear any talk about my being up here. If I do, I'll know where it came from. Understand?"

"Why sure, Billy."

"Good," said Walker, leaving the fat man with a foolish grin on his face.

He walked out into a darkening afternoon. A plank porch with an ornate wooden railing ran across the front of the old building. Billy perched on the railing and lit a cigarette. The smoke jetted through his lips and expanded into the cold air. His gaze drifted across the front yard and rested on a squirrel, sitting upright beneath a large oak. The squirrel clutched an acorn in its paws and stared steadily at the Captain. The AA rooms lay just over Billy's head and he heard the phone ring again. It rang once more before John picked it up. John Boles didn't know Susan's last name but the Captain knew. He'd heard it first from Baker Watson when the realtor had mentioned Nathaniel's daughter.

The preacher's wild kid, Donald's troubled lover, and Edwin Mayhew's victim were all Susan Briggs. Jenkins believed that Mayhew destroyed his girl, believed Mayhew's first destructive act was to provide her with liquor. How appropriate it would have seemed to pour whiskey on Mayhew's fatal wounds.

THIRTY-EIGHT

Cordelia reclined in her chair, her feet propped on the desk. "So Edwin Mayhew's thing for young girls may have led to his downfall."

"Yes," replied her boss, "or at least his thing for one young girl."

"Donald's girl. The preacher's daughter."

"That's right. Donald said he would pay a visit on Mayhew. I believe he followed through on that."

"He was going to 'make Mayhew suffer.' "

"According to John Boles, yes."

"A dangerous endeavor," said Hull. "I hope he took along more than a baseball bat."

"Perhaps he did."

"Like a twenty-two-caliber rifle?"

"And a bottle of whiskey," the Captain quietly murmured.

"So now, *mon capitaine*, our duty she is clear."

"Very clear. We find Donald Jenkins."

"I haven't been very good at finding people," came the rueful reply.

Walker gave her a smile. "Well, at least we know where Nathaniel's daughter is."

"Through no effort of mine. By the way, do we split up or search together?"

"Together, but not till Monday. You've got the duty this weekend and I'll be out of town."

"Okay."

"I'll be working, too," he added.

"Paying a little visit on someone?"

"Yes, I thought I might."

"Hal Jenkins or Susan Briggs?"

Walker gave his assistant an approving look. "Both, if possible," he answered.

Hull looked at her boss. "Think you'll get any sense out of Susan?"

"Maybe not, but it's worth a shot." Walker raised his eyebrows toward Cordelia. "Oh, did you find out anything from the preachers?"

"Nothing very factual. Both of them were full of praise for Nathaniel. A real man of God, according to them. They also said he was a very effective speaker and their parishioners loved him. Of course, nobody had a clue as to where Briggs is now."

"Anything more?"

"Well, they also praised the daughter. Described her as a 'real little lady.' Quiet. Polite. Well-mannered. Very helpful to her father. She handled the collection plate. She seemed the perfect daughter. Of course, all this was probably BM."

"BM?"

"Before Mayhew."

"Oh."

"And you know, Captain. That's the one thing I don't get."

"What's that?"

"How could someone like Susan come into contact with a man like Edwin Mayhew?"

The Captain gave his assistant a meditative gaze. "There's no reason that she should," he said, "at least not of her own volition."

"Right. They lived in two different universes. They should never have met. So what brought them together?"

"Not what, Cordelia, who? And that 'who,' " said the Captain, "is someone I'd very much like to talk with."

Thirty-Nine

Arkansas maintains two correction centers within its borders. Cummings, located in the southern part of the state, fits the everyday concept of a prison . . . large cell blocks behind high walls, a concrete exercise yard, and the grim daily activities that measure out an inmate's life. Tucker Farm, positioned further north, is very different. Single story, army style barracks house a not quite so dangerous or hardened population. Tall, wooden guard towers stand interspersed between the buildings, which also include a dining hall, a recreation room, and several administrative offices. The whole is surrounded by a ten-foot cyclone fence, topped by razor wire. And beyond the fence, stretching out in all directions, are the cultivated fields that give the place its name. Despite the wire, the scene seems almost pastoral and far removed from the dismal and dangerous Cummings.

Billy Walker drove along the two-lane blacktop and watched the cluster of buildings draw closer. He passed under an arched sign proclaiming TUCKER FARM and drew alongside the guard shack. A trusty studied his identification and waved him through. Billy was reminded that Tucker was virtually run by trusties, those inmates that had gained the warden's confidence. They supervised the other inmates, worked in the offices, and assisted the warden in almost all areas of prison operations. They even manned the guard towers.

The warden was Boss Bruler. He stood before his big bay

windows and watched Walker pull his unmarked police car into the office parking lot. Billy got out, looked around, and headed for the front door. Bruler smiled and went to open it.

"Well, I'll be goddamned," exclaimed the big man, as he stretched out his hand. "What in hell brings you up this way?"

"Came to see one of your boys, Roy. How've you been?" Billy didn't know it, but he was the only one here who called the Warden "Roy." Everyone else, including all the inmates, called him Boss, or the occasional Mr. Bruler. That was as it should be. Roy Bruler was boss and absolute boss of all he surveyed. Few questioned his authority or challenged his power. To his credit, the word "Boss" was usually used in a tone of respect, and even affection, rather than fear.

"Well, have a seat, Billy," said Boss, gesturing to a tan leather couch. He turned to a skinny young man, standing before a filing cabinet: "Bring us some coffee, Sam."

"Comin' up, Boss," The clerk strode into a back room. A moment later, he poked his head out and peered at the Captain. "How do you want yours, sir?"

"Black will be fine," said Billy.

The young man reappeared with two cups on a tray.

Walker noted that trusties still wore a special uniform . . . khaki shirt and pants with a red T over the left breast pocket.

Billy sipped his coffee and suppressed a grimace. It was very strong and very hot. Bruler took a large gulp and smacked his lips. He was impervious to things that discomfited most men, including scalding liquids. He sat down next to Walker.

"So who is it you need to see, Billy?"

"His name's Hal Jenkins. Came up on some burglary convictions about six months ago."

Bruler nodded to Sam. The trusty opened one of the filing cabinets and took out a manila folder. He walked over and handed it to the warden.

"Yeah, Jenkins, Jenkins," Boss murmured as he perused the contents. "He's in Barracks C. Got a good record, so far. Why does his name ring a bell?"

"He was on last month's T list, Boss," interjected the young man. "We discussed him at the meeting."

"Oh yeah."

"T list?" the Captain inquired.

"It's a list of prisoners who might qualify as trusties," said Bruler. "The trusties themselves make it up. Whenever a vacancy occurs, we go to the list."

"Did Hal make trustee?"

"No," replied the warden. "There were a couple of nays and the committee vote has to be unanimous. No big deal. He'll probably make it next time."

"Are all the committee members trusties?"

"Of course," replied the big man as he set his empty cup down. "You ready to go see young Hal?"

The two men walked across Bruler's parking lot and down the street toward Barracks C. A tower stood on their left. As they approached it, a guard appeared and rested a rifle on the ledge in front of him. Bruler waved and the guard raised his rifle barrel in salute. He wore a red T over his jacket pocket.

The building ahead of them gleamed in the winter sunlight. Nearing it, Walker saw that it had recently been covered with a fresh coat of white paint. They entered and Walker found himself in an anteroom with another small room opening to the left. A double door appeared at the rear. The anteroom held a filing cabinet and a metal desk. An older man with gray hair sat behind the desk and rose as they entered. A large paunch protruded over his belt buckle. He wore the ubiquitous T.

"Charlie, bring out Hal Jenkins," ordered the warden.

"You got him, Boss," said the trusty as he lumbered toward the doors. Before unlocking them he turned around and said,

"Permission to speak to the visitor, Boss?"

"Speak away, Charlie."

"How you doin', Captain? Remember me?"

"Of course, Charlie. How are you?"

"Not too bad, considering. Tell the boys I said hello."

"I'll do that," said Walker.

Charles Voss had worked for the Medford Sanitation Department, driving a street-cleaning vehicle. He was a conscientious employee and a tireless participant in church work. Everybody liked him. He was unfailingly courteous and obliging.

One day, Voss returned home early and found his wife in bed with a church deacon. He took a double-barreled shotgun from the wall and blew their heads off . . . one barrel for each head. Then he replaced the shotgun and dialed the police department.

The trusty reappeared, followed by Hal Jenkins. He pointed to the side room and Jenkins walked in and sat at a rough wooden table. Hal's face bore a worried look.

"Well, I'm going back to the office," said Bruler. "You gonna stop by before you leave, Billy?"

"Sure, Warden."

Voss went back behind his desk and Billy walked into the side room. He closed the door and sat across the table from the prisoner.

Hal Jenkins straightened in the chair. His hands rested in his lap. The prison barber had clipped his black hair short, and that, along with his thin face, made the dark eyes seem quite large. He peered at Billy, the expression serious and alert. Walker wondered if he resembled his younger brother.

"Hello, Hal."

"Morning, Captain. How's it going?"

"Fine," said Billy, taking out his cigarette pack. "You smoke?"

"I did before they put me in here."

Walker offered the pack but Jenkins shook his head. "No thanks. It was a good habit to lose."

"Yes," said Billy, "and a hard one."

"Yeah, but not as hard in here, especially if you're broke and don't like begging."

"Nothing came in from outside."

"Nah, my folks and me ain't on good terms and I guess my friends wrote me off."

"Even Bubba Hines?"

Jenkins chuckled and spread his hands on the table. "Ahh, Bad Bubba Hines," he sighed. "No, I don't think Bad Bubba wrote me off, but Bubba believes there's only one thing to do when a buddy's in the jug. Wait till he gets out and throw him a party. Till then, he's on his own."

"Well, maybe that won't be too far off," said Billy, thinking that Bubba wouldn't be throwing any parties for awhile.

"Hope not," said Hal.

"The warden seems to think you're doing okay."

"Oh yeah? That's nice to hear. I been a little worried 'cause I got passed over for trusty."

"I wouldn't worry about it," said Billy. "Keep yourself straight, you'll probably get it next time."

"Well, since I heard it from you, I'll count on it."

"Oh, I don't have anything to do with this trusty business," protested the Captain.

"Yeah, but I think you're right. In here it's like trying to get into an exclusive club of some kind. Some of the guys tell me you usually don't make it on the first vote." Hal tilted his head back and chuckled again. "You know, Captain, I don't think I ever had a goal or an ambition in my life. So now I got one and what is it? I want to move up in the ranks of the cons."

"Better than no ambition at all," replied Walker.

"Oh, I'm not treating it lightly," said Hal. "Like the man

says, 'it's all relative.' And in here, making trusty is important."

"You know, of course, how good that looks to a parole board."

"Oh yeah, but the main thing is what a difference it makes in here. The trusties are in a different world. Hell, they run the place and that's no joke."

"And the warden runs them."

"You got that right," said Jenkins.

Walker lit his cigarette and gazed at Jenkins. Hal looked back at him with an expectant look on his face.

"Hal, have you had any news from home at all?"

"No sir. No visitors. No letters. No calls."

"Your brother, Donald, has disappeared. People are starting to get worried."

Jenkins studied the Captain's face. "Disappeared?"

"Yes. Nobody knows where he is."

"Nobody at Medford Wholesale? How about our parents?"

"A close friend of Donald's has been asking around. I'm sure he's checked both places."

Hal straightened up and looked at the Captain with narrowed eyes. "He's been asking around? How about the police. Haven't they been looking?"

"No. We just found out. Nobody filed a missing person report."

"But you're looking now."

"Yes."

Jenkins examined his fingertips, then drummed them on the table. Walker could see the wheels go round. "Do you have any idea where he might be, Hal?"

The prisoner glanced at the policeman. "Captain Walker, I really don't. Donald and I weren't real close. Oh, we got along, but he didn't confide in me much. Now that's the honest to God truth, but there's something else I could add."

"What's that?"

"If I did know, I probably wouldn't tell you."

"Why not?"

"Because Donald is an adult and no missing person report has been filed. There's only one reason you'd be looking for my brother. You think he's connected with a crime."

"Maybe we just want to know what he knows."

"Yessir, maybe. But I still don't know where he could be."

Walker ground his cigarette out in a plastic ashtray. He leaned forward, and in a low voice said: "A little over a week ago, someone murdered Edwin Mayhew. They shot him four times in the chest and left him lying in his own front yard."

Hal Jenkins slumped down in his chair and his face grew pale. Walker continued in the same low tone.

"Your brother told you he meant to kill Edwin, didn't he? And he told at least one other person, a close friend, the same thing."

Jenkins voice was strained. "If he'd told me that, I wouldn't have believed him for a minute."

"Hal," said the Captain, "I've appreciated your honesty, so far, but don't jerk me around. Donald did say that. You know it and I know it."

"It was this girl," exclaimed Hal. "She had him all tore up."

"Did you know her?"

"Nah, I never met her. Like I told you, Donald and I weren't all that close."

"How did he come to tell you about Mayhew?"

Hal got up and walked over to a small window. A wire screen covered it. The clear sunlight shone through and made tiny crossed patterns on Hal's face.

"I dropped by Basil's Bar one afternoon," he said, "and Donald was there. We sat at a table and I ordered a drink. Donald was sipping on a Coke. Said liquor didn't appeal to him much anymore. I asked why and he said that it had fucked up his best friend and then his girlfriend. So I said something like, well, you can't blame it on booze. They just couldn't handle it, or they brought it on themselves, or something like that. And Donald goes, 'Maybe John brought it on himself, but Susan didn't. Someone brought it on her.' And I asked who? Who brought it on her? And Donald said, 'Edwin Mayhew.' "

"Go on," said Billy.

Hal stood by the window a moment longer. Then he came back and sat down at the table. "Donald said he was going to see Mayhew and confront him with what he did. And then he said, 'Mayhew has to pay.' That's all, Captain. He never said, 'I'll kill him.' He just said, 'Mayhew has to pay.' "

"What else did he say?"

"Oh, that's about all. Told me the girl had just been committed to Benton. I gave him some advice."

"What was that?"

"I said, Donald, do not mess with Edwin Mayhew. He is not just some dirty old man, and he will fuck you up. Donald just shook his head and I left. Right after that, I got arrested."

Hal gave the policeman a sad smile. "So that's why you came to me," he said. "You wanted to hear Donald's threat from my own mouth. You never thought I knew where Donald was."

"Well, I was hoping you'd have some idea."

"I don't. And I don't believe Donald killed Mayhew."

"Do you think he paid him a visit?"

Hal Jenkins sighed. "Knowing my brother, I'd have to say yes."

FORTY

The Captain stood beside his car for a moment and stretched his arms skyward. The sun had lost some of its brightness and was on a downward trek in the west. Walker had covered a lot of miles and still faced the drive from Benton back to Medford. His right leg tingled and he shook it a couple of times to restore the circulation. A cold wind gusted and blew against his back, driving dead leaves along the walkway in front of him. The building ahead had been constructed of red brick, as had all the two-story buildings surrounding him.

The Benton State Mental Hospital held the same visage as Tucker Farm, an institutional look, a look of confinement. The aged structures ranged out across a bleak, treeless ground and appeared blood-colored under the setting sun.

Billy walked toward the building that housed Susan Briggs. He'd called earlier from Boss Bruler's office and a Benton administrator told him that Susan would be available. He opened the door and entered a small waiting room. A youthful nurse sat behind a glass partition, talking on the phone. She smiled at Billy, hung up the phone, and came out into the waiting room.

"Captain Walker?" she asked.

"Yes," said Billy taking the outstretched hand.

"That was the superintendent on the phone. He wanted to know if you'd arrived."

"It was good of you to make time for me."

The young woman made an embarrassed gesture. "Captain, I'm sorry, but I'll need some identification."

"Of course," he replied, taking out his badge and card.

She led Walker to another door and softly rapped on it. In a moment, a voice from inside said, "Okay."

The nurse pushed it open and stepped aside so Walker could enter. She smiled again and let the door close between them.

Billy found himself in a long room. A row of bunks stretched down each side. Women of various ages were lying down or walking around the room. A few were gathered in front of a television set. The *Beverly Hillbillies* was on and the group would occasionally erupt in high-pitched laughter. Billy felt something pull on the sleeve of his jacket and looked down to see a short, older woman staring at him with a vacant smile. She was holding a doll.

"Betty, come here a moment, please."

Betty wandered over to the speaker, her doll trailing on the floor. The other woman, dressed in a starched uniform, led Betty to a chair. She then walked over to Walker. His eyes took in a rather large and matronly woman with a broad, expressive face.

"Hi," she said. "I'm Maude Campbell."

"Billy Walker," said the Captain.

"I understand you're here to see Susan."

"Yes ma'am," said Billy, looking around. "Which one is she?"

"Oh, she's not out here. I'm afraid Susan still has to be confined to a special room."

"Why is that?" asked the Captain.

"Well, she sometimes loses control a little and upsets the other patients. You know, a screaming fit or something like that. I don't think she'd harm anybody, but we feel she should be by herself for a little while longer." Maude gave him an appealing look. "I personally think she's shown a lot of improvement. I hope your visit won't unnerve her."

"I'll try to see that it doesn't," he answered.

Maude stared at the Captain, for a moment, and her face relaxed. "Please follow me, Captain."

Three doors appeared at the rear of the room. Maude walked to the middle one and inserted a key. She opened it and beckoned to Billy. He stood in the doorway and gazed down at the young girl, sitting on a cot. She wore a green shift and sat upright, both palms pressed downward on the mattress. Her large gray eyes stared up at the Captain, then darted to the woman at his side. Maude turned to go, but the Captain shook his head. Maude gave him an appreciative nod and let the door close behind them.

"Susan," she said, "guess what? Someone else has come to visit you."

The young girl's gaze returned to the Captain but she gave no sign of recognition. Walker returned her gaze and said nothing. Minutes passed and Maude shifted uncomfortably. Finally, Billy kneeled on one knee before the young girl and softly said, "Susan." He said it as if he were talking to himself, not addressing her at all. Susan made no response. The Captain rose, nodded to Maude, and quietly followed her from the room.

"Is she always like this?" he asked.

"Yes sir, but we haven't seen her hysterical in a long time. She never talks, though."

"Never said anything to you?"

"No, but once in a while she sings."

"Sings?"

Maude smiled to herself. "Yes sir, just one song. That old hymn, 'Yes, Jesus Loves Me.' She sings that. Must have learned it from her father. He's a preacher, you know."

"He was Susan's other visitor?"

"Yes, the only other one. He came up to see her once. Never

came back."

"Did you talk to him?"

"Just for a moment. He didn't stay long. Sat with Susan for a little while and then left."

"Did he say where he could be reached?"

"No."

"Did Susan say anything to him?"

"No sir. And he didn't say much to her. They just sat together for awhile."

They walked back to the exit. Maude was about to knock when she noticed the policeman was no longer at her side. She turned around and saw him staring back at the middle door. Standing there, he looked down at the floor and thrust both hands into his pockets.

"Captain," she called, "are you ready to go?"

The policeman nodded and came toward her. Maude gazed at him a moment and asked: "Do you have daughters, Captain?"

"Yes," he replied. "Do you?"

"Yes," said Maude, and tapped gently on the door.

A slight, balding man stood in the outer office. He held a paper before him and was frowning down at it. He looked at Billy and extended his right hand.

"Captain Walker, I'm Jimmy Hazlip. We talked on the phone."

"Yes, Mr. Hazlip. How are you?"

"Fine, Captain. I got what you asked for." He held out the paper. "The superintendent said bring it over."

Walker took Susan's admittance form and scanned the contents. The signature of Nathaniel Briggs was scrawled at the bottom. Under parent's occupation, he had listed "Minister." His address was for the house rented from Baker Watson. There was no other useful information. The Captain sighed and returned the form to Hazlip.

"Thank you," he said. "And thank the superintendent for me."

"Any time, Captain," said the administrator. He went over to discuss something with the nurse and Billy walked to the door.

Outside, the sun was sinking behind one of the brick buildings. Long, dark shadows stretched across the grounds and the winter wind moaned in low complaint beneath a rooftop.

Billy climbed into his car, made a slow U-turn, and headed back toward Medford.

FORTY-ONE

The two policemen swept past the Farmer's and Merchant's Bank and Cordelia glanced at its illuminated sign. Part of the sign read MONDAY, 9:00 AM. She looked over at her boss and said, "So, how was your Sunday?"

"Uneventful," said Billy. "So was Saturday."

"Yeah, well, the visits had to be made, right?"

"Yes."

He turned right on Fourth Street and followed it around a curve. An intersection appeared ahead. They passed under the green traffic light and Billy pulled over in front of a weathered wooden building. Loose pea gravel had been spread over the parking area and it crunched under their tires. A metal sign, hanging between two posts, read JENKINS GROCERY. Cordelia and the Captain got out and walked through the front door. A small bell above them gave off a cheery tinkle.

It took a moment for their eyes to focus in the store's dim interior. Two fluorescent fixtures hung from the ceiling, their light concentrated over the checkout stand and the meat counter. A man was working behind the meat counter and a woman stood at the cash register. She bagged a loaf of bread for a small boy and passed him his change.

"Thank you, Tommy," she said. "Tell your mama I said hello."

The boy clutched the bag and ran past the two policemen. Billy looked after him, then casually surveyed the store. Canned goods were displayed on two rows of free-standing shelves.

Bread, cakes, and snack items took up part of a wall, and tall coolers filled with beer, soft drinks, and milk occupied the remainder. A long counter, holding candy, gum, and the cash register, stood next to the opposite wall. The meat counter sat in the back. The woman closed the register and glanced at the cigarette display behind her.

"Carl," she called to the man in back, "when's the tobacco man due?"

"He'll be out tomorrow," replied her husband.

The woman turned her attention to the policemen and said, "Can I help you?" She wore a slight smile. A pencil was thrust through her reddish-brown hair and a pair of reading glasses rested on the end of her nose.

"I'm Captain Walker," said Billy, showing his badge, "and this is Sergeant Hull. Are you Mrs. Jenkins?"

"Yes," answered the woman, "and that's my husband, Carl." She lifted her chin to the man at the rear. "Carl, these folks are policemen."

Carl laid his meat cleaver down and walked up the aisle between the counter and the wall. He stood beside his wife and wiped both hands on his apron. He was tall, thin, and dark, and Walker was struck by the resemblance between him and his older son.

"This is Captain Walker and Sergeant Hull," said his wife.

"Pleased to meet you Captain, Sergeant." Carl did not offer to shake hands. "What can we do for you?"

"We'd like to speak to your son, Donald," said the Captain.

The wife sighed. "So would we. We haven't laid eyes on him in a month."

"What do you need to see him about?" asked her husband.

Cordelia glanced at her boss and said, "We just want to ask him some questions, Mr. Jenkins."

Jenkins frowned and folded both arms across his chest. "What kind of questions?"

The Captain's firm voice came from beside her. "Mr. Jenkins, we obviously need to see Donald on police business, and we'd appreciate your cooperation."

Mrs. Jenkins placed her hand on Carl's arm and looked up at him. Her husband slowly unfolded his arms and his shoulders slumped. She turned to Billy and Cordelia.

"Captain," she said, "we'll cooperate if possible, but we just don't know where he is."

A beer truck pulled up outside and the vendor came through the door. He pulled an order book from his hip pocket and he and Mrs. Jenkins walked over to the beer cooler.

Carl Jenkins spread his hands in an apologetic gesture. "That's a fact," he said, "and we ain't trying to hide him. We're both starting to get worried."

"You say it's been a month since you've seen him?" asked Cordelia.

"Yes, about that."

"And where was that, Mr. Jenkins?"

"Why, right here. Donald had give up his apartment and was staying with us."

"Why did he do that?"

"You mean give up his apartment? Well, he'd had girl troubles. They'd separated so he asked if he could move back in with us for a while. He was pretty tore up about it."

"Did he ever talk about the girl?" asked Walker.

"Oh yeah, he even brought her over a few times. At least he did at first. Later on, she didn't come by anymore. Pretty little thing and nice as could be. My wife really liked her. She and Donald would come over, and Susan, that's the girl's name, would help Lilly out in the garden. Later on, we'd ask about her and Donald would just say she was working or going to a class or something. We didn't press it. Figured it was none of our business. Lilly missed her, though." The thin man gave them a sheepish grin. "I kind of did myself."

Walker smiled in response. "What did your son have to say about her?"

"Aw, not a lot. He thought the world of her, but Donald wasn't much on talking about his feelings. Took after me, I guess. It was mostly just 'me and Susan' did that, and 'me and Susan' did this, and 'Susan said' that or the other. He was hers all right."

"What did Donald say about the breakup?" said Cordelia.

"Well," said the store owner, stroking his chin. "He was really close-mouthed about that. Kept saying it was due to an 'outside influence.' Me and the wife never pressed him on that at all."

"He never said what that outside influence might have been?"

"Nope, and we never asked."

The small bell tinkled again and they looked around to see the beer vendor leaving. Lilly Jenkins walked back and joined them.

"You folks want to sit down?" she asked. "There's some chairs behind the meat counter."

They walked back and Carl brought out some metal chairs from the corner. A side of pork lay on the butcher's table. Jenkins picked it up and placed it in a large freezer box. He came back and they all sat down. Carl lit up a cigarette and the Captain did the same. Mrs. Jenkins reached behind her and brought forth a tin ashtray.

"Did something happen to the girl?" asked Carl.

"What girl?" exclaimed Mrs. Jenkins.

"We was talking about Donald's girl, hon."

"Susan? Well, I sure hope nothing happened to her. I thought the world of that child."

"I'm afraid something did," said Walker. "Susan . . . ." Surprisingly, he felt the words fail him. His assistant gave him a questioning look and the Captain nodded.

"Susan started drinking," she said, "seriously drinking, and we believe she was also into drugs."

Lilly Jenkins's mouth formed a small O and her eyes widened. She shook her head back and forth.

"As a matter of fact," Cordelia continued, "she's now confined at Benton. Seems the girl lost her marbles completely." She immediately regretted her use of the phrase, "lost her marbles." Mrs. Jenkins's distress was evident.

"It's hard to believe," stated her husband, "especially the last part."

Mrs. Jenkins was shaking her head again. "No," she said, "I believe the last part."

Walker looked at her and said, "Go on, Mrs. Jenkins."

"It was in her family. Susan told me about it out in the garden one day. Her mother went crazy. Nobody could figure out what caused it. Susan said that her mama just started shutting everything out. Stopped talking, stopped working, and eventually just sat down and stopped moving. According to Susan, the woman finally got to the point where she didn't recognize her daughter or her husband. She died that way."

"Did Susan ever mention her father?" asked Walker.

"Couple of times. Bragged on him. Talked about what a good man he was. He's a preacher, you know."

"Yes," said Cordelia. "What we don't know is where he is."

"Well, can't help you there. You got any idea, Carl?"

"Naw, we never met him," replied her husband.

The little bell tinkled again and Lilly went to wait on a customer.

Carl Jenkins straightened in his chair. "Captain," he said, "it would relieve my mind some if you'd tell me what this is about."

Walker leaned forward and said, "We want to ask Donald some questions about the Mayhew killing."

Jenkins face blanched and he slid forward in his chair. Cordelia thought, for a moment, that he was going to fall.

"No," he whispered.

Cordelia placed her hand on the store owner's knee. "Mr. Jenkins, we're not saying that Donald did it. We don't even know if your son ever met Mayhew. But his girlfriend did, and we believe that Mayhew introduced her to the things that—"

"But she was just a beautiful child," interrupted Carl. "She was what we would have wanted if we'd ever had a . . ."

"A daughter?"

Carl nodded and turned back to the Captain. "You may not be saying Donald did it, but that's what you think, ain't it? You think he killed Mayhew on account of Susan."

"I think he's a suspect, Mr. Jenkins."

The men stared at each other and Cordelia watched the two dark faces. One calm and controlled, exuding authority, the other earnest and imploring.

"I've heard folks talk about you," said Carl. "You're Billy Walker. Everybody looks up to you. Captain, my boy didn't do it. It ain't in him. I got another boy. I imagine you know that. Hal's disgraced us a dozen times and broken his mother's heart. But Donald . . ." Jenkins swallowed and stared up at the ceiling. His eyes glistened.

"Carl," said Billy, "wherever Donald's name has been mentioned, I've heard nothing but praise."

Jenkins nodded his head. "Yes," he murmured and nodded his head again. "Yes."

"Can you remember what he said to you, the last time you saw him?"

"He just said he had to get away for awhile. On account of the girl, you know. Said he'd call us in a few days. I asked him where he was headed and he said he didn't really know, but not to worry about him. Donald had some money saved. He could have gone most anywhere."

Mrs. Jenkins came back around the meat counter. "Would you folks like some coffee?"

"No thanks," said Billy. "Mrs. Jenkins, when Donald told you and your husband he had to get away for awhile, did you take it he meant for a long while?"

"Oh no, Captain. Donald was coming back soon. I knew that." She glanced at her husband. "I still know it."

"When your son stayed with you, did he have a room of his own?"

"Yessir. We live in the back, but there's plenty of space."

"Do you mind if we have a look at it?"

Lilly turned to her husband, who gave an affirmative nod. "Come on back," she said, and led the way through a curtained partition. Carl remained out front.

The policemen found themselves in a well-furnished living room, surprisingly large. Broad windows appeared on one side. Sunlight shone through them and lit up the comfortable furnishings. An open door on their right led to the kitchen. Two doors at the rear opened into bedrooms. Lilly Jenkins took them through the one on the left.

"This is Donald's room," she said.

The bedroom was small and furnished with the usual dresser and chest of drawers. Two open doors on the left revealed a closet and a bathroom. A small nightstand stood by the twin-sized bed. A single book lay on it. The Captain picked it up and looked at the title: *R. E. Lee,* by Douglass Southall Freeman. He smiled and lay the volume back down.

Turning to the woman, he said, "Mrs. Jenkins, we don't have a search warrant, but I wonder if we could just look around."

"Yes, I guess it'll be all right, but there's nothing here that'll help you."

Billy glanced at the woman and her face reddened. "I went

through everything in here. Thought there might be something to, you know, give us a clue where Donnie might be."

"I see," said the Captain.

Cordelia searched the bathroom and closet. Nothing but towels, washcloths and a few items of clothing. Walker checked under the mattress and riffled through the pages of R. E. Lee. He noticed a small drawer, set under the table edge, and pulled it open. His eye fell on a red penknife and what appeared to be a photograph, laying upside down. He picked the photograph up and turned it over. Lilly Jenkins moved to his side.

Both gazed down at the picture of the two young men, smiling into the camera. They stood in front of a rundown house trailer, and a late afternoon sun cast their shadows across its concrete steps.

"It's Hal and Donnie." Lilly took the photo and smiled down at it. "That was taken about a year ago. Hal was gone from us by then. I mean he and his daddy . . . Well, we just didn't see each other anymore. Donnie was sort of the go-between for us. You know, kind of the link."

"Yes ma'am," said Billy. "Who does the trailer belong to?"

"Oh that's Hal's. He owns it. It's the only thing he ever did own, bless his heart. Since he's been . . . away, me and Carl go out and check on it now and then, make sure everthing's all right."

"Have you been out there recently?"

"Yes sir, we were out there about three weeks ago. Donnie had been gone a few days and we thought he might be, you know, holed up out there." She handed the picture back to Billy. "No sign of him, though. Carl checked all around and knocked on the door. No answer. We didn't expect one 'cause Donnie's car wasn't there."

"What kind of car does he own?"

"One of those foreign-made cars. What's the name of 'em?

Used to be called something else, then they changed it."

"A Nissan?"

"Yes, that's it. I think Donnie said it was a Sentra model. It was blue, a pretty little car."

"You and your husband didn't go inside the trailer?"

"No, Carl told me it was still padlocked. Donald had a key to it, but we don't."

"Where's the trailer located, Mrs. Jenkins?"

"It's kinda out in the country, Captain. What you do is head west on Court Street to the edge of town. Then you're on Old Town Road. Follow that for about five miles and the trailer will be on the right. It's easy to miss, though, 'cause it sets off the road a ways. Just keep looking to the right. You'll see it next to a grove of pecan trees. There's a gravel road leading up to it."

"Lilly," came Carl's voice from the front, "the Coke man's here."

Walker placed the photo back in the drawer. "Thanks for your help, Mrs. Jenkins. We'll be going now."

"Don't mention it, Captain. Maybe the next time you come by, Donnie will be here."

She followed them back through the curtain. The policemen shook hands with Carl and walked back to their car. Cordelia looked over at her boss.

"The trailer?" she asked.

"The trailer," he replied.

Forty-Two

This time Cordelia drove. They reached Court Street and headed west. The police station appeared ahead and she looked at her boss. He shook his head and they continued on by. They rounded a gentle curve and Cordelia saw the Razorback Cafe in the distance. She glanced at her watch and then at the Captain. He shook his head again and she pressed down on the accelerator, sweeping past the restaurant and around another curve.

Almost at once, they were in the country, with nothing but denuded cotton fields sliding by on either side. The two-lane blacktop narrowed into the distance. A dilapidated pickup met and passed them, the driver giving them a wave. Cordelia remembered they still did that in the country. The sky had turned overcast and the western horizon looked dark and threatening. Cordelia shivered, although the cruiser was warm. She glanced at the Captain. His face was set and grim as he stared off down the deserted highway. A quick current of alarm ran through her. Come on, she thought. Don't get superstitious again. He can't see into never-never land.

Walker reached over and picked up the mike. "CID One, Medford."

"Go ahead, CID One."

"Call Sheriff Hackett's office, please. Ask him to give me a radio call."

"Ten four, Captain."

Cordelia gave him a second glance.

"We're out of our jurisdiction," he responded. "We'll play by the rules."

"Okay."

She reflected that they'd ventured out into the county a bunch of times and Walker had never before informed the sheriff. Hell, the sheriff's office regarded Walker's CID as their office too. Hackett knew how to take advantage of a good thing. Every county case solved by the Captain, old Jimmy got part of the credit.

"Sheriff's office to CID One." It was a feminine voice. Cordelia recognized it as Juanita Parsons, the sheriff's secretary. She palmed the mike before her boss could move. Billy smiled to himself.

"Go ahead, Sheriff," she said.

"Cordelia? Is that you?" The voice sounded high and girlish.

Cordelia rolled her eyes. "Ten four," she replied.

"Now, Cordelia, you know this ain't the sheriff. It's Juanita."

To Hull, it sounded like "Wahneedah." Medford's Scarlett O'Hara, she thought.

"Is Captain Walker there?"

"Ten four."

"Well, put him on, Cordelia."

Cordelia grimaced and gritted her teeth. This lack of proper radio procedure was driving her nuts. The Captain had taught her better. She gave him a look. Oh yeah, he was enjoying her discomfort. "Go ahead," she answered. "The Captain is listening."

"Billeee," crooned Juanita. "How are you?"

Walker sat bolt upright and Cordelia handed him the mike. Her smile was much bigger than his had been.

"Fine, Juanita. Is the sheriff in?"

"Why no, Billy. That's why it's me that's callin'. He's down the hall, but he'll be back in a . . . Wait, he just came in." Juanita continued to hold the mike button down. "Jimmy, guess who's on the radio. It's Billeee."

Cordelia chuckled and Walker shot her a look.

"Go ahead, Captain," came the gruff voice.

Thank God, thought Hull. At last we're back to business. She could picture James Hackett standing at his secretary's desk, one meaty hand pressing the mike button. The sheriff was a big, bear-like man, and his personal uniform of tan khaki shirt and trousers was invariably rumpled. His face seemed always in need of a shave and his hair a comb, but Hackett was a professional right down to his fingertips. She would never understand why he put up with Juanita.

"Sheriff, we're headed west on Old Town Road. Do you have a deputy handy?"

"Yeah, Deputy Hansom's over at your station, picking up some mug shots. You need him?"

"Ten four. We'll be at a trailer house on the right, about five miles out of town. It's off the road a bit, next to a grove of pecan trees."

"Okay Billy, but you know when it comes to the CID, my county is your county."

Cordelia smiled and nodded her head. She liked to hear her boss advertised, and this was going out to every cop and deputy on duty.

"I appreciate that, Sheriff," said Billy, "but maybe we better have a deputy this time."

"You got it," replied Hackett. "Go ahead and use Hansom."

"Thanks, Jimmy."

"Any time."

Billy waited a moment and pressed the mike button again. "Did you copy all that, Sally?"

"Ten four, Captain," came the dispatcher's voice. "Deputy Hansom was listening. He's headed out the door."

Cordelia figured they should be getting close to Hal's trailer. She kept an eye peeled and finally a stand of pecan trees appeared on the right. They drew closer and she could see the trailer. It sat at the edge of the grove. A gravel road led from the front yard back to the highway. They were almost to the turnoff when she saw the small blue car. It had been parked to the left side of the trailer and its shiny color seemed alien in that drab winter landscape.

"Pull over," commanded Walker and Cordelia pulled onto the loose gravel shoulder.

"Donald Jenkins's car," she breathed.

"Yes," said Walker, and Cordelia got that old feeling again. The Captain was out there ahead of her somewhere, ahead of everybody.

"What do you want to do?" she asked.

"We'll wait for the deputy."

Hull reached over into the back seat and pulled the .38 Chief's Special from her purse. She glanced at Billy and stuck into her coat pocket. Walker was staring at the trailer. They sat silently. Finally, a car appeared in her rearview mirror. It drew up behind them and stopped, its long rear antenna whipping back and forth. The driver's door, with SIMPSON COUNTY SHERIFF'S DEPARTMENT lettered on the side, opened and the deputy got out. He walked around to the Captain's side, opened the rear door and got in.

"How you doing, Captain Walker?" he said with a brief smile. The teeth were small and even.

"Fine, Mark. You know my assistant, Sergeant Hull."

"Sure thing. How you doing, Sergeant?"

"Good," said Cordelia, taking the proffered hand.

"How can I help you, Captain?" inquired the deputy.

"We're going over there," said Billy, nodding at the trailer. "If someone named Donald Jenkins is inside, we'll take him in.

Why don't you go first and drive around back. Sergeant Hull will cover me from the front. We'll take it slow and easy."

"Yes sir," said Hansom, and returned to his car. He swung around them and turned down the gravel road. Cordelia followed close behind as they slowly approached the trailer. Hansom turned to the right and disappeared behind it. The two policemen came to a halt and gazed through the windshield.

Hal's trailer looked old and uncared for. Rust had formed along the roof line and was creeping down the sides. Two windows appeared on each side of the door. There were no curtains or shades and the windows faced out like dark square caverns. Cordelia's eyes darted back and forth, looking for signs of movement. Concrete steps led up to the door. The door was partly open.

She pulled closer and parked with the driver's side away from the trailer. Getting out quickly, she pulled her revolver and laid it across the car roof. She sighted down the barrel and continued to scan the windows. By this time, Walker was out and walking toward the front door. He stood at the doorway for a moment, then looked down at his feet and back along the ground to the little blue car. He took a few steps toward the car before coming back to the door again. He pushed on the door and it swung easily back into the trailer's dark interior.

NO! Cordelia almost screamed the word. What was Walker thinking. He'd of skinned her for doing what he was doing, standing quietly in front of the open doorway with daylight illuminating him, a perfect target. She flinched when she heard him call the deputy.

"Mark! It's all right. Come on around."

He turned toward her and beckoned once with four finger tips. Hull placed the revolver in her coat pocket and walked around the car. She'd only taken a couple of steps before the reek of rotten flesh burned into her nostrils. She wondered why she hadn't smelled it sooner because the odor fairly boiled from the open doorway. She saw Mark Hansom out of the corner of her eye. He walked toward the Captain, then stopped as the stench hit him. He began breathing through his open mouth. Walker nodded toward Jenkins's car and Cordelia walked over to it. She looked in the driver's side window and saw the thick accumulation of dried blood. It covered most of the front seat and floorboard. She turned around and saw the trail of blood leading up to the trailer. Hull watched Hansom come up and stop beside Walker. He held a handkerchief to his face. The Captain stood watching her. She started toward him and toward the darkness beyond the trailer door.

FORTY-THREE

What had once been Donald Jenkins lay facing upward across the narrow bed. The body was clothed in a blue, slipover sweater and tan slacks. The right pants leg had turned a rusty brown and looked stiff as cardboard from the dried blood. Jenkins's eyelids were open and the eyes had turned to gray mucous. The bloated face swelled around them. His whole body had swelled and stretched the tan slacks taut. The skin was the color of bread mold. It seemed to glisten, and that overpowering stink, emanating from the body, grew stronger and more awful as they stood there. Cordelia turned away, but then her eyes caught movement and she turned back again. The body had moved. No it hadn't. Only Donald's sweater had moved. It rippled downward across his stomach. Then Cordelia saw the hairy rat. It clambered from under the sweater and squatted on top of the corpse. A string of putrefied flesh hung from its jaws. Scrambling up the body, the rat paused on Jenkins's face and turned to look at them before disappearing over the far side of the bed. Cordelia made a weak, groaning sound and stumbled out the trailer door. She bent over the concrete steps and let this morning's breakfast gush from her open mouth. She heaved and heaved and tears poured from her eyes and she thought she'd never stop heaving. Then she felt the Captain's hand laid gently on her shoulder. His handkerchief came round in front of her. She took it and wiped the bile from her lips. Straightening, she squared her shoulders and nodded her head. The

Captain stepped aside and Cordelia led the way back into the trailer.

Mark Hansom stood over the body, the handkerchief still clutched to his nose and mouth. Billy walked over and murmured something to him. The deputy nodded and headed outside to his car.

"He's calling the coroner," said her boss.

Billy reached into his pocket and pulled out a small jar. He unscrewed the cap and Cordelia caught a whiff of something pungent, a medicinal smell, maybe Ben Gay. Where had he gotten it? Was it already in his pocket? Cordelia quit thinking about it. The Captain walked over, dipped his thumb into the jar, and spread the fragrant salve under her nose and down the sides of her mouth. The scent cut through the foulness like a breath of mountain air. Cordelia could still detect the stink, but it was bearable now. Walker spread some under his nose and offered the jar to Hansom, who'd come back in behind them. All three walked over to the bed and stood looking down. They didn't see the writing until then.

Donald must have finally realized that he was bleeding to death. He'd dipped his index finger into the fatal wound, the gushing arterial wound, and scrawled his final message to whoever might find him. The bed was covered with a white sheet so the letters written on it showed plain and legible.

"I'll be damned," said the deputy in a low voice. "Looks like a woman did it." Billy Walker and Cordelia Hull said nothing.

They simply stared at the writing.

"Yep," he continued, "they must have got into it somewhere else and she shot him in the leg. Must have hit a vein. He managed to drive out here and fall across the bed. But he wrote her first name before he died. May! I wonder how many women named May live in Medford. Do you know any, Captain?"

"A few," Walker replied.

Cordelia looked up at her boss and they exchanged looks of perfect understanding. She glanced back down at the bloody word . . . no, the bloody half word. The tail of the Y was trailed out, and no wonder. Jenkins's wasn't finished. He was trying to complete the word, to make an H. But Hansom was partly right. Donald Jenkins had tried to write down the name of the person who killed him.

Mayhew, she thought, and the name filled her with a sudden rage. Mayhew! You evil, treacherous, murderous son of a bitch.

FORTY-FOUR

Walker waited for a lumbering John Deere cotton picker to pass in front of them before pulling out of the Jenkins' gravel drive and onto Old Town Road. Cordelia slumped in her seat and stared across the flat, vacant fields. She felt empty and it was more than just her stomach, voided by vomiting. She was empty of the rage and every other emotion. She felt like telling the Captain to take her home or maybe let her out of the car so she could take a long, solitary walk. Cordelia Hull did neither. Instead, the young woman straightened up, squared her shoulders, and looked at her boss.

"So where does all this leave us?" she murmured.

Billy swept around the cotton picker and increased his speed. He placed a cigarette between his lips, lit it, inhaled deeply, and sent smoke cascading against the windshield. "Well," he said, "it leaves us with one less suspect."

Cordelia wished, for a moment, that she also smoked. Maybe that would clear out the stink, still lingering in her lungs.

While waiting for the coroner and ambulance, she and Walker had given the trailer a thorough search, and had turned up nothing. Finally, Donnie Reed arrived and they left. They did not mentioned to Reed or Hansom the real meaning of Donald's scrawled message. As yet, they hadn't mentioned it to each other.

Now she asked, "How do you envision the meeting between Jenkins and Mayhew?" If anybody could retrieve the scene, her boss could do it.

"Oh, I think that Donald confronted Edwin with what he knew. One of Donald's friends says that the boy wasn't capable of murder. I tend to believe that, but I also believe that Donald intended to do Mayhew harm."

"He went there to beat him up?"

"I think so."

Cordelia turned toward her boss. "That was bad planning."

"Yes. Mayhew shot him and Donald managed to get back to the trailer before he bled to death."

"Bad planning," Cordelia muttered for the second time. "Donald Jenkins had only two options, really."

Walker raised an eyebrow at her.

"Either leave Mayhew alone or kill him."

"Yes," said the Captain. "Too bad that Donald could do neither."

They saw Medford in the distance with a few lights starting to come on. The Medford Water Reservoir lay off to their right, and in the twilight, Cordelia watched a flight of wild ducks bank steeply above it. They slanted in and splashed onto its surface.

"We never found a gun at the liquor store," she stated.

"I don't think Edwin would have held onto it. He was too smart for that. Still, we need to follow up and make sure."

They swept back past the Razorback Cafe. Cordelia glanced at it and shook her head. It seemed years since she'd last seen it. Darkness was settling in. They passed a strip shopping center as its parking lot lights flicked on. Beyond and on the left, Mayhew's Liquor proclaimed itself in neon to all the passing traffic. Billy parked near the entrance and he and Cordelia walked inside.

"Evening, folks. Business or pleasure?"

Only one person could own that voice and that tone. Billy

glanced to his left and saw Josephine Harvey standing on a stool and holding a decorative bottle of Wild Turkey in each hand. One container was formed in the likeness of Elvis Presley's head and the other depicted Abraham Lincoln, an incongruous duo. Jo placed the bottles on a top shelf and stepped down from the stool. She smiled and glided toward them.

"Business," said Billy, "but it'll only take a moment."

"You want to go back to the office?"

"Is Lavonia back there?"

"Um hm."

"Let's go back. There's something I want to ask both of you."

Lavonia sat behind her brother's desk. Her left hand finger traced a row of figures on an invoice. The right fingers pecked at keys on a calculator. She glanced up and smiled at Billy.

She looks livelier, he thought, and credited it to her new-found occupation. Hull was thinking the same thing. They were both right.

"Billy, Cordelia," said the old lady. "What can we do for you?"

Cordelia cleared her throat and asked, "Do either of you know where Edwin kept his pistol?"

"I've no idea," said Jo. "It's been years since I've seen him."

"I know he owned at least one," said Lavonia. "Tried to give it to me, you know, for protection. I told him to keep it. I could take care of myself without shooting somebody."

The image of a certain plumber, cowering beneath a bush, flashed through Walker's mind. "Do you happen to know the make?" he asked.

"Edwin said it was a Smith and Wesson thirty-eight."

"Do you know where he kept it?" asked Cordelia.

"No. I've been all through his room since he died, and it ain't there. I know he didn't carry one on him. Maybe it's here in the store."

Both policemen turned to Josephine.

"Well, you've both searched his office and his little boudoir," she said, "and I've been all over the front. There's no gun there."

"Edwin probably got rid of it," said Hull, and mentally kicked herself. She didn't usually slip up like this.

Lavonia frowned. "Why would he get rid of it?"

"Oh, you keep things for awhile and then you get tired of them. Your brother might have sold it." She didn't sound too convincing and Lavonia's frown remained.

They followed Jo out of the office. "Sorry," Cordelia muttered under her breath. The Captain shrugged.

The store had gained a half dozen customers, all dressed in heavy work clothes. One stood at the checkout counter arguing with the cashier. The cashier listened with a resigned look on his face. Billy remembered that Jo had called him Robert.

"Now look here, Robert," the customer was saying. "The sign over this bottle of Old Charter said six fifty a mamaleeter, or whatever they call a fifth nowadays. Now you tell me it's eight fifty."

Robert gave a faint smile. "That sign's for the whiskey above it, Luther. The price signs are always below the bottles. He emphasized the word "below" and pointed downward with his index finger."

"Well, it's damn confusin' is all I got to say," muttered Luther, fumbling at his hip pocket. The man's words were slurred and he swayed back and forth as he sought his wallet.

Walker recognized him. Luther Hollings had slept off several drunks in the Medford PD's holding cell. Billy remembered Officer Pruitt's report on his last arrest. The charges on that one had included disorderly conduct. The Captain realized, to his dismay, that Hollings had recognized him also and was now shuffling his way.

"Cap'n," he called, and was seized by a fit of coughing. After a moment, he wheezed, "How's it goin', Cap'n?"

"Very well, Luther. Are you all right?"

"Yessir. Damn bronchitis gets hold of me ever once in a while."

"Sorry to hear it."

"Aw, it passes," said Luther. Then with a smirk, "I jist got me some cough syrup for it."

The Captain said, "Well, don't let it go to your head."

"I won't. I won't. You know I don't cause no trouble, Cap'n, and I ain't got no car so I ain't a danger."

"Well, I hear you were causing a little trouble a few nights ago," said Walker.

"Oh, you mean that thing over on Seventh Street?"

"The cops say you were harassing the customers."

"Naw, jist one customer. I seen him in the liquor store and I followed him out to his car." Luther lowered his chin and peered up at the Captain. "There wasn't no reason to call the cops."

Billy made no response.

"And he deserved some harassin'," Hollings added.

"Why were you bothering this particular person?"

"Well Cap'n, I'd been drinkin', true enough, but that man needed a good talkin' to."

Cordelia had walked past Hollings and was waiting for Walker to follow her to the door. Walker started toward her, then slowly turned and faced the intoxicated man. "Why was that Luther?" he asked. "Why did he need a good talking to?"

"Because he was a preacher for God's sake. And there he was buying a quart of booze." Hollings straightened and squared his shoulders. "So I walked up to him and I says, 'Brother Briggs, what do you plan on doin' with that whiskey?' And he says . . .'"

"What did you say?" Cordelia's voice cut in clear and sharp.

"Brother who?" She took a step toward Hollings. Several customers looked over their way.

The Captain took Hollings's elbow and guided him toward the door. "I want to hear more about this, Luther," he murmured. "Let's talk about it in the car."

Forty-Five

Cordelia got behind the wheel, started the engine, and turned on the heater. Warm air flowed from the vents and filled up the car. Luther Hollings sat in the middle of the back seat and leaned forward, his whiskey clasped in both hands. Walker got in beside Cordelia. He placed an arm on the seat back and turned to look at Luther. Hollings gave Billy a plaintive look.

"Cap'n you ain't fixin' to arrest me, are you?"

"Why no, Luther. Why do you ask that? Have you done anything illegal?"

"No sir, but ever time I've been in the back of a police car, that's what's happened."

"Tell you what," said Walker. "How would you like a ride home?"

"Hey, I'd like that fine," Hollings answered. His fingers crept to the top of the bottle and tapped on the cap.

Billy noticed and said, "Take a sip if you want one."

Luther nodded, unscrewed the cap, and took a large swallow. He leaned back, shook his head, and chuckled. "Man oh man," he said. "I never thought I'd be ridin' home in a police car and drinkin' whiskey on the way." The liquid revived him and he sat a little straighter. "What else did you want to know, Cap'n?"

"Do you know Briggs's first name?"

"Yeah, it's Nathaniel. You know, like in the Bible. I remember thinkin' it was a fit name for a preacher."

"And what did this preacher say when you asked him about

the whiskey?"

"He stared at me with them black eyes of his and then he said it wasn't none of my affair."

"And?"

"Well, that sort of set me off, Cap'n. I mean him answering me that way."

Cordelia eased the patrol car forward and pulled onto Court Street. She glanced over her shoulder and asked, "What's the address, Mr. Hollings?"

"Eleven-oh-four Sixth Street."

"Go on, Luther," said the Captain.

"Well, he started out the liquor store door and I followed him. Like I said, I'd had a few drinks, and the more I thought about Briggs's attitude, the madder I got, especially when I remembered the last time I heard him preach."

"When was that?"

"About two weeks before. He was guest preacher at my church, and I have to say he preached a damn good sermon. He sure has a way with words. Anyhow, part of the sermon was about drinkin' and druggin' and how the Lord despised them both. Briggs said he surely hated them, and with good reason, but that his hatred was nothing compared to the Lord's."

"With good reason? Those were the words he used?"

"Yessir, that's what he said, 'with good reason.' I figured it must be somethin' personal. Anyway, he went on and on about it, especially the drinkin'. I sank down in my pew and just felt sick and small. Briggs could do that to you."

Suddenly, Hollings stiffened and his florid face flushed a darker hue. "Then after all that, I catch the bastard buying a quart of liquor and telling me that it's none of my affair."

Cordelia turned onto Sixth Street. Luther leaned forward and pointed to a small frame house on the right. "The one with no lights on," he said. Hull pulled to the curb and cut the motor.

"Go on, Luther," said Walker.

"Well, there ain't much more to tell. I followed him out to his car and give him some of my opinion on liars and hypocrites."

"Did Nathaniel say anything else?"

"Well, yeah." Luther rubbed a hand across his mouth and stared out the window at his house. "He was about to get in the car, but he turned around and said, 'I didn't buy this to drink, Brother Hollings.' So I said, 'Yeah, well what did you buy it for, Brother Briggs?' "

Luther was silent for a moment, remembering. "Then that preacher said the damndest thing."

"And what did Brother Briggs say?" asked the Captain.

"He said he'd bought it to baptize a demon."

Billy looked out the windshield into darkness, not noticing Cordelia, staring at him with her mouth slightly open. He pulled a cigarette out and lit it, letting smoke curl from his nostrils.

"Well, I wanta thank you for bringin' me home," said Luther. "Much obliged." He fumbled with the door latch.

Cordelia finally noticed and murmured, "You can't open it from the inside, Mr. Hollings. I'll get it for you."

She got out and walked around the car. Her boss had not moved. Hull opened the rear door and Luther climbed out. A dog commenced barking inside the house. It sounded like a small one. Her mind flashed back, for a moment, to another boozer and another dog and Mayhew's baseball bat.

"That's Lucy," said Hollings. "She knows when I'm close." He shambled up the sidewalk, whiskey bottle in hand. Cordelia watched him for a moment, then turned back to the cruiser. Walker had lowered his window.

"Luther," he called.

Hollings turned around, the streetlight shining on his face.

"What kind of car was Briggs driving?"

"It was an old one, Cap'n Walker. American make. Might've been a Chevy. I remember it was a four door 'cause the left back door was all caved in."

"What color was it?"

"Don't remember. Don't think it had much color at all."

Cordelia got back in the car and they both watched Hollings walk away. The barking grew louder as he approached the front door.

"I didn't think Briggs owned a car," she muttered. It was a throwaway statement. The car didn't really matter now that they knew what they knew.

"I don't believe he did," said the Captain, "but he got one from somewhere. On that night, Nathaniel had need of a car."

The two policemen entered their office and Cordelia placed a chair in front of the Captain's desk. She slumped into it and closed her eyes. Walker sat down and punched a button on the phone in front of him.

"Yes, Captain," came the dispatcher's voice.

"Paul, get a bulletin out for me, please. Let it read: 'Be on lookout for older model, four-door sedan with damage to driver's side rear door, possibly a Chevrolet, color unknown.' "

"Anything else, sir?"

"Not on the car. That's all the description we've got and it's pretty general. The officers will have to use some discretion. If the driver is identified as Nathaniel Briggs, he's to be brought in and held for questioning. Consider Briggs armed and dangerous."

"Ten four."

"Get that out to the highway patrol and the sheriff's department also."

"You got it, Captain."

Walker leaned back, placed both hands behind his head and gazed at the ceiling.

Cordelia slipped off her pumps and wiggled her toes. She glanced upward and sideways at her boss. Her lips formed a smile, and Billy was reminded of all the coquettes he had ever known.

"It's him, isn't it?" she whispered.

"Yes," he replied. "It's him."

"So all our work came down to accidentally running into a drunk at Edwin's liquor store."

"That's what happened," said Walker, "but sooner or later our work would have brought us to the preacher."

It's true, thought Cordelia. All their actions had been correct. The Captain had seen to that. They were headed for Nathaniel Briggs all along. They'd simply done what was necessary, clearing the path. "Did you always believe it was him?"

The Captain smiled and shook his head. He'd long known that his assistant was convinced he possessed intuitive powers. Others, included Uh Oh Earl, believed the same thing. Walker never thought about it.

"No," he answered.

"But you suspected it."

"Later on I did. After all, there were certain indications."

"The unpaid loan."

"Yes. That was the first one. I think Nathaniel would have repaid that loan no matter what. Unless he came to feel that Mayhew was . . ."

"Unworthy?"

"Yes, and also evil."

"Easier to kill when you're in that frame of mind."

Walker nodded. "He maybe felt that someone that evil had to be killed."

"All on account of what Edwin did to his daughter."

"And perhaps what he himself also did."

Cordelia stared at her boss, a puzzled frown on her face. What did Briggs do? And then the light came on. She sucked in her breath and slowly blew it out.

"So that's how it happened," she whispered. "He brought them together."

She had wondered how Susan, the innocent and virtuous daughter, ever came into contact with someone like Mayhew. Mayhew's loan to Briggs was the link. The preacher was the link, and, of course, Walker had suspected this for a long time. Cordelia wondered why she had not.

"But," she said, "Nathaniel wouldn't have offered his daughter to . . ."

"Of course not," replied Billy. "I'm sure he never imagined the outcome. He believed in his daughter. He trusted her."

"Then how did it happen?" asked Cordelia.

"I think he sent her to the liquor store on some errands. Nathaniel didn't drink so that wasn't the reason she was sent."

Cordelia gave the expected reply. "She went to deliver the payments."

"Yes, I think so. Briggs would not have wanted to be seen there."

"So Edwin went to work on her and eventually ruined her and Briggs had to live with his part in it."

"Yes, with the knowledge that his pride, his vanity, had helped bring it all about."

"Sweet Jesus," breathed Cordelia.

The Captain gazed at her before replying, "And that's not the whole of it. Briggs indirectly brought about the death of Donald Jenkins. Remember, Donald confronted Mayhew with what he knew to be true. He knew it because he'd been told by 'someone who wouldn't lie.' "

"A preacher wouldn't lie."

The Captain didn't respond. Perhaps this one wouldn't, he thought. But he would kill. And that killing would come out of guilt and revenge and an incontestable compulsion. His own zealotry had called on him to do it. And his own personal God.

FORTY-SIX

For a long time afterward, whenever Cordelia Hull looked back on the remainder of that week, she would remember the weather. The gloomy overcast disappeared and was replaced by fluffy patches of cumulus and a bright cerulean sky. And the sun, huge and yellow, sent down its warmth.

The next morning, when she and the Captain met at the police station, the temperature had already risen. The Captain wore only a light windbreaker. Cordelia had traded her coat for a cotton jacket. They climbed into the police car, already heated by sunlight through glass, and she unbuttoned her jacket. Then she remembered where they were going and gave a little shiver.

"I wish we had done it last night," she murmured.

"This morning will be better for them."

Yes, she thought. It will be. Better than the night. Better than the darkness. "You suppose anybody has let it leak out? Maybe they've been told." The Captain had made certain arrangements, and Donald's death was known by only those who had to know. They had promised silence, but you never could tell.

"They don't know," he said. "I called them this morning to tell them we'd be over. They asked if we'd found Donald."

Carl and Lilly Jenkins had a ledger laid out on the counter beside the cash register. Their heads were bent over it and Carl was making an entry. They both looked up and watched the two policemen enter. Lilly Jenkins removed the reading glasses from her nose and started around the counter, Carl following after.

They stood before the Captain like mute disciples while he told them what they had to know.

That day and the next and the next passed in endless sunshine and unbroken routine. The news of Donald Jenkins's death came out in the paper and everybody wondered who "May" was.

May Daniels sat with the newspaper in her lap. She'd gone to high school with Donald and they'd worked on a science project together. She'd worn braces back then and usually felt clumsy and unattractive around boys, especially Donald. But he was unfailingly kind and considerate toward her and now she knew he had felt something more. They'd spent a lot of time alone together in a effort to construct a robot arm. She remembered Donald gazing at her occasionally and the prolonged hug when they won second prize at the exhibit. As far as she could tell, she was the only "May" he knew. Her eyes misted when she reflected how his innermost feelings must have emerged at the time of his death. May shivered and hugged herself and resolved to always keep silent about their love for each other. Maybe she would whisper the word "Donald" when she drew her last breath.

The Captain went to Judge Harvey Wilson and obtained an arrest warrant for Nathaniel Briggs. This time it had not been easy. Wilson was usually quick to oblige the Captain, the two reasons being that, first, his charges were always borne out, and second, because he was Billy Walker. However, on this occasion, Wilson observed that there wasn't much here to incriminate Briggs, and he was right.

"Billy," he'd said, "all you've got is a belief that Briggs hated Edwin on account of what Edwin did to his daughter, and that's conjecture. And your idea as to why he didn't pay off the loan, that's conjecture, too. It's just all something you see in your mind. And that thing about him buying the whiskey, what in hell is that supposed to mean?"

So Billy had told the judge about their holdback.

"Well, I'll be damned," said Wilson. "That's downright weird." He sighed and pulled the warrant across his desk. Pulling out a plain Bic pen, he signed it at the bottom. "Hope you can make it stick," he muttered.

"I think we can," replied Walker. "I believe that Nathaniel will confess."

"Oh?" inquired Wilson. "Why would he do that?"

"Because that's what he wants to do." replied the Captain.

Judge Wilson watched the door close behind the policeman, then steepled his fingers under his chin. It had never occurred to him to ask how Walker knew that Briggs wanted to confess. The judge reflected that in that area Billy Walker's perceptions had always been dead on. And that was why he had signed the warrant.

There had been no response to the Captain's bulletin, and no one had come forth with information about Briggs. It seemed they'd come to a standstill, but Cordelia remembered that through those last balmy days there was a certain tension in the air. Well, maybe not tension. No, she remembered clearly. It had been expectancy.

On Wednesday a reporter visited Walker (Cordelia suspected he'd been invited) and the Captain told him about the warrant on Briggs. There was no mention of whiskey. The story came out in Thursday morning's paper.

The two policemen went about the routine business of the CID. No felonies were committed that week, but they continued their investigations on a couple of old burglaries and an armed robbery. Cordelia remembered she'd been tense and impatient during the week. Maybe working under a layer of expectancy did that to you. The work had been slow and tedious, and dammit, she did sense that something was going to happen.

The Captain evidently did not. He went methodically about his work, and even took an afternoon off to play golf with Sheriff Hackett. What Cordelia had come to think of as "the whiskey killing" seemed to have passed completely from his mind. They waited.

On Friday morning, two weeks to the day from Mayhew's murder, the phone on Billy's desk rang and the Captain picked it up. He listened for a moment, murmured something that Cordelia couldn't make out, and slowly replaced the receiver.

"That was Carl Jenkins," he said. "He's coming up to see us."

And somehow Cordelia knew that their wait was coming to an end.

FORTY-SEVEN

Carl Jenkins came into the office and gently closed the door behind him. Slowly, he walked past Cordelia and headed for the rear desk, his eyes on the Captain. Billy stood and nodded toward a chair. Carl drew it toward him and sat down heavily. Billy was struck by the man's appearance. He looked years older, and to Walker's eyes, he seemed to have somehow lessened. His dark hair was carelessly combed and he hadn't shaven that morning, or probably the morning before. Tired, vacant eyes stared out of a vacant face. Walker remembered that when they'd heard about their son, Lilly Jenkins had faced him and asked the necessary questions. It was Carl who sagged and had to be assisted to a chair.

"Good morning, Captain." The voice sounded hoarse.

"Good to see you, Carl."

Jenkins half turned toward Cordelia. "Good morning."

"How are you Mr. Jenkins," she gently asked. "Can I get you a cup of coffee?"

"No ma'am. Thanks anyway." He pulled a pack of cigarettes from his shirt pocket and offered one to the Captain. Billy shook his head. Carl placed one between his lips and lit it with a match. The hands began to tremble and he flung the match on the floor. The flame expired and a thin line of smoke drifted upward. The Captain and Cordelia waited.

"I need to tell y'all something," began Carl. "I should've told you before. At the time, I thought I had good reasons not to.

Anyway, I was wrong."

Billy leaned forward and placed both hands on his desk. He slowly nodded to Carl.

"When you came looking for Donald, you asked if we'd ever met Nathaniel Briggs and I said we never had."

The Captain nodded again.

"Well, the truth is, I had met him. I knew the preacher."

"I see," said Walker. "And Mrs. Jenkins?"

"No sir." Carl was emphatic. "She never saw him and she thinks I never did either."

"Go on," said Billy.

"It was just between me and Donald. We got to talking one day and he broke down and told me what had happened to Susan. It all came out . . . the drinking, the doping, and all the rest. He said the Susan he knew was gone, and what was in her place was just something wild, something crazy. I couldn't believe he was talking about the same little gal who used to help Lilly in the garden. I said, 'Don, is the booze what you meant by an 'outside influence'? And he said, 'No Daddy, I was talking about a man.' So I asked him who the man was, and Donald said he'd let somebody else tell me, somebody who could tell it better than him."

Carl Jenkins leaned back in his chair and stared at the ceiling. He kept his eyes there while he muttered, "And that's when I first met the preacher."

"Where did you meet him?" asked Walker.

"Nathaniel was staying out on Norris Street. I don't remember the house number. It was one of Baker Watson's old rental houses. That's where Donald took me."

"How long ago was this?"

"Oh, about three months ago, I guess. Donald had just come to live with us."

"Go on, Carl."

"Well, we got out there and the preacher came to the door. Donald told him who I was and he invited us inside. He was real polite. Went out to the kitchen and brought back two glasses of cold buttermilk. He'd got a glass of ice water for himself.'"

Jenkins smiled. "I asked him didn't he like buttermilk and he said he preferred water, called it 'Adam's Ale.' He was always making little jokes like that. Anyway, we sat and talked for awhile, and finally Donald mentioned Susan." Carl stubbed out his cigarette in the Captain's ash tray. "Then, you should have seen that preacher change."

"Change how?" asked Cordelia.

"I mean something just came over him. He'd been relaxed and friendly, but all of a sudden his face froze and them black eyes of his just seemed to bore a hole in you. I thought he was gonna kick us out, but he just looked at Donald and said: 'I take it you want your father to know what happened.' I thought that was real smart in the preacher, because Donald hadn't said anything, even though that was the reason for us going out there. Anyhow, my son nodded his head and Briggs told the story."

Cordelia sat riveted on Carl as he related what was said.

It seemed that when Briggs and his daughter first moved to Medford, times had been hard. He couldn't find much carpenter work to do and he hadn't established himself as a preacher. There were days when he and Susan went hungry. Borrowing money was out of the question. Nobody he knew had any to loan, and of course the banks would have laughed at him. Finally, a man he'd done some roof work for told him about Edwin Mayhew. Nathaniel didn't want to borrow from someone like Edwin, and at first it looked like he wouldn't have to. The carpenter work picked up, and the pastor at a nearby church, who needed to be out of town, offered Briggs a fourth of the donation to fill in for him one Sunday. The congregation had loved the sermon and they spread the word. Two other churches offered invitations at the same rate.

Then, misfortune hit. Susan came down with a kidney disorder and had to be hospitalized. Nathaniel was faced with, what to him, were enormous bills. He picked up a phone in the hospital waiting room and called Edwin Mayhew. To his surprise, Edwin offered to come over to the hospital and talk to him. They sat in the cafeteria and Briggs told him about his problem. It seemed Mayhew already knew that Nathaniel was a carpenter and part-time preacher. He appeared especially interested (and amused) about the preaching. Nathaniel said he kept asking about that.

In any case, he said yes to the loan, and to Briggs's amazement, pulled the money from a coat pocket and gave it to him on the spot. Susan left the hospital that day and the preacher paid the bill.

Things started to look up again. Briggs continued to do carpenter work, and his reputation as a preacher was spreading. He started to think about maybe getting his own church. People encouraged him to do it. Nathaniel realized these same people might not be nearly so supportive if they saw him in a liquor store making payments to the notorious Edwin Mayhew, and Mayhew insisted that he make them in person. What to do? Susan had the solution. Mayhew surely wouldn't object to her showing up in her father's stead. She would make the payments and get the receipts. People were much less apt to recognize her, and she promised her father to go right in and come right out.

The preacher agreed to it and walked with his daughter into sorrow.

Carl placed both hands on his knees and slowly shook his head. "Nathaniel told me once that he'd come to believe that Mayhew was a demon or something else not quite human. He thought maybe Edwin had sold his soul to the devil in return for special powers."

"Special powers," said Billy.

"Yes sir. Nathaniel had watched Susan change, and he couldn't stop it. Even as a man of God, he couldn't stop it. And it had happened so quick. He believed that Mayhew was the devil's disciple. How else could he take a person like Susan and do to her what he did."

"And where was Susan when you visited the preacher?"

"She was there," said Carl.

"There?" said Cordelia. "There in the house?"

Carl turned to face her. "When we were getting ready to go, the preacher asked if I remembered Susan and I said, of course, and I told him how much my wife thought of her. And Briggs said, yes, but did I remember how she was? And I said, sure, a kind and pleasant girl, a pretty girl. Then Briggs asked me if I'd like to meet her again, and he led us into the bedroom. Well, if I hadn't already been told who it was, I never would have believed it was Susan. Her hair hung straight and stringy and she appeared to have lost twenty pounds. Her face was pale and lifeless. She just sat on the edge of the bed and stared at the wall, didn't notice that anybody else was in the room. Her father spoke to her, but she never so much as blinked an eye. I couldn't stand it. I started backing out of the room. Donald walked over and placed his hand on her shoulder. She didn't look up so he followed us out the door."

Jenkins turned back to the Captain. "The preacher was talking to me, but it was a moment before what he was saying sunk in."

"And what was that?" asked Billy.

"He said it was better when she was like this, because he hated to hear her scream."

The office was silent for awhile. Cordelia watched Walker

light up a cigarette. Both men sat looking at each other. Finally, Carl said, "The preacher told me she'd been like that for days and that she barely ate or drank. Said he was taking her down to the institution at Benton. Planned to leave her there for awhile. I told him I thought it was a good idea."

"I think you were right," said Cordelia. The Captain continued smoking.

Jenkins stood up and walked over to Cordelia's desk. On it stood a clear glass vase, holding a single rose. He reached out and touched it with his fingertips.

"Nathaniel didn't have a car so I lent him an old Chevy we kept out back. When he got back from Benton, I told him to just keep it awhile. We never used it anyway."

"That was generous of you," said Billy.

Carl walked back to his chair. "I liked the man," he said. "As time went by, I liked him more and more. And I always respected him. If you'd known him, Captain, you'd have felt the same way. And like I said, that car was old and beat up. We never used it anyway."

"Is the left rear door smashed in?"

Jenkins sat back down. "Yes sir," he said. "It's the one you're looking for."

Billy leaned back in his chair and gave the store owner a thoughtful look. "Go ahead and finish, Carl."

"I know where Nathaniel Briggs is," said Jenkins. "I came here to tell you."

Cordelia gave a start and stared at Jenkins. "Where?" she demanded.

Walker raised a cautioning hand. "Earlier, you said you had good reasons not to tell us all this. What were they?"

"First of all, I admired the preacher, like I said, and I didn't want any harm to come to him. Donald felt the same way and I didn't want him mad at me. Up until Tuesday, I supposed my son was still alive. Oh hell, I guess, deep down, I suspected Briggs had shot Mayhew, but the preacher never said he did and I didn't ask. And I'll tell you something else, Captain." Carl's face darkened and Billy could see the pulse beat in his temple. "I read the paper and I know what my son was trying to tell us when he wrote out 'May . . .' with his own blood. When I saw that, I wanted to hug Nathaniel for what he'd done. I was glad I hadn't told you."

Cordelia, feeling slightly subdued after her boss's gesture, watched his face and waited for his lead. In his face, she could discern only sadness.

"But now, the situation has changed, hasn't it?" he said.

"Yessir. I read there's a murder warrant out for the preacher, and I'd be an accessory, wouldn't I?"

"Yes, you'd be charged with harboring him. You are harboring him, aren't you, Carl?"

The store owner stared at his feet before answering. "The wife and I own a little cabin over close to the river. It ain't much. We go out there on weekends sometimes. I do a little fishing. Lilly does craft work. She likes the place but I haven't been able to take her for awhile."

"How long has Nathaniel been out there?" asked Billy.

"Since right after he delivered Susan to Benton. All he'd do was sit and stare. Didn't want to do any carpentry. Didn't do any preaching. Donald and I couldn't bear to see him in that old tumbledown shack. Cold weather was setting in and he didn't even have a heater. I took him to the cabin. Every week I take him a few supplies, see how he is."

The Captain slowly got up and reached behind him for his jacket. Cordelia arose and slipped on her coat. Carl looked up at the two policemen. "You're going now?" he asked.

"Yes," said Walker, "and we'll find the place quicker if you come along. Do you feel up to it?"

"Yes, I'll go," murmured Carl. "I need to see him. I need to explain."

"Explain what?" asked Cordelia. She felt she knew the answer.

"Explain why I became his Judas," said Carl.

Cordelia hit the light switch and they left the darkened room.

FORTY-EIGHT

Crowley's Ridge runs north and south between the town of Medford and the great Mississippi River and is largely covered by thick forest. Few people live on this long, narrow range of hills, although the east side of Crowley's Ridge, sloping down to the river, accommodates a few fishing shacks and weekend cabins. A gravel passage, called the "Low Road," winds across the Ridge from Medford, draws near the river, and then turns left, heading northward until it dwindles and disappears among the wooded hills.

The unmarked police car was the only vehicle to be seen on the Low Road this morning. The Captain drove and Cordelia sat beside him. Carl Jenkins was sitting in the back, gazing out the side window and watching the trees slide by. Dry leaves covered the ground, stirred occasionally by a random breath of wind.

Miles passed before Carl pointed to a dirt road, branching off to the right. They turned onto it and headed downhill. Cordelia began to glimpse parts of the river through the trees. An aluminum gate came up on the left and Carl leaned forward.

"That's the entrance," he said. "I'll have to unlock the gate."

"How far is it to the cabin from here?" asked Walker.

"Just a short walk. About a hundred yards."

Billy drove slowly past the closed gate and pulled off the road. He cut the ignition and turned to Jenkins. "Let me have the key, Carl."

Jenkins gave him a questioning look.

"I want you to stay in the car," said the Captain. "Don't move until Sergeant Hull and I get back."

The store owner nodded and handed over the key. "Will I get to talk to him?" he asked.

"Yes," said Walker. "The preacher will be coming back with us."

He and Cordelia walked around to the car trunk and the Captain unlocked it. He withdrew a twelve-gauge shotgun and handed it to his assistant. Cordelia took it, jacked a shell into the chamber, and nodded at her boss. They walked over to the gate. It was secured with a rusty piece of chain and a steel padlock. Walker inserted the key and the lock sprang open.

They stood on a narrow dirt road which ran ahead for a short distance before turning right and disappearing down a slope. The smell of wood smoke came to them even before they saw it, curling above the trees.

"That must be the cabin," murmured Cordelia. She felt her stomach knot. The sweat broke out on her palms and she grasped the shotgun tighter.

They walked toward the curve and had almost reached it when the sound of singing rose to meet them. They froze in their tracks and listened.

> Ohhhh, precious is the flow,
> That makes me white as snow o,
> Noooo, other fount I know,
> Nothing but the blood of Jesus.

The voice, a deep man's voice, stopped as abruptly as it had started. It was as if the forest's immense silence had surrounded the sound and swallowed it up. Only the silence remained.

Up ahead, a gigantic oak spread its branches across the road. Billy signaled Hull to remain still, walked over to the tree, and peered around the trunk. He watched something in the distance, then walked softly back to his assistant. "Go take a look," he said.

Cordelia did as she was told, and stood for a long moment, studying the scene before her.

On the left side of the road, at the bottom of the hill, stood a rough log cabin. An uneven plank porch stretched across the front and a cedar roof covered both cabin and porch. The smoke they'd seen was issuing from a metal stovepipe, sticking above the roof. An old Chevy sedan, rusty and covered with leaves, rested beside the house. The left rear door was caved in. Cordelia observed all this, and then she saw the preacher. After that, she had eyes for nothing else.

Nathaniel Briggs sat on a wooden stool beside a cypress tree. His back was turned to her and he was gazing out across the river. As she watched, his chin dropped and he gazed down at his knees. He appeared to be reading something. Cordelia was sure of it when she saw the left hand move to turn a page. He looked up and the baritone voice rang out again, while his right arm waved back and forth, keeping time in the air.

> Ohhhh, he walks with me,
> And he talks with me,
> And he telllls me I am his own.

The singing stopped and Briggs began reading again. Cordelia backed away and returned to the Captain.

"Is his back still to us?" he asked.

"Yes sir." The "sir" came out unbidden and she wondered about that. Well, maybe the occasion demanded it.

The Captain brought his face closer and said, "We'll go around the curve together. When we start downhill, move as far away from me as you can. We'll stay abreast, but keep that space between us."

Cordelia nodded and he added, "Don't point the shotgun at him, but keep it ready. I'll start talking to him when we get close enough."

"Do you think he's got a weapon?" she asked, and was ashamed of the tightness in her voice.

"I didn't see one, but if he comes out with a gun, shoot him quick. The double-ought buckshot will stop him."

Hull looked down at the shotgun and swallowed. The swallowing was audible. Billy laid a hand on her shoulder.

"Just stay cool. I don't expect any trouble, but don't take your eyes off him for a second."

Hull took a deep breath and said, "I'm okay. Are you ready to go?"

Walker smiled at her and nodded.

They walked back to the oak tree, circled around it, and were now standing in the open. Both started to move downhill, following the narrow road.

Briggs still faced the river, absorbed in what he was reading. He wore a dark corduroy coat and some sort of work pants, also dark, with the legs disappearing into a pair of shabby, high-topped boots. A slouchy felt hat sat atop his head, and thick, black hair hung beneath the brim and curled down over his coat collar. He sat motionless.

Billy and Cordelia's approach had been without sound, but as they drew nearer, they saw the preacher's head come up. He softly closed the book and watched the river for a moment. Then he slowly turned around on the stool, his feet making little side steps as he turned, until he was facing the two policemen. They both stopped walking. The man's hands remained in his lap and Cordelia could see he was holding a Bible. Briggs calmly looked from one to the other. His eyes lingered on Cordelia, for a moment, and he said: "You won't need the shotgun, officer. I don't mean to harm you."

Hull stared into anthracite eyes that reflected no light. They seemed huge and unnatural in the preacher's wan face.

"That's good to hear, Reverend Briggs," came the Captain's soft voice. "We were hoping to have a little talk with you."

Cordelia gave Walker a surprised look. She'd assumed the next step would be to cuff Nathaniel and lead him to the car. The Captain resumed walking, and so did she, still keeping space between them and the shotgun barrel depressed. They stopped in front of the seated man.

"There's a couple of chairs on the porch," he said, and started to raise up.

"That's all right," said Walker. "I'll get them."

He came back with a chair in each hand. They both sat down in front of Nathaniel, Cordelia a bit further away. She placed the shotgun across her knees.

"How did you know Sergeant Hull was a police officer," asked Billy.

Nathaniel gave him a tired smile. His teeth were even and white. "Well," he said, "she's with you, Captain Walker, so it seemed logical."

"And how is it that you know me, Reverend?"

"Oh, folks have pointed you out to me. And I've seen your picture in the newspaper." The black eyes narrowed. "How did you know where to find me?"

"Is that really important, sir?"

Briggs slowly shook his head. "No, I reckon not."

"Nathaniel Briggs," intoned Walker, "before we ask you any questions, you must understand your rights." And he began the queries: "Do you understand that you have the right to remain silent?"

"Yes," answered Briggs.

"Do you understand that anything you say can be used against you in court?"

"Yes."

And the litany continued.

After the preacher's final affirmation, Walker paused and said, "Nathaniel Briggs, you are charged with the murder of Edwin Mayhew."

Cordelia kept watching Nathaniel. Something's not right, she thought. He's too calm. Why isn't he more defensive?

Both men sat quietly facing each other. In the stillness, Cordelia could hear a faint gurgling from the nearby river current. Somewhere in the distance, she heard a woodpecker hammering. Finally the preacher spoke: "So, the formalities are over, Captain. And now you can make your arrest." He cocked his face to one side. "But you want something from me, first. What is it?"

Billy Walker withdrew an undersized tape recorder from his jacket pocket and placed it on his knee. "I want you to tell me about it," he said.

Briggs regarded the Captain, then sighed and said in a low voice, "Ahh! I see."

"I'd like you to tell me about it in your own way."

"Like a story," said the preacher.

"Yes."

"How about one with only one sentence? It goes: I have nothing else to say and I want to see a lawyer."

The Captain nodded and a slight smile played around his mouth. Nathaniel saw it and gave a short chuckle.

"Oh, you've read me my rights, Captain, and now you'll have your story, I've been waiting to tell it, as you know. It's a good story. It might even make a good sermon, because it's all about how false pride led the innocent and good into the presence of that which was evil. And how that evil presence destroyed the good and innocent one."

Briggs straightened and the ebony eyes glowed, and suddenly

it was apparent to Cordelia that this preacher had found his proper calling. He sat there on his rude, three-legged stool, and the pale face came to life and radiated force and confidence and an unshakable dignity. His voice rose up deep and strong.

"And I'll tell you the part that's certain to interest you most, Captain. It's the part where God takes the one with false pride and makes unto him an instrument of divine justice. Created to seek out the evil one and purge him from the earth."

Captain Walker pushed the RECORD button.

FORTY-NINE

Rec: Nathaniel Briggs . . . homicide . . . Edwin Mayhew . . . date and time appearing on reports. Stated in the hearing of: Captain William R. Walker, CID, Medford Police Department and Sergeant Cordelia Hull, CID, Medford Police Department . . . Nathaniel Briggs . . . his voice.

I came back to Medford, Arkansas, in the month of September, riding in a Greyhound bus with Susan sitting beside me. We'd done a lot of traveling together, my daughter and I, working awhile in one town, then moving on to another. My wife is dead, been dead these many years. She lost her mind and only the body and soul were left. The body could not endure without a mind to direct it, so the body died and went into the grave and the soul ascended to heaven to dwell forever with our Lord. Her name was Sarah. I have thought of her and missed her every day of my life.

Susie and I were gypsies over the earth, never thinking about staying long in one place. I had no need to seek a regular job, because I am a good carpenter and there was always carpentry tasks to be done. That was my work. Then one day, while I was repairing a roof, God spoke to me in a clear voice and called upon me to also do His work, and I became a preacher. I've preached all over the South and carried my carpenter tools with me, and in that at least, I became as our Savior, who was also a preacher and a carpenter.

Susie was always with me and her devotion to me never faltered. And she was happy. I know she was happy, and knowing that, I was content. Everything she did cheered me and gave me comfort. I took a great pride in my daughter.

In all the towns we visited, I never worried about our welfare, and there was no need to. Time after time and in town after town, the Lord provided for us. I practiced my trade and preached His word and Susan was my helpmate. It was enough, Captain. My calling, my daughter, and my work were enough, and I believed they would always be constant. And so they were until we came to Medford.

Things started out the same as in other towns. I found a place for us to live and began doing carpenter work. After a while, I found myself preaching an occasional Sunday sermon at a local church. The Lord saw to that. I never had to seek out congregations. I was drawn to them as they were drawn to me. God's will.

Then Susie, who'd never been sick a day in her life, grew seriously ill and ended up in the hospital. She stayed there a week, and when they gave me the bill, I got weak in the knees. I couldn't believe it was that much. You know, Captain, I'm getting to be an old man and I've never in my life worked for a salary. I've always worked for myself. Even so, I've paid my debts as they accrued and I never left a town owing money. The Lord says we should 'forgive our debtors' and I do, but I would not be a debtor myself. Now, I owed an amount that I didn't see how I could pay. I asked to make monthly installments but the hospital refused. They wanted their money before Susie was released.

Somebody had once told me about a liquor store owner who made loans. I talked to this man and he handed over the money without hesitation. The terms of the loan were hard, but not impossible. I settled up with the hospital and began to repay

Edwin Mayhew. And oh, Captain Walker, the length and width and weight of what I finally paid is past imagining. The debt became, for me and mine, a monstrous thing, dangled over our heads by a monster. And out of this loan came my own black act of sin, the knowledge of which has rived me and burned me, and perhaps made me mad.

I sent my precious daughter into the pit. I sent my own harmless lamb before that ravening wolf, and I did it for reasons so trivial, so . . . For vanity and pride, to preserve what I conceived to be my image, I sent Susie to act as my emissary, and thereby face destruction by the Demon. And even after her destruction began, I blindly allowed her to return again and again, until she herself cried out for help and told me what Mayhew had done.

Do you know that's she's in an insane asylum, Captain? I think you do. I think there is much that you know. But you wanted to hear it all from my own lips and so you shall.

My friend, Carl Jenkins, is a decent, Christian man, and this property belongs to him. After I left Susie in Benton, he and his son brought me out here. It's here that I planned the killing of Mayhew, but Jenkins had no knowledge of that. Carl has brought you to me, I know, but I don't fault him for that. The Lord led him to do it. It was right and necessary that he do it, so things come could come to their proper end.

I imagine, Captain, that you're ready to hear the pertinent details, an accurate account of the act. Well, how long has it been? Two weeks? Why this is Friday, isn't it? It's been exactly two weeks. Seems longer. Seems almost years since I confronted the Beast.

First, I watched him for awhile. I watched his comings and goings and I learned his habits and it wasn't long before I pretty much knew how and where I would do it. Mayhew visited many places in the evening, but he always returned to close his liquor store at midnight. Then he would drive home. Sometimes he would spend the rest of the night there and sometimes he would go out again, but he always went inside first. Two weeks ago, on Thursday night, I parked Carl's car in the alley behind Mayhew's house. I waited for midnight to arrive and then I got out and walked across the Creature's back yard. I carried my rifle and a bottle of whiskey. The liquor was important to my plans as well as the rifle. I intended to use them both on Mayhew. I crept up to the back of the house and waited.

The night was cold, made colder by a north wind, steadily blowing. It kept swirling dead leaves around the corner of the house and into my face. The sky was clear with only a few shining clouds hurrying across it. And oh yes, there was a full moon, one of the largest and brightest I've ever seen. I pulled on a pair of jersey gloves and stuck the whiskey in my coat pocket. I kept looking up at the moon.

Finally, a pair of headlights appeared in the distance, and a few moments later, Mayhew came driving up the street. He parked in his usual place and started across the front yard. I walked around the corner of the house with the rifle gripped in my hands. He stopped when he saw me and I walked up very close to him. The full moon shed its cold light down upon him.

He kept twisting his head from side to side, trying to see my face, but I wore the same hat I've got on now. As you can see, it's got a wide brim and my face was hidden in shadow. We were both bathed by moonlight, but I don't think he ever recognized me. Or maybe I'd become transfigured into someone or something else, transfigured by grace. I felt as light as the air, but at the same time, as substantial and immovable as a slab of granite. When I raised the rifle, it seemed no heavier than a toothpick in my hands. I glanced out at the street and it was deserted. The blood-red moon shone down and nighttime clouds raced across its surface, but nothing moved in Mayhew's yard. Even the wind had ceased to blow. The Creature himself grew still, and stayed that way, even after I'd pressed the rifle muzzle against his chest.

When I shot him the first time, his arms stiffened and he gave a little shudder. I shot him again and he sank to his knees. I'd hoped that placing the muzzle against his body would deaden the sound and it did.

He knelt before me, for a moment, and then with knees still bent, he fell onto his back. I leaned over and once more placed the rifle muzzle against his chest. The Creature looked up at me with his dull, pig eyes and then he squinted them shut. He knew what was coming. I pulled the trigger and moved the barrel a little ways over and pulled the trigger again. Mayhew jerked his legs straight out after the last bullet struck him and I knew that was enough. I didn't want it to be enough. I wanted to keep shooting him over and over, but that would have been for my pleasure and not in accordance with God's instruction. There were four patches of blood on the Creature's chest. They looked black beneath the moonlight. I stepped over him and uncapped the whiskey bottle.

He had given my daughter a living death. I gave him death in return. Susie's destruction began with whiskey. Whiskey would conclude my destruction of Mayhew.

I poured the liquor down upon his face and over his open wounds. A baptism from Hell for a hellbound demon. God's will.

I left him lying there and drove away.

End of NBriggs rec.

FIFTY

Stretching back from the sweeping river, the forest lay vast and still. In its midst, the woodpecker hammered again and found a juicy larvae under some bark. He swallowed it and then fell backward off the tree trunk, spreading his wings to catch the air. Banking to the left, he sailed through an avenue of trees and passed over a small cabin, nestled near the current. Three people sat in the cabin's front yard. They didn't look up and the woodpecker paid them no mind. He had his eye on a large elm, towering just ahead. The woodpecker knew there were fat grubs under the elm tree's bark. He'd been there before.

Nathaniel folded his hands and looked from one policeman to the other. The Captain put the tape recorder away and all three sat silently. Walker gazed past Briggs's shoulder to the wide flood beyond. Cordelia's eyes remained on the preacher. Her mouth hung slightly open. The silence lengthened. She tried to think of a question to ask, but she couldn't come up with anything. There was really nothing to say.

Suddenly Nathaniel asked, "How is the boy? I haven't seen him for awhile."

"The boy?" said Cordelia.

"Yes, Carl Jenkins's son. Carl comes up once a week, but I never see Donald."

The policemen exchanged glances.

"He's a fine young man," Briggs continued. "I thought the world of him. So did Susie before . . ." Nathaniel lowered his

284

head in thought. "He would not abandon her. No matter what she did, he stuck by her. All the way up to the time she . . . left us."

The Captain cleared his throat and leaned closer to Nathaniel. He would not conceal what he knew from the preacher. "Donald is dead, Brother Briggs."

Briggs's head remained lowered and for a moment Cordelia thought he had not heard. Then his voice came forth, muffled and low. "Tell me about it, please."

"We found his body last Monday," said Walker.

"Where?"

"Out at his brother's house trailer. Seems he'd been staying there." The Captain paused. "The boy had been dead for several days. His body was . . ."

"Yes," said Nathaniel. "Tell me, Captain Walker. How did he die?"

"He was shot in the leg. The bullet hit an artery. Donald had enough strength to drive back to the trailer. He made it to the bed and then he bled to death."

"And you know who shot him, don't you Captain?"

"Yes, I know who shot him."

"Please tell me."

"Donald used a bloody finger to write a message on his bedsheet. We believe he was trying to write the name of his killer."

The preacher raised his head and regarded Walker with dark, smoldering eyes.

"The boy wrote out 'May . . .' on the bedsheet," said Walker. "Clearly, his strength gave out before he could finish the word."

"Maaayhew." The word issued forth in a long, drawn out, croaking sigh from the preacher's throat.

"Yes," said Billy. "We believe that Donald confronted Edwin. He may have tried to beat him up. That was foolish. Edwin Mayhew was a very dangerous man."

"I should not have waited so long," whispered Briggs. "I should have shot him sooner." And Cordelia reflected that this man could also take a prize for "dangerous."

Nathaniel's chin dropped to his chest. "Shot him sooner," he repeated, and gave a brief shudder.

Finally, he looked up and held them in a wide-eyed gaze and they both witnessed the fearful, fateful, transformation of Nathaniel Briggs. His body twisted and his face took on a stricken look of grief and pain. He gave a violent shudder and the great voice of the preacher rang out in infinite remorse.

"Oh heavenly Father," he cried. "What am I saying? Oh merciful Jesus, what have I done?"

Cordelia's eyes moved to her boss, to his dark, unreadable face. She was still looking at him when a shout rang out from halfway up the hill.

"Brother Briggs!"

She jerked her head around and saw Carl Jenkins standing on the dirt road above them.

"Forgive me, Brother Briggs," he called. "I hope that you will forgive me."

Jenkins took a stumbling step forward, then stopped and gaped at the preacher. He raised both arms in front of him, the palms of his hands facing outward, and cried, "NOOOO."

Watching Carl, Cordelia sensed movement behind her and knew it was the preacher. Walker's last words of instruction flashed across her consciousness: Don't take your eyes off him for a second.

She whirled to face Briggs, bringing the shotgun up and half rising from her seat. The preacher remained on his stool, but now he was grasping a rifle. It looked as big as a cannon. As the shotgun came to her shoulder, the complete image of Briggs and the rifle finally imprinted itself on her boiling brain . . . and Cordelia froze. He's holding it backward.

Briggs sat with the weapon's muzzle pointed at his own forehead. His left hand gripped the barrel, the right hand enfolded the trigger guard, and his thumb lay against the trigger.

She lowered her gun and yelled "No," the cry echoing Carl's, both equally futile.

Nathaniel exchanged a look with Walker. Billy remained seated. Giving a barely perceptible nod, the preacher leaned forward and his right thumb pressed the trigger.

CRAACK!

The sharp report echoed against the hills and faded across the river. A round, gray hole appeared in the middle of Nathaniel's forehead and a crimson stream of blood shot from the rear of his skull. The preacher tumbled backward off the stool and lay face up, the rifle resting on his chest. His Bible fell with fluttering pages to the ground. One thin leg stayed draped over the stool, a tattered boot dangling from the edge. Cordelia's eyes lingered on the boot for a moment. The front part of the sole had worn completely through. She could see Nathaniel's toes.

The Captain rose and walked over to the body. Nathaniel's open eyes stared upward at eternity. Using his thumb and forefinger, Billy knelt and closed them. He picked up the rifle and regained his feet.

Carl stumbled up and stood staring at the preacher. He reached down, gently removed Nathaniel's leg from the stool, and placed in on the ground. Then he sat down on the stool and quietly regarded his friend.

"Cordelia." The Captain stood facing her.

She blinked her eyes at him but couldn't get them focused. Her face felt numb.

Walker reached over and took away the shotgun. Hull gave a slight shiver and pointed at the rifle.

"Where did it come from?" she asked. "He got it so quickly. I didn't have time to do . . . I couldn't . . ."

"He'd placed it behind the tree," said Billy. "It was leaning against the trunk, just a few inches from his hand. We had no way of seeing it, and he was very fast. It's not your fault," he added.

"Want me to get on the radio?" she asked.

"No, I'll do it. You stay here with Jenkins. I'll bring back the car."

Cordelia watched the Captain trudge up the dirt road. He moved slowly, the shoulders slumped, his head lowered. He disappeared around the curve.

She stepped down to the river's edge. Looking out over the expanse of water, she tried to clear her mind and make room for rational thought. She had known this river all her life, had never tired of looking at it. The vast flood of muddy water moved quietly by her, the surface full of swirls and eddies, hiding all that lay beneath. Cordelia wondered, not for the first time, what it would be like to lie beneath this river, lie on the very bottom, way out in the middle of it, with a half mile of current flowing by on either side and tons of water sweeping overhead. It would be dark, she knew, and very cold. And very, very lonely.

And you, my captain, she thought. My river. What are your waters like? And what would I behold if I looked below your currents?

The man lying behind her had said he was glad that they had found him, "so things could come to their proper end." The Captain had heard those words and he before all others would have understood the meaning. She remembered the arrest of Bad Bubba Hines when Walker drew his gun. She remembered the blurring speed. She really didn't think the preacher could have matched, much less beaten such a movement.

Yes, my captain, my river. You knew. When Briggs reached for his weapon, you knew what he intended. Had you thought otherwise, Briggs would have died from a .38 Special instead of a .22 rifle.

Nathaniel had nodded to the Captain before squeezing the trigger. Cordelia had not marked it then, but now she remembered it and understood that nod in all its terrible aspects. The preacher was giving a sign of acknowledgement to someone who understood everything, and who was willing to sit quietly, so things, all things, could come to their proper end.

The vast, amber waters continued to surge past, washing south from a frozen northland down to a warmer sea. The young woman watched a moment longer before she turned away. The forest's utter silence filled her ears. She walked back to the cabin and stood waiting for the Captain.

EPILOGUE

The following Thursday brought a cold front into Medford. It swept in just after midnight, carrying wind and rain and falling temperatures. And along with all that, this Thursday brought Thanksgiving.

Billy Walker slept late. He finally awoke to the smell of coffee and the sound of Sammy in the kitchen. He lay motionless, while the last two weeks played out in his mind. It's time once again, he thought, to say goodbye to a case. Goodbye to the whiskey killing.

And a special farewell to those who did not survive it. To the gentle Leonard Simpson, and the homicidal Eddie Partee, and the gallant Donald Jenkins, all resting under the sod.

And to the Preacher, resting there of his own volition. He had not asked his God for forgiveness as he prepared to commit that final, aberrant act. He had asked only for the Captain's acquiescence. I would not interfere that you might end your pain. Goodbye.

And Edwin Mayhew.

Walker arose and took a shower. He dressed quickly and joined Sammy in the kitchen. She kissed him on the lips and handed him a cup of coffee. They sat down at the breakfast table. A large wicker basket, covered in white cloth, rested on the floor beside them. Walker took a sip of coffee and gave his wife a fond look.

"Did you tell the girls?" he asked

"Yep. They understand. We'll get together next Thanksgiving."

"Of course."

"Lavonia Mayhew was in the flower shop yesterday."

"Oh?"

"Um hm. She told me about the reward and about Carl Jenkins turning it down. Said she decided to put it into a trust fund for the girl. Was that your idea?"

"No, Lavonia suggested it after learning the whole story. I told her she couldn't have made a better choice."

"I agree."

Billy smiled and said, "By the way, who was Lavonia buying flowers for?"

"Look in the basket," said Sammy.

He reached over and raised the cotton cloth. A bouquet of violets lay across the homemade bread.

They backed out of the driveway and the Captain headed down the glistening street. The gutters on either side were filled with rushing water. At the first intersection, they turned right and followed Marlan Avenue to Medford's city limits. The asphalt highway stretched dark and straight before them. It led all the way to Benton.

Billy stopped by the roadside and Sammy turned to secure the basket, resting on the rear seat. She placed a hand on her husband's shoulder and they remained quiet for a moment, savoring the silence and the aroma of fresh-baked bread. Finally the Captain started the engine and sat looking at his wife. She nodded and they drove westward through the rain.

ABOUT THE AUTHOR

H. R. Williams was born in Marianna, Arkansas, and grew up on Crowley's Ridge, a line of hills and a geographical region that figures prominently in many of his stories—an area he refers to as his own "Yoknapatawpha County." He was a paratrooper with the 101st Airborne Division at Fort Campbell, Kentucky, and later attended Austin Peay State University in Clarksville, Tennessee. He is husband to Nora Lee ("long suffering, eternally patient") and the father of four children.

Williams has sold short fiction and essays to many national publications, including *Southern Outdoors, Safari, Curriculum Vitae, Woman's World,* and *American Hunter.* He has won numerous prizes and awards, and *The Whiskey Killing* was awarded first prize at the Arkansas Writer's Conference, a branch of the National League of American PEN Women. His western novel, *Harris: The Return of the Gunfighter,* was sold to Treble Heart Publications.